SKIN
and
BONES

The Jones Brothers

Derec Jones

OPENING CHAPTER

First Printing, 2020
Reprinted with minor updates, 2024

ISBN 10: 1-904958-73-7

ISBN 13: 978-1-904958-73-4

published by

Opening Chapter
Cardiff, Wales

www.openingchapter.com

For the Backfields crew

CHAPTER ONE

SKIN

I was too tired to drive for much longer. It was around midnight, most of the early wave had been ferried home and there was the usual lull in trade before the clubs emptied, so I decided to pick up one more fare before packing it in for the night and getting back on the controls to give Mandy a break. She was more exhausted than I was, poor thing. It wasn't easy for her, working so hard and not being able to see much of her parents, especially now that they were both suffering from the after effects of the virus, long Covid as they called it. My own father was the same, although in a worse condition due to the lung disease he'd acquired after more than 40 years of smoking, but at least I was able to visit him regularly, seeing as he lived so near.

As luck would have it, the fare's destination was one of those new executive houses up by the motorway, you know, all red brick and hardwood with wide metal gates and leaded windows. They were only a mile past my dog-eared semi in Bont Road, a quiet street a couple of miles outside town.

She looked freaked out, this girl, freaked out and tired. She sighed as she sat down in the back seat, then started talking in a nervous hyped-up way. I didn't mind, I was used to it. Anyway, it passed the time in the cab to indulge in a bit of amateur counselling, and it worked, I'd seen it happen, believe me. I'd cheered some people up so much that by the time I got them home they wanted to go out again. But not this one.

After a long ten minutes I parked up on the road outside the address and waited for her to pay. She stopped talking but didn't move.

"We're here," I said.

She sighed.

"All right?" I asked.

"Um . . ." she said, "don't go yet, can I stay in the cab for a while? I'll pay."

I shrugged. "No problem."

"What's your name?" she asked.

"Harry," I said.

"That doesn't tell me much. Who are you Harry?"

"Harold Jones. There's some business cards in that holder on the back of the seat, if you ever need a ride, you can call me direct."

She giggled self-consciously, then took a breath. "Harold? That's a funny little name, doesn't really suit you. You don't look like a Harry either to be honest."

"Tell me about it, but I'm also known as Skin, that's what people call me."

"Oh, did you say Skin?"

"Yeah, ever since I was a kid."

"Um . . ." she hesitated.

"What?"

"Um, I mean, how old are you Skin? Early thirties?"

"OK, yeah, that'll do, something like that."

"Cool," she said.

"Ready to go in yet?"

"Yes – no, I can't."

She shivered.

"What's up?" I asked.

"It's complicated."

"OK."

"My sort-of ex is a Jones."

"Ex?"

"Yeah, sort of."

"Fair enough. There's a lot of us about."

"I know."

"Does he live here?" I asked.

"No, this is my father's house. This is where I live. For now."

"Must be hard, living with your parents with all that

2

family stuff. It'll do you no good. You want to get out of there."

"It's only temporary. I've lived away for years."

"Oh yeah, where?"

"All over, Manchester, London, Bristol."

"I like Manchester and London. Bristol's all right too."

"I'm in retail."

"What type?"

"You know, shops and stuff."

"Of course," I said, feeling stupid.

"I'm ready now. Is cash all right?"

"Yeah sure," I said, "whatever's best for you."

She got out of the car, leant back in and gave me a twenty pound note. I took the money bag from my pocket and looked down to count the change.

"Skin," she said, in a cute sexy voice.

I looked up and she kissed me full on the lips. I couldn't speak, she was very pretty, beautiful, and she tasted of strawberry lipstick and Pernod. I didn't know how to react.

"I like you," she said. "Keep the change."

I laughed it off, like you do, and thought about Mandy. She'd be waiting to go to bed.

"I'd better go," I said.

She smiled and stood back from the car.

I watched her in my rear-view mirror as I turned out of the close. She was still standing on the edge of the pavement, staring at me as I drove away. 'Wow!' I whispered to myself. 'That was surreal.'

BONES

It was late Friday night. We'd just come back to the station after a pointless couple of hours of surveillance. I was supposed to be writing up reports but couldn't be bothered, that investigation was dead in the water anyway. The Chief reckoned we needed to bust a few people to make an example of illegal-substance takers, to put the shits up everyone else, but why anyone would care about a couple of dozen drugged up tossers plotting a secret rave in a closed-down pub was beyond me.

"Cup of tea?" Chunky asked.

"Aye, why not. Might as well take advantage of the overtime."

"I might pop over to the club to see Jan in a bit, if it's ok?"

"Course it is Chunks. Just watch she doesn't take advantage of you again," I joked. "You couldn't walk properly for two days after the last time."

"Shut up Boss, it's not like that," Chunky laughed.

He waddled over to the kettle. He was much too fat to be a copper. I'd have sacked the useless bastard years ago. The detective game was all about thinking, on your feet, you had to be quick, and fit.

"And don't fuck it up this time you fat fucker. One sugar, not two."

He looked at me in that pathetic hurt way of his. What did he want me to do? He was a fat fucker, and he was fucking asking for it. Get over it. I ignored him anyway and stared back at the computer screen. I was selling some stuff on e-Bay, nothing spectacular, just some bits and bobs that had come my way over the years, like they did in my job.

My phone rang. I ignored it, but Chunky picked it up from the edge of the desk and handed it to me.

"It's him," he whispered. "Big Bill."

I sighed. What the hell was he after? He should have been tucked up in bed after one of his dinner parties with his poncey bent friends.

"Yes Bill," I said into the phone, with just the right amount of enthusiasm I thought, not too much, considering it was after midnight on a Friday.

"Is she with you?" he asked.

"Who?" I mumbled, but I knew the game was up.

"Don't give me that shit Jones. I know she's been seeing you."

"Um, well, sort of. I mean . . ."

"Never mind that, just get over here straight away."

4

"Where? Your house?"

"Where else!"

As I disconnected the phone Chunky handed me the tea, expecting an explanation.

"I've got to go and see Bill Mason," I said. "You drink it. You could do with the fluid."

"I'd better come with you," he said, gulping his own tea.

"No, fuck off. I need a bit of social distancing – from you anyway. You stay here and make a start on the reports."

"Do I have to? I'm knackered."

"Just pretend to work then, you're good at that."

I passed that twat of a brother on the way there. There he was in his cab, self-important prick, like a big-shot businessman or something. Who the fuck did he think he was, poncing around in his mangled heap? If he wasn't my brother I'd have busted him ages ago. Then we'd have seen what sort of an entrepreneur he was. I'm sure he synchronised his shift patterns with mine, just to get up my nose.

Anyway, I ignored him and he ignored me, just like I liked it. Except what I really would have liked to do was to pull the bastard over and put him in his place with a good slapping, show him who was boss, like I used to do when we were kids on the estate and he got too cocky.

I got to the house and Bill Mason let me in. The stupid fucker was in his dressing gown, a silk paisley affair in dark purple. Prick. I stepped towards him.

"Keep your fucking distance," he said. "God knows what shit you're carrying, with all the wankers you deal with in your job. And put your fucking mask on."

I'd forgotten that he was still freaked out about the Covid. "Jeez," I said, "you're a bit paranoid, aren't you? Didn't think you were the sort of bloke to buy into all that crap."

I fished in my pocket and yanked out the manky disposable mask I kept handy to satisfy the idiots who believed the bollocks.

5

"There," I said, looping the mask behind my ears. "Happy now?"

"Shut up Jones. She hasn't come home," he snarled, looking down his nose at me as if I was his poodle's turd.

"I haven't seen her tonight," I said quietly. "It's been a while."

"Don't fucking lie to me," he said, "we argued earlier and she admitted it all. It stops now. It's finished, do you understand?"

It wasn't worth arguing with him. I looked down at his feet, ugly as fuck they were, with dirty brown claws for nails and half covered in peep-toe slip-on mules, like an old tart.

To tell the truth I was glad he was forcing me to stop seeing his daughter. She was getting boring, too fucking possessive and jealous.

Ah who was I kidding, I knew deep down that the reason I couldn't keep seeing Moira was not because she was boring, she was anything but. No, I couldn't keep seeing her because I was afraid. Yes, I was afraid of her father because of the potential damage he could do to my career and of course to my physical wellbeing if I got in any deeper. I was also afraid because I'd realised I was falling in love with her, whatever that meant, and she scared me a little bit herself because she could be unpredictable and obsessive. I hadn't had feelings like that since my marriage to Lindy ended years earlier. I didn't want to feel that pain again.

And then there was Jill. She'd been very good for me. She was kind and loving and was one of the rare people who actually got me. I'd loved being in her company, there was simply no stress, not until I called it a day anyway. She had visibly crumpled when we finished, and crept away, head down as if she had a sack of spuds on her shoulders. I'd almost caved and called her back, but my feelings for her weren't in the same league as those I'd had for Lindy, or even for Moira, who I'd just met at the time. Anyway, I'd kept Jill in reserve, told her that maybe I just needed some time, so there was still a chance we would get back together.

"Do you understand?" Mason repeated forcibly.

"Yes I do."

"Good," he said, "but for now I want you to find her, and when you do, bring her straight back home to me."

I nodded. "She was upset? You argued?" I asked.

"Don't give me that CID crap here son, just find my daughter and bring her home."

"Yes Bill," I said.

SKIN

I passed my brother on the way back to base. I often saw him when I was working, but then I did work at all times of day and most of the night. I felt the nasty vibes before I noticed it was him, staring through the windscreen of the dark blue Beamer. I nodded in acknowledgement as he raced past, but he didn't reciprocate. Perhaps he didn't notice me?

I decided to take a detour to fill the car up before heading home. After I left the all-night petrol station a big black MPV pulled out suddenly from a lane, no indicators, no lights even. It clipped my headlight and I stopped instinctively, but it was gone before I had a chance to get a good look. Luckily I found a spare bulb after rummaging about in the boot for a few minutes. I'd still need a new lens and would have to sort out the scratch on the wing. Fair enough, it was an occupational hazard, but it didn't stop me getting annoyed.

When I got back in, Mandy gave me a grateful kiss on the cheek and went to bed yawning as I took her place in the office. By about half one I started getting a buzz from the boys in the cars, little snippets they'd picked up, rumours about a missing girl and increased police activity. At three o'clock they found her dead under the motorway junction, her face kicked in and looking like pulverised grapes, according to Len anyway.

I started to feel queasy as soon as I heard the first rumours but waited until I was sure before phoning the cops.

"Hello," the voice said.

I couldn't speak, all of a sudden the image of that girl's

face came into my mind, about as vivid as you can get with images coming into the mind, and that's quite vivid, especially at three o'clock in the morning after what amounted to a twenty hour shift.

Anyway, there was that gorgeous vision, very pretty, very sexy, strawberry and Pernod, and her eyes, promising a fantastic creature of playfulness and light, and the feel of her lips on mine and . . .

"Hello, can I help you?" The voice was bored.

Then there was the imagined scene of a young woman lying dead in a mess of blood and loose flesh under the motorway.

"Sorry," I said, "um, yes. It's just that I'm a taxi driver and I heard about the girl, you know, the one that was found. We get to hear things you know."

"Yes sir."

"Well, anyway, I think I picked her up earlier, around midnight, and took her to a house on that new estate up by the motorway."

"Hold on sir, I'll put you through to CID, it's in their hands."

Oh shit, I thought, I hoped it wasn't him, my horrible miserable-chops brother.

BONES

I left the old bastard's house and drove back to town. What was Moira playing at? I tried phoning her on the way but it went straight to voicemail. I didn't leave a message.

I phoned Chunky to see what he was up to. He'd already made his way to the manager's office of Taffies Club. When I got there he was chatting up Jan. She was the co-owner, a large bleached blonde woman with a mouth like an angry bulldog. He liked them a bit rough.

"Come on Chunky, we've got work to do."

"OK Boss," he said, knocking back a shot of brandy.

Fucking upstart. I only put up with him because he could

be useful, plus he knew how to keep his mouth shut.

"Well get a move on then, we haven't got all night."

We went out the back and into my car.

"What's it all about Boss? Some dickhead nicked Big Bill's pushbike or what?"

"It's not fucking funny Chunks. There's a girl missing – it's Mason's daughter."

"Fucking hell, do you mean Moira Mason? Your Moira?"

I got angry then, stuck my face right in his and shouted, showed him who was boss. "No, you stupid fat twat, she's not MY Moira, she's anybody's Moira, ok, she's a fucking tart."

"Sorry Boss, cool head, that's too close, I don't want to catch the Rona."

"Oh jeez, not you as well. OK sorry. I haven't got the fucking Rona. Anyway, I'm not seeing her anymore. I've been with you all night."

"Yes Boss, except when you went . . ."

"Shut the fuck up fatty. Now, we're going to find her."

My mobile rang, it was Mason, demanding an update. I told him we had six men on it, making discreet enquiries. He seemed satisfied with that.

Me and Chunky toured the clubs and the late bars and asked around a bit. It wasn't all that busy for a Friday, so it didn't take long. We went back to the station for a break. Then the call came in. A traffic cop had found a woman's body under the motorway bridge.

Fucking hell, what a mess. I knew it had to be Moira.

I popped up the motorway, secured the scene, couldn't face a close look at the body, and drove back to the nick to start the ball rolling.

That's when the phone went.

"Elchurch CID," I said.

It was Rob on reception.

"I've got some bloke on the line, it's about the murder," he said yawning – stupid pratt.

"Go one then, put him on."

"Hello. Is that, is that you? Bones?"

Oh shit, that voice.

9

"Yes," I sighed.

"It's me, your brother, Skin."

"What the fuck do you want?"

I waited while he got the words out; he'd always been a little wimp when he was under pressure. Twat! I hoped he had something important to say, something good. Perhaps the old man was dead at last. That would be nice.

SKIN

Bastard. Why did he always get me like that? Just the sound of his voice was enough, like a feral dog's threatening snarl. There was something dark in it, something to be scared of.

"It's that girl," I mumbled.

"What fucking girl?"

"That girl, up by the motorway. I had her in my cab earlier."

"Oh fuck, you'd better come in."

"OK, sure, give me fifteen minutes."

I put the phone down and went upstairs to see how Mandy was. She was out for the count. I kissed her cheek. Her skin was glowing with a warm energy, she was so soft, so trusting and so relaxed. I started to feel guilty, because only a few hours earlier my lips had touched another woman's lips. That touch had thrilled me more than warmed me, like the kick of an expensive drug.

I drove down to the police station passing a few desperate stragglers as I hit the streets of the town centre. One of the idiots nearly killed himself when he stood in the road in front of my car. That's the problem when you drive the company car on private business in the taxi game, you never get any peace. But I couldn't afford a separate vehicle for my personal use so had to put up with it.

I wondered if my brother had softened a bit in his old age, it was about time he grew up, he was nearly forty, a good four years older than me, a couple of inches taller and a fair bit thinner. He was pretty good-looking, but his head was screwed inside and his bite was as bad as his bark.

Skin and Bones – The Jones Brothers

"It's been a while," I said, as he led me into his office.

We were both on edge. I could see he was only just managing to keep himself under control. I didn't understand why he was always so angry with me. I decided to play it as diplomatically and as cool as I could.

"Everything all right?" I asked quietly.

"Yeah, yeah," he said, "now about this girl."

"Yes, I picked her up just after midnight, left her on the pavement outside her house, then went back home to relieve Mandy."

"Yes, well, is that all?"

The anger was still there, he wouldn't look at me directly, so to avoid unnecessary conflict I lowered my head in false deference. Whatever his problem was he'd have to sort it out himself.

"She seemed fine," I said. "Pretty girl too, something about her, but she obviously had things on her mind."

"Just tell me exactly where you picked her up and where you put her down."

"Who was she?"

He sighed impatiently. "Her name was Moira Mason."

"Mason?" I said. "That name's familiar, and that address come to think of it. She's not Bill Mason's daughter is she?"

He nodded.

"Shit! How's he taking it?"

"Just keep your fucking mouth shut for now," he said. "Until it's official, ok?"

"Of course," I said.

BONES

It looked like the old man wasn't dead, more's the pity. But that stupid bastard of a brother had got himself tangled up in Moira's death. I asked him to come in. I had to try and stay civil with him, but he started to get too personal, too familiar, so I had to slap him down.

I stood up and turned my back on him and his stupid

needy face, or else I really would have slapped the bastard.

"Listen," I said, "I haven't got time for all this shit now, just tell me where you picked her up and where you dropped her off."

He looked away when I turned around, he knew when he was beat. He told me what he knew and then I showed him the door.

CHAPTER TWO

SKIN

Boy was I glad to get out of there. What was his problem? Our dad reckoned he used to be jealous when he was a kid, jealous of me and jealous of the other boys he hung around with. Something had gone wrong in his life, or in his perception of his life. My dad was a wise old codger, but I still didn't get it.

By the time I got back to the house again it was nearly four o'clock, so I shut the system down and went to bed. I didn't bother setting the alarm, I'd be up by half nine anyway, I always was, even on a lie-in day.

I got up at about ten, did the usual ablutions and then a breakfast of tea and toast with marmite and peanut butter. Mandy had woken up before me and gone out somewhere, probably browsing the few shops that were open on the main road. Since the early days it had become a ritual to switch everything off on Saturday mornings, including the phones, and Mandy liked to go out and pick up on the local chit-chat, there was always someone to slag off or feel sorry for, especially with all the crap going on in the world. She'd been distracted and had seemed tired and fed up for a while, so it did her good to chill.

She was a darling was Mandy, one of the best, always level-headed and always ready to help anyone, but she had this thing, she thought she was never going to be able to have kids. I'd told her often enough, it was just a matter of time, the best thing to do was to relax. Sometimes she did.

Then about eleven, Mandy was still out so I walked to the Co-op to get a newspaper. I enjoyed a good read on a weekend, and over the previous year or two had started buying the real physical version of the Saturday Guardian, it was a bit of a wade but it was good to have a break from a screen, and it had the occasional interesting piece.

While I was picking up the Guardian I noticed the headlines on the early edition of the local evening paper. There it was, a report on the girl's body found near the motorway. *Body Under Bridge*, was the headline, and the sub-heading was *Police Launch Murder Inquiry*. There was an old photograph of the victim but it had none of the spark that the real woman had when I'd dropped her off less than twelve hours earlier.

I'd pushed it all to the back of my mind with the routines of the morning. Funny thing, when I saw that headline, my heart seemed to skip a beat, I started to miss her, as if I'd known her and loved her for years, but of course, that was stupid, she'd been just another random fare.

BONES

Because of the relationship I'd been having with Moira Mason there was a conflict-of-interest situation brewing. It could get difficult and complicated. Not that I couldn't deal with difficulties. In fact, I prided myself on being able to handle any situation, however complex, that's why I was good at my job as a CID officer. Give me a mystery and I had a knack of finding the fastest and most hassle-free way of getting a solution to it. My father used to say I was lazy, cunning he called me – prick.

I managed to get to bed about eight, I reckoned I would have at least five hours sleep ahead of me, but I'd have to be back on the ball by two, because by then, the preliminary forensics would be complete, and the plods would have done a lot of the initial donkey work. Besides, I had to get some kip, because I knew I had a long afternoon and night ahead of me.

I didn't sleep very well, but it was good enough. Chunky picked me up from my flat. I wasn't in the mood for driving, besides, I wanted to keep an eye on the fat bastard – he knew too much and he was stupid.

"Now Chunky, not a word about me and Moira, or fucking Mason, not a fucking word. Understand?"

"Cool head Boss, what the fuck do you think I am?"

He looked genuinely offended. I thought I'd better keep him on side for the time being, he could cause a lot of damage if I pissed him off too much.

"OK," I said, "sorry, now just drive, come on."

"What's the latest Boss?"

"How the fuck should I know?"

"They've given it to Adams, Boss."

"That arsehole, I should have known. Never mind, he hasn't got a fucking clue."

"What are you going to do? You're in a bit of a pickle, as my old girl used to say," Chunky chuckled.

I gave a feeble imitation of a laugh to humour him. How did the dumb bastard keep his job?

"Do you know how it went with Mason?" I asked.

"Aye, good mun. The old tart started blubbing like a girl when they told him. He had some kind of pull, they had to call the Doc."

"How's fucking Adams behaving?"

"He's all right, harmless enough."

My mobile rang, I looked at the screen. Fucking Adams. Better answer it I thought. Better be polite, well at least in a colleague-to-colleague kind of way. He was a meticulous bastard, a stickler when he wanted to be.

"Hi Gerry. How's it hanging?" I couldn't help myself.

"Where are you?"

Cheeky twat, what did he mean 'Where are you?' What fucking business was it of his? I took a breath. "I'm in the car, on the way to the station. With Chunky."

"Oh, sorry to bother you. Would you mind coming up to the Mason house instead. There's something I need to talk to you about, about last night. I know you must be tired but it is important. Do you know where the house is?"

My mouth went dry but I managed a weak response. "OK Gerry, no problems."

I hung up, threw the phone on the dashboard, and stared through the windscreen at the drizzle.

"What's up Boss?" Chunky asked.

"Huh? What's that?"

"You're staring Boss. What's up?"

I had to front this out. Show any weakness and I was dead. Couldn't let the bastards get me, not now. I'd find a way, I always did.

"Change of plan Chunks, we're going to meet Adams at Mason's house."

"Why? What's up?"

"Nothing's fucking up. Just fucking drive will you."

Chunky shrugged and pulled over. When the road was clear he did a U-turn and we headed off up towards Mason's place near the motorway. It wasn't much more than a ten-minute drive, just enough time to get my story straight.

SKIN

I was in the kitchen trying to read the reviews in The Guardian. I like to keep tabs on the latest films and books and all that. Not that I get much chance to go and see any films or to read any books, not with my job, but it's nice to know what the latest cultural buzz is. But it was no good, I couldn't concentrate. I looked again at the local paper, I'd already read the report about the murder at least six times. There was something about it that didn't make sense, I couldn't work it out.

Mandy came back in, I hadn't seen her since getting up.

"Morning," she said. "Are you compos mentis yet, after your late night?"

"Yeah," I said. "I've been up ages. How are you? You must be knackered yourself."

"I'm fine, but you do look shattered. Fancy a coffee?"

"Yeah, OK. Thanks."

Mandy kissed me on the top of my head and fussed with the jar of instant, the kettle, and the cups. While the water was boiling she picked the local newspaper up.

"I see you got the Guardian again," she said, "don't know what you see in it myself, too many words, and this, the local rag – anything interesting? Ah! Look at that, lots of gossip in the shops about it, shame, a pretty girl."

"Yeah, I know, she was in my cab."

"My god, when?"

"Last night, before I knocked off."

"You didn't say anything when you got in."

"There was nothing to say then. Just another passenger. My last one of the night, as it happens."

"So where did you drop her off? When? You might have been the last person to see her alive, besides the killer that is."

"I know," I sighed.

"You'll have to tell the police."

"I already have."

Mandy poured the boiling water into the cups and stirred.

"What did they say?" She sat down opposite me and pushed my cup across.

"Thanks," I said, sipping the coffee. "Nice. Um, it was that twat of a brother."

"Barry?"

"I've only got one twat of a brother," I snapped.

"No need for that. Why do you get so upset every time his name comes up?"

"You know my history as much as anyone. You know what sort of bloke he is. The less I have to do with him the better."

BONES

I started getting the jitters about halfway to Mason's. It wasn't like me. Normally I can handle everything, well, nearly everything, but to be honest the old bastard rattled me, especially since I'd started shagging his crazy daughter. Anyway, I thought it would be better if I calmed my nerves before fronting up to Adams.

"Hang on Chunks," I said, "I'm busting for a piss, pull over in the car park of the Carpenters, it's just around the next bend."

"Sure Boss, I know where the Carpenters is, but what about Adams? Shouldn't you wait until we get there?"

"For fuck's sake. How do you think that would look? You can't piss in someone else's house uninvited, especially when their daughter has just been done in. I won't be long; I'm just going to have a piss and maybe a takeaway innit."

"Ooh, I fancy a burger."

"Not that sort of takeaway you plonker."

"Ah," he said, as if he knew what I was talking about.

Chunky teased the big Volvo into the small cramped car park and switched the engine off.

"You wait in the car," I said as I got out. "Play with your fat cock or something." I laughed, trying to show that I wasn't bothered, that I was still in control.

Chunky shook his head and chuckled. He knew me well enough, but he probably would get one of his porno mags out of the glove compartment and he might even have a sneaky wank under the dashboard. He might also guess that I'd be knocking back a couple of possibly illegal whisky lemonades, so he'd probably give me twenty minutes or so before coming in to get me, unless Adams nagged me first that was.

The bar was more or less deserted, just a tired-looking middle-aged couple sitting nervously with two half pints, at a round table, and a skinny blond man, who I knew too well, at another. Fred, the landlord, had started doing takeaway food during the pandemic, but it never caught on, probably on account of the fact that he couldn't cook, and was too tight to pay a proper chef to do it for him. Shame, he could have done all right for himself, there wasn't another decent café for a mile or so, and it was a fairly well-populated area. Mind you, his prospective client base consisted mostly of tossers from the estates who were either broke or on the rob. I knew them well enough, I'd busted enough of them in my time.

Fred beamed through a set of cracked brown teeth, I suppose that was another reason nobody wanted to eat his chicken curry.

"Bones my boy. Long time no see."

"Aye Fred. How's it going?"

"Scotch and lemonade?"

"Nah Fred, never mind the pop, I'll just have the scotch. A double."

He turned to fill a tumbler from the optic. I looked around the bar. The middle-aged couple were sitting by a window, the woman was looking through it at the traffic passing on the main road outside. The man, I couldn't be bothered to dig his name out of my brain, all jeans and manky T-shirt looked at me and smiled guiltily. I ignored the bastard. The only other drinker was the skinny blond man wearing a smart checked sports jacket, white shirt and thin blue tie, bit posh for him.

Fred slid the tumbler across the bar and waved away my token attempt to pay him.

"On the house, always glad to support you lot. Never know when I'll need you."

I grunted at him and turned away. I think he was relieved. No one wanted to make small-talk with a copper, they never knew what would slip out. Jackie Mann, the blond, was not so lucky though.

"Mind if I pull up a pew Jackie?" I asked, already dragging a stool into place at the small round table he was sitting at.

He shook his head nervously. "No Mr Jones, always a pleasure. I see you've got a drink, can I get you another?"

"In a bit maybe. You're looking smart today, what's up? Can't be court – it's a Saturday."

"Very funny."

I drank half the contents of the tumbler in one gulp and put it down on the table.

"What's new? What's the buzz?" I asked him.

"I don't know nothing Mr Jones. Keeping my head down these days, you know that."

"I do Jackie, I do. But people talk and you've still got ears I assume."

"Are you involved in that nastiness up by the motorway

then Mr . . ."

"Who's asking the questions?" I laughed. "That's my job. Do you know anything about it then?"

"Who? Me? No sir, never sir. Fred was telling me earlier. Pretty girl, he said, shame innit?"

"It's always a fucking shame innit," I mocked, and slugged back the rest of the whisky. "You can get me that drink now. Fred knows what it is. And get me some of that burnt pig-skin stuff too."

"Huh? What's that?"

"Pork scratchings you dumb bastard."

Jackie laughed. "Very funny Mr Jones, very funny."

I didn't really want the scratchings, but what the hell, you had to show them who was in charge, didn't want them getting too fucking complacent. Always squeeze that little bit more out of them, even if it was only the most disgusting pub snack ever invented.

SKIN

"Do you think you can manage the town centre love?"

It took a few seconds for Mandy's words to register. I'd been sitting in the armchair for about half an hour, the main section of the Saturday Guardian still unopened on my lap. "Yeah, of course. What were you thinking?"

"No problem if you can't, I know you had a long night and you're back driving in a few hours."

"Nah, it's all right. Could do with a change of air. Just as good as a rest they say."

"Thought we could just pop in, have a look around, get some of those plum tomatoes you like, from the market. Could get some laverbread too, if there's any there. We haven't had any for ages."

I folded the paper over the arm of the chair and stood up. "Just need a quick slash. Are you ready?"

"I wish you wouldn't use words like that."

"Piss then," I said grinning.

She was a pearl was my Mandy, but she could be a little bit too uptight at times. I kissed her on the cheek as I left the room. She smiled and shook her head.

Fifteen minutes later and we were in the wholefood shop. Mandy was clutching a large bag of lentils and hovering near the smelly soap that she liked so much. I couldn't understand it myself, all the soaps smelled the same anyway, but what did I know. The young woman who ran the place seemed to do all right out of it. She was a natural, just as charming to me as she was to Mandy, and a sexy voice that reminded me of the poor girl who had been in my cab the night before. Besides the lentils Mandy ended up paying more than eight quid for three small bars of soap.

"I could spend all day in there," she said as we left.

"Hmmm, you could spend everything else you've got too," I said.

"Very funny. But wasn't that girl lovely?" she said, as we emerged into the busy street.

"I suppose," I said.

Somebody big bumped into me, it was a proper shock, my fault I suppose, I was thinking about the dead girl again.

"Sorry mate, you OK?"

The big guy had almost knocked me down, but sounded genuinely sorry. I was a bit winded but no real damage.

"Don't worry about it," I said. "I'm fine."

"Crikey," he said, "it's you isn't it, Skin?"

I looked at him more closely. He stepped back and stared at me with a silly grin.

"Shit!" I said, "Shane Hughes. I thought you'd disappeared years ago, abroad somewhere, wasn't it? What are you doing back in Elchurch?"

"Oh, this and that, looking up a few old pals, that sort of thing."

He looked good. He'd always been a hunk, tall and well-built with tight blond curls, like a Greek god reincarnated as a prop-forward. In fact he had once been a promising rugby player, played for the seconds for a couple of years, until he went off for his police training. Never picked it up again. Trained with that prick of a brother of mine. They used to be good friends, until he fell out with Bones over a girl. Disappeared somewhere not long after that.

He was in good shape, older of course, but a couple of stone lighter than he'd been when he was younger, with a nice tan that complemented his hair and his blue eyes. I was aware of Mandy at my side and wondered if she was admiring him as much as I was.

"Oh, this is Mandy," I said, "my missus."

Mandy shrugged and raised her eyebrows high, a habit she'd acquired when wearing a face-mask was normal.

"Well sort of," I said.

"I remember Mandy from around the place. I recognise those lovely eyes." He beamed a charming confident smile at her. "You were very young when I saw you last. You haven't changed at all."

Of course it was bullshit, Mandy was a good-looker, but hardly his type, didn't stop her from lowering her head in embarrassment though.

"Aw thanks," she said quietly.

To save her, and my, blushes, I changed the subject. "So, visiting old pals is it?"

"If you mean that brother of yours, forget it, sorry, but I don't think we'll ever be friends again."

"Don't worry," I said, "it's not like me and him are ever going to share a spliff."

Mandy nudged me. "Ssh Skin, stop it."

Shane laughed. "Fancy a coffee? You can fill me in on the local goss."

"That would be nice, why not."

I'd always liked Shane, he'd been more of an older brother to me than that bastard who shared my blood, before he fucked off that is. Never kept in touch though, who could blame him?

"Coming Mand?" I asked.

"No, I'd better not, got to get a few things, I'll catch up with you later. Where you going?"

"I dunno, maybe the Tinworks Arts Centre, you can usually find a quiet corner in their garden, and they do decent coffee. Fancy that Shane?"

Shane nodded. "Great, could do with a bit of culture."

"You'll be lucky the way things are at the moment," I said.

Shane shrugged. "You never know."

"See you both in a bit then," Mandy said as we walked away.

"I do have an ulterior motive Skin," Shane whispered. "I hope you don't mind."

BONES

Sure enough, Chunky came into the pub after twenty minutes. I must have looked pissed off, because he motioned for me to stay on my stool and went to the bar. Jackie Mann was just leaving, he didn't know it but he had left me with some very useful information, very useful indeed. Chunky came over to the table with another whisky for me and a pint of lager for himself.

"Thanks Chunks."

He winked and smiled at me. Sometimes he could be all right, and he did have good instincts, perhaps he was a decent copper after all, of a sort anyway. He handed me my mobile.

"You left it in the car Boss," he said. "Adams phoned again. I told him you had a sudden lead, had to follow it up, you can always tell him it came to nothing."

Thank fuck for that. I relaxed. Chunky was right in a way, I did have a lead, and it might come to nothing, but then again who knew.

CHAPTER THREE

SKIN

Shane went to the counter to order the coffees. I sat down at a table just outside the rear entrance and waited. I looked across at him through the glass wondering what his 'ulterior motive' was. He caught me staring and smiled. After he ordered he walked back towards the table still smiling at me. He was an impressive looking man and I couldn't help but smile back.

Shane sat down. "Did you want a cake or a biscuit with the coffee? Sorry, I should have asked."

"Nah! I'm all right thanks." I patted my stomach, "besides, I promised Mandy."

Shane laughed. "You look all right to me."

"Um . . ," I mumbled, not sure how to react.

Shane laughed again. "Don't worry, you're not my type."

I smiled and shook my head.

"Now that," Shane said, nodding towards a young Johnny Depp lookalike who was brewing coffee behind the counter, "is where I'm coming from."

I'm not going to say I wasn't surprised, but working as a taxi driver you learn to absorb surprises so I didn't show it. I nodded knowingly and smiled at him again.

Young Johnny Depp came outside and placed the coffee cups on our table, Shane exchanged a flirty glance with him. I picked up a sugar packet from the bowl, tore the top off and tipped the amber crystals into my Americano.

Shane sipped his double Espresso neat. "So, how has it all been?"

I shrugged. "Much as it always is I suppose. Nothing much happens round here."

"Good old Elchurch," he chuckled.

"I don't know about the 'good' bit."

"And what about that brother of yours? Still nicking all the baddies?"

"I suppose he must be," I shrugged, "truth is, we don't have much to do with each other, although, last night . . ."

"Oh yes?" Shane's eyebrows lifted. He waited.

"A girl got murdered last night," I sighed.

"Yes, I saw something about that, on the internet, in the hotel, this morning."

"Hotel?"

"More of a guest house really, it's only temporary, just for a couple of nights. What has the murder got to do with you?"

Shane listened quietly while I explained, nodding and sighing as appropriate. I paused. Suddenly, I couldn't speak. I was overwhelmed with a deep feeling of sadness.

"You OK?" Shane asked gently.

"Yes," I nodded, taking a deep breath.

"OK. I see what you mean about your brother, and all this must have got to you more than you thought," he said softly.

"Sorry, I don't know where that came from. Anyway," I shook myself, "what about you, you said there was another reason . . ."

"Never mind that now. Tell me more about the girl."

I described her again. He looked puzzled.

"Sorry," he said, "did you say her father's name was Bill Mason?"

"Yes, he's a well-known local character, proper dodgy. Why? Do you know him?"

Shane shook his head. "Never mind that now, carry on."

"That's about it," I shrugged.

Shane took a deep breath. "OK, it's like this, you know I went to serve in the Jamaican Police?"

"Yeah," I said, "Sort of."

"Well, I still work for them, but now I am a Special Investigator."

"Oh!" I forgot about the girl for a moment and waited eagerly for him to elaborate.

Shane continued. "I wouldn't, shouldn't, normally tell anyone else this, but I'm on my own here, and when I bumped into you it occurred to me, and I'm shooting from the hip, so don't worry if you can't, but I thought you might be able to help."

I recoiled instinctively. Me? Help the cops?

"I'm not sure about that," I said.

"No, don't worry – listen, I wouldn't ask. It is bad stuff, but all I need from you is a little local info."

"I'm not a grass," I shook my head, "besides I don't know anything about anything like that."

"OK, no worries, but please don't tell anyone else about this conversation. I can manage."

I was relieved but also ashamed that I'd let him down, then I thought that if he really was alone . . . why couldn't he hook up with the local police?

Shane continued. "It's not something I can share with anyone," he said, "including Bones of course, so, if you see him."

I needed to know more, it sounded sort of exciting. "What is it you want?" I asked. "Maybe I've been too quick."

"If you're sure, but remember," he pressed his finger against his lips. "Ssh!"

BONES

"Another? Boss?"

"Nah Chunks. Suppose we'd better get on with it aye?"

"Aye OK. Three pints is about my limit for a daytime, unless it's a day off of course, then I can . . ."

"Yeah yeah, that's enough." I didn't want to encourage the fat bastard. There were lines, mustn't let him take the piss, get too familiar.

Chunky went to the car and I went to empty my bladder. Bit fucking stupid I know, but I couldn't stop fiddling with my phone, checking if it had a decent signal and making sure I hadn't missed a text or a call. Perhaps it wasn't that crazy girl Moira under the bridge after all. I shook myself, I had to get that mangled-up image of her out of my head.

I zipped up, ran my hands under the cold tap for a second then wiped them in my trousers. I checked the phone again on the way across the car park – nothing.

As I put the phone back in my pocket it shrieked the Mission Impossible theme tune. It took me by surprise and I fumbled and dropped it onto the tarmac.

"Fuck!"

I leaned down to pick it up, probably fucking Adams, or . . . no it was that old twat Mason.

"Yeah," I said with a slight snarl.

"Is that fucking you?"

"Yeah, of course."

"Now listen."

"I'm on the way to your house now."

"Just fucking listen."

I listened.

"I'm on the toilet," Mason whispered. "That fucking woman detective is here with Adams. How the fuck am I supposed to operate with her asking stupid questions, for fuck's sake, who does she think I am? Get rid of her, I don't care what you do, just get her off the case, she's cramping my style big time. I don't need your mates sticking their big beaks into this. I'll do it my way, just get fucking rid of her."

"I thought DCI Adams was dealing with it all?"

"He's no bother, he's a pussy compared to that fucking woman. Sort it out."

He rang off before I could object, thank fuck, but how was I going to respond to that? Who did he think I was? He must have been talking about DI Rebecca John, Reb. She was a good officer and was probably running rings around her boss Adams.

I put the phone back in my pocket and walked slowly towards the car. Chunky turned the ignition as I approached.

I got in and shut the door. "Hang on," I said. "Turn the engine off."

"What's up? Who was that on the phone? Was it Adams again?"

"No, it wasn't him. Let me think."

Chunky grunted and fidgeted as we sat in silence for a few minutes. I had more or less the same opinion of Adams that Mason had, that he was all front but when it came to it he was a pushover, Reb on the other hand was tough and wasn't going to budge if she didn't want to, and I didn't have the pull I used to, not since old Davies retired and Bob 'Bastard' Brent took over the division. I didn't know if I'd be able to 'sort it out' as Mason wanted, truth was I felt trapped. I'd have to find a way out, even if I couldn't sort it out.

"Fuck it, let's drive." I nudged Chunky.

SKIN

"OK," Shane said, "I can't give you too much detail yet but there's some seriously bad people involved. I'll tell you if you want but I promise you the less you know the better."

I sighed. He was right; I didn't need or want to know the details, but maybe I would help him after all.

"All I need is some local backup from someone I can trust," Shane explained. "I may not even need you to do anything, just be there if needed. It wouldn't harm to keep your eyes and ears open too."

"All right then," I said. "Just let me know when and where and I'll be there, that's my job after all."

Shane laughed. "That's all I ask, thanks. Did I say there might be a few bob in it?"

"What?"

"Don't panic, just for expenses, loss of earnings, that sort of thing."

I laughed. "Two hundred dollars a day plus expenses," I said in a mock American accent. The idea of acting like a private eye appealed to me a lot.

Shane shook his head. "I do appreciate this," he said, "but please don't take any risks – OK?"

"Don't worry, it's all good," I said smiling, even though I was already having doubts.

BONES

Mason was a very dangerous man, probably a psychopath, or a something-path at least. Sure, I believed he loved his daughter, at least he seemed to care about her a lot going by how aggressively protective he was of her. But there was something about him that didn't chime. If I had been a better copper, or a braver man, or a foolish man perhaps, I would have taken him on years before. As it was, he frightened me, scared me to the core, so I tried to keep a distance, knowing that was just what he wanted, but I was no lackey. If only I'd been able to keep my dirty paws off his daughter. She wasn't worth it in the end. I didn't want to have to deal with all that, but there it was, deal with it was something I had to do.

Mason was still in the same manky dressing-gown he'd been wearing the night before. He still had the same attitude too.

"Where's Adams?" I asked quietly as he ushered us in.

"Fuck Adams," he hissed. "He's not the problem, it's his sidekick, that blonde, get rid of her, she's asking the wrong sort of questions. They're on the patio."

"Reb you mean?" Chunky said. "She's all right."

Mason looked uglier than ever in the harsh daylight. He obviously hadn't slept and the bags under his eyes were as black as his heart and as big as his arse. He was emotional sure, but the emotion was pure anger.

"Someone is taking the piss out of me big time, and that just cannot happen. Do you hear me?"

I moved my eyes to acknowledge.

"Good," he spat the word out and with it a shower of his own spit. Good thing he was paranoid about social distancing or I would have been soaked.

"Good," he said again, turning away. "Now, go and sort it."

Adams and Reb were sitting at a glass table on Mason's patio like they were the Rees-Moggs surveying their estate. The lawn rolled away towards the river at the end of the garden, the whole place was landscaped and manicured like

Buckingham Palace.

Reb was all right; yes, she was Adams' partner against crime, and she was blonde, but she was all right. She was a couple of years older than I was and a proper good cop. If she hadn't been a woman she would be Chief I was sure. I liked her, and it helped that she was gorgeous too. She turned and smiled at us when we approached. I nodded at her.

Chunky looked down at his feet and mumbled something that was probably hello. I think he was intimidated by Reb, strange bloke, he could have crushed her with his big toe, and he could handle his female doppelganger Jan, from the club. well enough, even though she was almost as big as he was and twice as hard.

Reb motioned for us to sit down, but Adams stood up abruptly.

"Well Jones?"

"I'm here aren't I? What do you expect? I was up most of the night."

"Sit down. I'm a bit concerned about something Mr Mason told us."

I stayed standing, so did Adams.

"Is it true that you were having a relationship with the victim, his daughter?"

"Strictly speaking sir," Reb said, "the victim hasn't been identified yet."

"Yes Rebecca, I'm sorry."

"What's the delay?" I asked.

"He says he can't do it, and there doesn't seem to be anyone else, except you perhaps?"

"No, I can't do that, she's nothing to me, not any more anyway. What I mean is . . ."

"It's true then?"

"I wouldn't have called it a relationship, it's finished anyway."

"Why did it finish?"

"It never really got started. She was just a girl, just another girl."

"It should be easy for you then. You can identify the body."

I shrugged.

"And I'll need to speak to you later, all right?"

"All right," I echoed.

"You'd better get going. You know the procedure I'm sure, the body is at the usual place. I'll see you back at the station. As soon as the uniforms come back we're on our way, there's a lot of work to do."

"Bye boys," Reb smiled at us again.

I winked and Chunky mumbled again.

Mason was standing outside near the front porch puffing on a big cigar.

"My only vice," he laughed. He didn't look too distressed.

"Adams and Reb are leaving soon," I said, "but there will be a uniform nearby, and a liaison officer will probably turn up at some point."

"Those I can handle," Mason said, pushing the cigar deep into the soil of a container plant. "And you will go and identify . . .?"

"Yes," I said.

"Make sure you let me know as soon as you're sure. There's a lot at stake here, you know what I mean?"

Chunky drove me back to my flat. I told him to fuck off to the beach or somewhere. I needed to sort the ID of Moira's body by myself, I didn't need anyone else to start analysing my reactions.

I went into my flat, had a piss and a shot of brandy, shook myself, took a deep breath, and headed out to my car to drive to the morgue.

CHAPTER FOUR

SKIN

After taking Mandy home I decided to do a short shift on the cars. Saturday afternoon, and I'd get a couple of fares, probably just carting some old biddies shopping home for them, but it would be good to hang around with the other drivers for a bit. The ranks would be buzzing with gossip, and I might pick up something worthwhile. The chatter was always at its loudest soon after an event, especially after something as dramatic as a murder.

I drove to the rank near the big mall on Wheel Street. Stu was there, and Dave, along with at least a dozen others. Dave was one of my drivers, Stu was an old friend, though we hadn't had much to do with each other since I moved in with Mandy, he was more of a pub mate I suppose and I didn't get to the pub much after I shacked up with her.

Stu was a nice guy, a bit of a Buddhist, always going on about mindfulness or something. Dave used to be a roadie for some mid-list bands in London, but he was a better musician than most of the people he lugged for. No confidence you see.

Dave was the first to greet me. "Hi Skin," he said.

I nodded. "How's things? What's going on?"

Dave shrugged. "It's been quiet so far. Any more on that girl?" he asked.

"Yeah, I had her in the car last night."

"We know," Stu said.

I wasn't surprised, there wasn't much got past them. "Of course, pretty girl too," I said.

"Bastards," Stu said.

"What happened?" Dave asked.

"Some bloody bloke no doubt," Belinda chipped in.

"I don't know Bel, I suppose so."

"You'd better be careful love," Dai Honda, an unpleasant toad of a man, offered his usual feeble attempt at humour.

"Shut up Dai," I said. "It's not funny."

"I wasn't being funny."

"Shut up anyway."

"What's your problem?"

"For Christ's sake boys, give it a rest will you, a girl is dead," Bel said angrily.

"Sorry Bel," I said.

Dai Honda struggled not to react, then slunk back to his car and pretended to take a mobile phone call.

"Wasn't it that bloke's daughter, that bloke who owns the Beach Hotel?" Bel asked.

"Mason, Bill Mason," Stu said.

"Dodgy Bill," Dave added.

"Mad Mason," Belinda said.

"All those things," I said, "and yes, it looks like it was her."

"What was she like?" Bel asked.

"Well," I said, "pretty, like I said. Nice, yes, very nice."

Again I felt that dark rush of emotion. I coughed and looked away to cover my reaction. Then I realised that coughing had taken on a lot more meaning since the pandemic started. I turned back with a smile.

"Something caught in my throat," I said.

Bel and Dave stared at me with puzzled looks. I shrugged.

Suddenly all the drivers sprang into life and hurried to their cars. It was a bit of a surprise.

"The early Bingo," Bel said, touching my arm, "chucking out time."

"Ah yes," I said. "Life goes on."

A couple of minutes later and I was driving a pair of disappointed middle-aged sisters towards the new flats down by the estuary. The women were funny and chatty in the back seat, it sounded like one of them, at least, was a winner, but the flats were ugly, like bad teeth springing from the ground, saved only by external paintwork in bright Mediterranean colours, though, even that was peeling. It must have looked good on paper.

As I drove I decided I'd slope off after that one fare. It was early and there was a lot of business still to come later on that Saturday night, dead girl or not, but hell, half a day earlier, she'd kissed me on the lips with her Pernod and strawberry. That had to be worth a couple of hours off or something.

I didn't feel like making elaborate excuses to Mandy, so I told her I had to go and see my old man, he hadn't looked too good the last time I'd seen him. I switched the radio off and went to see him anyway, it had been a while.

BONES

Jason, a greasy chubby fuckface, moved the trolley into the light. I'd dealt with him a few times before but never like that, never when I was the identifier. He was an idiot, always playing weird classical music.

"What's with the crappy tunes?" I asked

"They like it," he said, waving his arm around the sterile dead room. "Some like jazz but most like . . ."

"Oh, for fuck's sake. Just get on with it," I snapped. I don't have time for this shit."

"I beg your pardon, sorry sir."

He pulled the sheet back.

Its face was grey, it had been tidied up, but was still a bloody bruised mess. Moira's swollen features were obvious.

"Yes," I said, "I'm sure it's her – Moira Mason."

He nodded and covered her up.

SKIN

The old man lived alone in a council bungalow in a quiet cul-de-sac around the corner from the house I grew up in. The front door, as usual, was unlocked. Eric, my dad, was in the compact galley kitchen, sitting on a bar stool stirring a pan of porridge as it spat and bubbled on the gas hob.

He looked around as I entered. "I knew it was you," he said.

"You always say that."

"That's because I always know. Do you want some porridge?"

"Is that all you've got? Do you need some shopping?"

"There's nothing better."

"A man cannot live on porridge alone you know."

"Do you want some? I made too much. I was going to make it with oat milk, then I thought that's daft, it's already oats, so I made it with water, oh and a pinch of salt."

I shook my head. After what he'd been through and was still going through I was surprised he could sound so relaxed.

"Hmm! Yes then," I said, not wanting the porridge but wanting the chance to spend some time with him in case he took a turn for the worse again.

He smiled. "It's just about ready. Pass me a couple of bowls from that shelf over there. The spoons are on the draining board."

We sat in the armchairs in the living-room, bowls on the coffee table, squeezy bottle of golden syrup to hand, and gorged ourselves. He really had made too much.

"How are you?" I asked, hoping for the usual vague response. It was nice to see him but I didn't want the gory details.

"To tell the truth, not too good. Everything is aching, inside and out."

"Have you got enough tablets or whatever?"

"Oh sure, but they don't seem to work as well as they used to, so I have to take more, but it's ok. I'm very lucky really."

I shook my head. "You worry me sometimes."

"Hah! I'm seeing the doctor next week, I can cope. It won't last forever. What about you? How's the lovely Mandy?"

"Good," I said, but it wasn't Mandy's face that came into my mind.

"Are you sure?" He'd noticed I was distracted.

"Yes of course. She's fine, we're fine. Busy. Look, I'm sorry, I haven't been much use lately, just so much to do."

"It's ok. It's nice to know you're busy. Can't be easy with everything that's going on out there, everyone's feeling it, businesses shutting down and people losing their jobs every day," he sighed, "I wonder if it will ever end."

"Ha, you just said it won't last forever."

"Yeah well, both are true, in a way. Everything changes, it's always the same."

I laughed and shook my head.

"Are you doing ok? Keeping your head above water?" he asked.

I hesitated. He didn't need to know the gory details either. It wouldn't do any good for anyone, especially him.

"I worry about you, coping on your own," I said.

"Ah, I'm all right. I've been on my own a while now. I know how to look after myself."

"Five years," I said.

"Doesn't seem that long. By the way, have you seen your brother lately? Is he still as miserable as he always was?"

Again I hesitated, but it came out anyway. I told him about the murder and how I'd seen Bones in the early hours. I kept it simple.

Dad grunted.

"He was just doing his job," I said.

"I never see him."

"Why is that? Do you know?"

He hesitated, stared into space and shook his head. "Nah. He's always been the same, bit of a mummy's boy if you ask me. Anyway, as long as he's all right. Is he still with that woman you told me about? Jill isn't it?"

"I don't think so. But he doesn't really talk to me, I just hear things sometimes, on the grapevine."

"That's a pity," he said. "I don't like to think of him being on his own, he's not as tough as he looks."

"I did bump into his old mate Shane earlier though."

"Shane? Which one was he?"

"Come on Dad, you must remember Shane, they were best friends for a while, he's a cop as well."

He winced with pain. "Ah, that Shane, I know, big bloke. Never really took to him, that one. Something about him."

I was surprised. "Seems like a great bloke to me. Is it because he's gay?"

"Is he? I didn't know. Why do you think I'd be bothered by that anyway, I didn't come down in the last shower you know."

He winced again.

"Are you sure you're all right Dad?" I touched his arm. "Sorry," I said, withdrawing my hand quickly.

"Don't be daft," he said, taking my hand in his and squeezing it. "Just tired. I usually nod off in the afternoon."

"I'd better go anyway. An empty taxi is an empty pocket. I'll call in tomorrow, see how you are, or Monday perhaps. Do you want a lift to the surgery?"

"Don't be silly, it's only down the road, I'm not quite on my last legs."

He pulled his hand away. "Now get going, and if you see that brother of yours . . ."

"What Dad?"

"Nothing really, I'd just like to see him before . . . you know."

"OK," I said. "I'll try."

BONES

I phoned Reb and then Mason to tell them I'd identified the body, neither of them wanted to talk, thank fuck. I sat in the car for ten minutes smoking and tried to get that image from my mind. It wasn't really Moira, not any more at least, just an empty shell, discarded and decomposing. I would need help to shake that off.

SKIN

The old man insisted on seeing me to the door. I walked outside and down the path. When I got to the car I turned and waved.

He smiled. "Great to see you, thanks for coming."

I smiled back, knowing that he was in great pain. By the look of him, unless a miracle happened it was just a matter of time. Poor bugger, he hadn't had it easy. Sure, he used to be an arsehole at times, but aren't we all?

BONES

I needed a drink, needed to kill a few brain cells; hopefully they'd take those images with them. If only I could target them individually, but a cluster bomb would have to do. I decided to drive back to the Carpenters, perhaps even get the bonus of nicking, or at least putting the shits up, one of the hoodlums from the estate on the way. They needed a bit of a slap, been getting far too matter of fact lately. It was easy to fuck them up, that's what the drug laws were for, kept them on their stinking little toes, stopped them thinking about proper crime.

I drove slowly through the quiet streets of the estate, just one or two stragglers clutching 4-packs, heading home before the damp coldness of the night kicked in. Fucking morons. Cheap booze, a ten quid deal, and Ant and Dec, kept most of the twats subdued, and I always knew where to find them. They were creatures of habits, bad habits.

And there he was, standing shiftily at the side of the off-license, my very own Jackie Mann. Maybe it was time to poke him a bit harder, to get him to elaborate on what he'd hinted at earlier. I drove a hundred metres along the road, parked the car and walked softly back towards the shop. I was on him before he knew it.

SKIN

I still couldn't face Mandy so drove to the beach road and parked up in a little spot where I could watch the sea through the windscreen. It was a place I often came to breathe for a while. It didn't usually take long, ten minutes in the car, then another quarter of an hour walking to the edge of the sea and back, depending on the tide of course, and the time of day.

It was too cold, too damp and too overcast to get out of the car, so I sat there checking the news on my mobile phone. But I couldn't focus, it was all just a meaningless blur of pixels. I threw the phone down and it bounced into the gap between the seats. Damn!

I reached into the gap but couldn't get a good grip of it. Reluctantly, I got out of the car and opened the rear door. When I leaned in to reach the phone I noticed something else peeking out from under the front seat. I teased it out with my finger and sat back in the driver's seat to get a better look at it. I thought it was a pocket diary at first but it turned out to be a notebook. I had been too tired to clean the car that morning but had cleaned it the day before, so, of course, I thought it could be hers – Moira's.

I tried to read it in the weak internal light but it didn't make sense. It was half-filled with scribbles and doodles and I couldn't see any clues as to its origins. It didn't look important so I shoved it in the glove compartment with the rest of the flotsam intending to check it out another time.

BONES

Ha ha! The shocked look on Jackie Mann's face almost made me give the game away by laughing out loud, but I kept up the pretence of being a serious police officer. It was the part I played in the cat and mouse game of keeping the streets safe for the average law-abiding citizen.

"Mr Jones. Um," he said fidgeting.

His hand disappeared behind his back. Did he think I hadn't seen that action a thousand times before? He shuffled to obscure my view but the wisp of smoke gave it away. I leant down and picked up what looked like a fairly well-constructed half-smoked spliff.

"Well, well, well, what have we got here," I said. I lifted the spliff to my nose and sniffed.

"Hmm," I said, "primo skunk by the pong of it. Home grown?"

"No, it's not mine Mr Jones . . ."

"You're a proper fucking joker Mr Mann," I said, grabbing his collar and keeping him at arm's length, didn't hurt to be a bit careful even if most of the virus crap was total bullshit.

"Let me see now," I said.

I cupped my hand around the spliff and took a long drag without touching it with my lips – I didn't want to catch anything. I exhaled into his face. "Nice," I said, "what is it? Better than that Vietnamese crap I usually find around here."

"Like I said, I don't know."

"Like you said? Like you said? That's funny that is, your word is gospel isn't it Jackie? Well isn't it?"

I squeezed his collar more tightly. "Now come on, tell me what it is? Hindu Kush is it? White Widow? Old school Skunk? Come on tell me. I could do with a bit of that. Have you got any spare?"

The little polecat tried to struggle free. I squeezed his collar more tightly.

"Stop. Let go. I can't breathe."

I dropped my arm and patted the pockets of his trousers. There was a substantial bulge. I shoved my hand in and pulled out a compressed zip-lock bag the size of a fat satsuma.

"Hmm," I said, turning the package over in my hand, "I'm sure we can sort this out."

"Yes Mr Jones. Anything."

"Good boy Jackie, good boy. But not here. Come on, let's go

and have a quiet chat in the Carpenters, my car is just down the road."

We started walking towards the car. He became agitated and hesitant.

"Sorry, look, please can I meet you there Mr Jones?" he begged. "You know what it's like on the estate, too many eyes."

"No can do, you'll just leg it . . . hmm, on the other hand. Here, give me your phone. I'll drive on, you can have it back when you get there."

Reluctantly, he handed me his phone, a brand new gizmo-laden beast by the look of it.

I nodded. "Impressive. Now fuck off for a minute. I'll see you in the pub."

SKIN

I phoned Mandy. She was OK, quite chirpy really. I told her I was going back to work for the night. I drove to the railway station, there was an Intercity due in. When I got there, there were already a few other drivers waiting including Bel and Dai Honda. As usual Dai was sulking behind the wheel looking pissed off because he wasn't first in line. I pulled up at the end of the queue, walked up to Bel's car and tapped on her window, it slid down.

"Hi Skin," she said. "How are you, you know, after all that?"

"Yeah, I'm cool," I said. "Anything happening?"

"The train is late, of course. Still, it gives me a chance to catch up on my Sudokus," she chuckled.

"Can't get to grips with them myself," I said.

"Good exercise for the brain mun, you should have a go. How's Mandy, I haven't seen her for a while."

"She's good."

"Yes, she is a good woman, you're a lucky man. Come to think of it, she's a lucky girl too, if you know what I mean."

She winked at me.

I laughed. "I'll keep that in mind," I said. "You never know."

I liked Bel, I'd known her a long time, but couldn't imagine getting with her in that way, and of course there was no way she would ever leave her beloved Charlie, aging Hell's Angel and the most honest mechanic I'd ever met. What I did imagine though, was walking hand in hand with Moira Mason, strawberry and Pernod, wind in her hair, her soft skin against mine. I just couldn't get her out of my head.

"You sure you're OK? Bel asked. "You were miles away then. Is it that girl?"

"Um no. I mean, yes, sort of."

"Must have been a hell of a shock for you."

"Yes," I said, "but you get used to that sort of thing in this game. Don't you?"

"Yes. Fucking game it is too."

"You're right. Hey, I forgot to say, guess who I bumped into earlier, literally."

"I dunno."

"Big Shane, remember him?"

"Oh fuck," she said. "Fuck, fuck, fuck!"

"Steady on Bel," I said, "What's up?"

"Bollocks," she said. "Are you sure?"

"Yeah, we had a coffee together and everything."

"Bugger."

"What do you mean?"

"Well, you know that time, before he disappeared, well, we had a thing, nothing serious, but I'd just started going out with Charlie and well, you know, that was the last time, but Charlie, he got very upset, forgave me though, eventually."

"That's funny," I said. "He's gay."

"Huh, well he wasn't gay then, believe you me."

"Yep, straight up," I said. "Deffo."

"I suppose it can happen, good thing in a way. But I hope he doesn't bump into Charlie, you know what he's like, heart of gold, but a mad dog when the heat is on."

"Ah, don't worry, all that was a long time ago."

Dai Honda got out of his car and walked towards us. Bel

grabbed my sleeve.

"You want to watch that one," she whispered. "Just be careful."

"Who? Him?" I asked, nodding towards Dai.

"No, not him. Shane – the big bugger."

"Why?"

Dai was drawing closer.

"Remind me later," she said. "Can't talk now."

BONES

The Carpenters was almost as dead as the morgue – that suited me. I'd be able to have a quiet chat with Jackie Mann, if he turned up. I wondered how much his phone was worth. I still had his bag of weed of course, so I didn't think he'd let me down.

Fred nodded as I entered. "Thirsty day? He asked, already reaching for a whisky glass.

"Aye Fred aye."

I sat at the bar. Fred looked disappointed but resigned to the idea that he had to talk to me. What the fuck did he expect, it was a pub-lic bar.

SKIN

"What's happening boyo . . . and girlo, if that's the right thing to say," Dai Honda chuckled at his own pathetic attempt at humour.

"Don't give up the day job," I said.

"Uh?" he didn't understand.

"What do you fucking want Dai?" Bel asked impatiently.

"Cool head girl . . ."

"Enough of the girl stuff. You might be five years old, in the head at least, but I'm a woman, thank you."

"Cool head woman then," Dai said. "Is that better?"

"Hmm!" Bel grunted. "Bit of respect goes a long way."

"Bit of respect from you would be welcome too," he said.

"Fair enough," Bel said reluctantly. "But what do you want?"

"Just a catch up, we are in the same game," Dai turned to me. "All right Skin?"

"Yep."

"What about last night then? I knocked off early so I missed it all. You found the body didn't you?"

I shook my head. "Nope, I picked her up in town and took her home, that's it."

My phone rang. I stared at the screen, it was an unfamiliar number. I swiped and put the phone to my ear.

"Hello."

"Mr Jones?"

"Yes."

"Ah, it's DCI Adams here, Elchurch CID. Can you talk?"

"Yes," I said walking along the pavement to a quieter spot. "Carry on."

"Can you come to Elchurch Central Police station as soon as possible, I can send a car if you like."

"I've got my own car thanks," I said. "Give me ten minutes."

I disconnected the call and walked back towards Bel and Dai Honda.

"Sorry," I said as I passed them. "I've got to go."

"What's so urgent?" Dai asked as I rushed past.

I ignored him.

BONES

I was just about to go on the hunt for the weasel Jackie Mann when he crept into the pub. I left the bar and walked over to a corner. He followed me. We sat down and I put his phone and his weed on the table between us.

"I suppose you want these back?" I said, looking into his shifty eyes, just to rattle him in advance of any line of questioning that might develop. It was always good to keep those people on their toes, it got them all defensive and sometimes made them babble like a baby.

He lowered his eyes and stared at his stuff hungrily.

"Right then," I said, "let's get down to business. Me and you are going to come to a tidy arrangement. I leave you alone, and you help me and do as you're told. It's simple see."

He looked up at me warily.

"And . . ."

His fucking phone crashed into life with some awful tinny rendition of a techno dance tune. His hand reached out automatically but he stopped himself grabbing hold of it – wise move. I reached across and dismissed the call, it was from someone called Scotty.

"Who's Scotty?" I asked.

"No one," he said.

I laughed.

My own phone rang. I pulled it out of my pocket – it was Adams. I stood up and walked a few steps away from the table to answer the call.

"Can you come to the station, now please," he said. "We need to get on with the investigation and I've got your brother coming in to have a chat, best if you were there. I'm going to need help with all this anyway."

Wow, Adams asking me for help. I was kind of flattered, and a little bit excited. It would be good to be at the heart of things, that way if anything dodgy came up I would be on the plot to limit the damage. This was personal and I didn't want anyone else turning over the wrong rocks.

"Of course," I said. "Give me ten minutes."

I disconnected and went back to the table where Jackie was trembling. I couldn't work out whether he was scared of me or just strung out and needed whatever drugs he normally used to shut his demons up.

"You're off the hook, for now," I said. "Keep your shit, I'll catch up with you again. Watch how you go."

I winked at him. He looked bewildered.

Less than ten minutes later I was sitting in an interview room with fucking Adams, twiddling my thumbs as he was fucking around with his tablet computer pretending to read the various reports coming in from all the strands of the investigation.

There was a tap on the door and Sergeant Elena Jackson came in, ushering my idiot brother before her. I smiled at Elena, I liked her. Skin looked shocked when he saw me. I scowled at him and narrowed my eyes, a warning not to mess with me.

Adams looked up from his tablet and stood up.

"Thanks for coming in," he said. "Please sit down."

Skin looked at me for approval. I shrugged. He sat down.

"I'm just trying to build a picture of whatever happened last night," Adams said. "It's early days of course and while we must move quickly, we also have to be meticulous, so if there's any little detail, whatever it is, it will help us build an accurate picture."

"Sure," Skin said.

"I've seen your initial statement, for what it's worth," Adams said. "Though there's not a lot of detail." He looked disapprovingly at me. "So I just want to start at the beginning, if that's all right?"

"Of course."

CHAPTER FIVE

SKIN

I didn't expect to see Bones when I was shown into the interview room. I was being naïve I suppose, of course he was involved, it was his territory after all.

The Chief Inspector asked me to tell him everything that I remembered about the previous night, perhaps he didn't trust his colleague, my brother.

I repeated everything I'd told Bones, I still didn't mention the strawberry kiss, there was no point complicating things. When I finished, Adams scribbled some notes on a pad and looked up at me.

"Tell me all that again please, particularly about what happened when you dropped her off," Adams said. "Take your time and try not to leave anything out, even if it seems insignificant."

I sighed, what was the point of that?

"All right," I said.

"Thank you," he said.

I repeated what I knew about what were probably the last few minutes of that girl's life. I don't think I said anything new and I still omitted the kiss, I don't know if I was ashamed or embarrassed or both. But then what was there to be embarrassed or ashamed about? It was just a friendly gesture, no more than a peck on the cheek really. Yet still . . .

After Adams was satisfied I left the police station and walked back to where my cab was parked on the road at the rear. I got in and put the key in the ignition. Before I started the engine I took a deep breath in and out in one big sigh. I sat back and closed my eyes, trying to centre myself by focusing on my breathing, like Mandy had tried to teach me many times.

It didn't work. All I could think about was Moira Mason, if I'd been a bit younger and wasn't shacked up with Mandy . . . ah, but Moira was dead of course . . . but then . . .

I was yanked from my imaginings when my car started shaking. I looked up and stared through the windscreen into the hateful eyes of my brother Bones. He was standing at the front of the car, leaning on the bonnet and glowering at me.

I got out of the car and confronted him.

"What's going on Bones? Why are you so angry with me?"

He turned his face away from me before snapping back. "Do you know how weird this is?"

"Everything's weird," I said. "Living, breathing, eating, sleeping, it's all weird."

"Shut the fuck up Skin, you pratt."

"No need for that, I'm just agreeing with you. Yes, this is weird. I don't know how we got here and I don't know how to get back, or at least how to get back to some state of being that isn't weird."

"For fuck's sake," Bones said, "I meant it's weird that every time I turn around lately, you're there fucking things up for me. I've tried my best, with you and with our bastard father. You're like a stupid double-act."

"I wouldn't call him stupid," I said. "Anyway, he's always asking about you, he doesn't understand why you never bother with him. He's quite upset about it."

"Bollocks," Bones said. "He's never been bothered about me, not in that way anyway . . . so just fuck off with all this amateur psychology crap. Just keep out of my way. What I do or don't do is nothing to do with you. You know nothing about my life."

"We used to be close," I said. "You always looked out for me. We told each other everything."

"Well, I grew out of that quick enough."

I thought about my encounter with Shane and almost blurted it out, I don't know why, probably in the hope that it would somehow re-establish some connection with my brother. I didn't like the animosity between us . . . but the solution to that was out of my reach.

"Ah well, I can see there's no point in talking to you," I sighed

"Good," Bones said. "Now fuck off."

"That's what I'm trying to do," I said quietly, defeated.

But then . . .

BONES

I thought stupid bastard Skin had finally got the message. He was staring down at his feet whimpering like a dirty dog.

"Off you pop," I said, and stepped back to let him get in his car.

I waited. He was breathing erratically, as if he was struggling to control himself. He looked up at me. His eyes were hard and cold. Before I could react he pushed me down backwards onto the bonnet and his stinking breath was leaking into my face. His hands were on my neck and I couldn't breathe. With all the strength I could manage I shoved him away. He staggered backwards and for a second it looked like he was going to topple over.

I took the chance and lunged towards him but he sidestepped and it was me who ended up on the floor, still gasping for breath. I looked up at him, hoping for enough time to recover before showing him how bad a mistake he'd just made.

SKIN

What had I just done? What was happening to me? Bones was struggling to get up, a look of pure hate in his eyes. I couldn't blame him for that, I wouldn't have blamed him if he hunted me down and banged me up in one of his stinking cells. But I had to get out of there, get away and take some time to regain my sanity. This was serious, I'd never been so violent before, it was like some crazy maniac had taken control of my body and was using it to destroy everything including myself.

I got back in the car, turned the ignition and drove away in a daze. Ten minutes later I was parked near the bridge that crossed the estuary. It felt as if every one of my nerves was screaming, my hands were shaking involuntarily. I felt sick and my head was throbbing with searing pain.

The skies were dark as I stumbled out of the car. I forced myself to walk towards the marshy wetlands that edged the waters where the sea mingled with the river.

I stared out at what was visible of the gently lapping waters of the estuary and across at the darkened coastline on the opposite bank. It was a different country across the tide, populated by small farms and campsites that edged against the much-praised golden beaches and rocky shoreline.

I thought about how, more than two decades earlier, when I was a young teenager, Bones, who was only eighteen years old himself, let me join him and his friends on a weekend camping trip over there. My father had tried to stop me going but Bones took him aside and said something magic that made him change his mind.

The campsite was not far from the sea in one direction and probably too close to The Bard's Arms in another. I sat outside the pub with Bones and his friends late on the Saturday afternoon. I was drinking shandy and they were knocking back cheap beer, but as the day turned into evening Bones insisted that I go back to the tent with him, leaving his friends to continue drinking themselves into a stupor.

That turned into a memorable night when I walked happily between the dunes with my brother and we chatted like proper friends until it started getting dark. We returned to the campsite again and made a magnificent meal of baked beans that we warmed up in the can over a camping stove and sprinkled with crushed salt and vinegar crisps.

A couple of weeks later Bones left home and went to live in a flat near the police training place. We hardly spent any time together after that, so the memories I had of the dunes and of the crispy beans was a precious one.

What the hell had happened to us?

Maybe my dad Eric would be able to help. I decided to go back to his place and talk to him.

BONES

I managed to get to my feet and watched Skin's car speed away. What the fuck had happened to us? We used to be close. I was proud to be his big brother once, but he turned into a prick. I noticed it when I got my first posting back in the old home town of Elchurch. By then he was already a very busy taxi driver, doing all right, I thought.

Maybe it was because of that time when he got the stupid idea that I was chatting up his missus, although he'd not long met her then. I wasn't coming on to her anyway. Yes, she was cute, and looked quite beautiful in photographs, but there was something dark and mean in her face, and she was the sort of woman who wanted to nail a man down and suck the life out of him. I couldn't be doing with that.

Well, fuck her bullshit, and fuck his too.

I decided to put all that on hold and let things calm down a bit. I'd have to tolerate his nonsense for a little while longer, and I might have to pretend to apologise in some way, but then, when the time was right . . .

Truth was I was rattled by his ferocious attack and the feral look in his eyes. For the first time in my life I was afraid of my younger brother.

My head needed a rest and I was hungry so I phoned Chunky and asked him to meet me in the Tinworks for a quick bite, the place would be empty at that time of day and we could find a quiet corner. I would try to be nice to the wanker, I needed all the support I could get.

SKIN

I knocked the door gently and waited. I guessed it was probably unlocked but wanted to give my old man Eric time to sort himself out. I waited a bit too long and he came shuffling up the passage. He looked very weak when he opened the door, his face was drained and his breathing was laboured. He managed a thin smile.

"Oh, hello," he said. "This is an honour, twice in one day."

"Don't be daft," I said. "It's an honour for me."

He winced. "You wouldn't say . . . never mind, are you coming in?"

What was he on about? But he was already turning to walk back inside. I followed him. He sat down heavily in one of the small cottage armchairs. I'd grown up with those chairs. I remembered my mother had crocheted white doilies to lay over the back to protect the fabric from oily hair stains. The doilies had long since disappeared and the red floral pattern on the upholstery was pretty much faded and grubby all over.

"Take a pew," he said. "I'll make a cuppa. Or do you want a proper drink, I think there's some gin in the cupboard. Not that I can drink any more – not with all the tablets."

"I'll make the tea – you relax."

He sighed.

I went to make a cup of tea for each of us, then sat down in the other chair.

"Well, what's up?" he asked.

"Um, nothing important, just fancied a chat, it's been a weird day."

"What do you mean?"

"Since last night, you know, the girl . . ."

He nodded and took a sip of the tea.

"And I saw Barry just now, when I went into the police station to talk about last night."

"How was he?"

"To tell the truth he was in a really bad mood and I'm sorry to say but I acted very badly too."

"Don't blame yourself. I'm not sure what his problem is, but it's not yours," he sighed. "He used to be such a good kid."

I noticed a tear in the corner of the old man's eyes. It was such a shame that he was so ill. He wasn't really old at all, but it was easier to think of him like that to be able to accept that he might not have long to go, by the way he looked he'd be lucky to reach his sixtieth birthday, poor bugger.

"Your mother used to worry too much about him, he always was a wild card, ever since he left home at least. He hardly saw her even when she was dying."

"I remember that," I said. "He didn't hang about after the funeral either."

My father nodded. He wiped the tears from his eyes. "Did you have a chance to talk to him . . . you know . . . about me?"

"No, sorry. He won't listen to me anyway. When was the last time you saw him?"

"Um," he said, "it was a long time ago, nearly five years."

"God, that is a long time. That's when Mam died."

"I know, I haven't seen him since the funeral."

"Oh, sorry, I didn't realise that."

He shrugged. "We all have our own lives to live I suppose."

A wave of black sadness flooded through me, bringing tears to my own eyes. How could I not have noticed the misery of those that were close to me? I'd been so preoccupied with my own pathetic ambitions of building my business up that I'd been completely negligent. And Bones, he couldn't just be a bastard, could he? He was as much a human being as I was, and with almost identical genetics, so he couldn't possibly be the bad person I thought he was. I was determined I'd confront him properly, in a sympathetic way and try to find out what had gone so wrong for him.

"I'll talk to him, I promise," I said. "I'll make sure he listens."

"Do you want anything to eat," my father asked, "it's nearly supper time for me."

"Nah," I shook my head. I'd better get back to it, it's Saturday after all. Going to be busy tonight."

"Yes," he nodded. "You're a good boy."

BONES

"What's happening Boss?" Chunky asked as he sat down.

I'd already bought two pints from the bar and had ordered two bowls of fries and some extras that I knew he would appreciate. I knew Chunky would love them – anything to feed his fat face or his beer belly always went down well and put him in a receptive mood. I wasn't sure what I expected to get out of the visit to the Tinworks, a bit of goodwill at least I suppose.

"Cheers," he said as he lifted the glass to his mouth. "I was getting a bit thirsty."

"I just wanted to go over where we are so far with the Mason case."

"I thought Adams was in charge of all that."

"He is, at least he thinks he is, but he won't get anywhere without me, I mean, he won't get anywhere without us, me and you, we're like a pair of superheroes."

"Ha ha, that's funny. Can I be Batman boss?"

"Don't be daft Chunks, I'm the boss. You can be Robin, I'll be Batman."

"Fair enough, age before beauty."

"Watch it," I joked, "or you'll be Alfred the butler."

Chunky laughed again and took a long gulp of his beer.

A waiter brought the fries I'd ordered to the table.

"Starters," I said. "Hope you don't mind."

Chunky was already shoving them into his mouth. "Cheers Boss," he mumbled through the chips.

"What else do you fancy?" I asked Chunky.

"You know me," he shrugged. "Whatever's going."

"Good," I said, I've also ordered a jacket potato and veg chilli each for us. Is that all right?"

"Are you joking? Double spuds, yum!"

We talked as we ate. I made a good show of sounding as if I was concerned for him and his life, and weirdly, the more I pretended to be a nice guy, the more I enjoyed it. Hmm, that was something I would have to think about, but for now . . .

"All right Chunks," I said. "This is important. We, me and you that is, know what's going on around here. We know who's who and what's what, isn't that right?"

"Yes Boss."

I nearly lost it when he shovelled a giant forkful of food into his big fat gob. He didn't care what I was saying, I was wasting my time. He would do whatever I told him to do. I didn't need to buy his compliance with anything more than an endless supply of food to top up his fat gut.

I took a breath and forced a smile even though by then I knew I could drop the pretence.

"So, listen now, as I said, this is important."

"Yes Boss."

I needed just one more slow breath to steady myself. I didn't bother with the smile.

"From now on, don't talk to anyone else at the station about what we're doing."

Chunky shrugged. "Fair enough Batman, you're the boss."

It was too easy. I decided to leave it at that but would have to keep a close eye on him.

I was satisfied that I knew how to handle the big bastard. We finished the meal in near silence, except when he asked me if I was going to eat the second half of my baked potato or not. I wasn't. He was pleased with that. I hope I wasn't underestimating him, but he seemed to have the appetite and the brain of a dog.

While he ate I thought about what had happened. Moira's smile came into my mind. Perhaps if I'd been braver and looked after her better she wouldn't have been there, at that time. Why the fuck was I thinking like that? It was going to drive me mad if I carried on. I needed a drink, a serious one.

"I'm off Chunks," I said. "Got to get a bit of kip – a nap at least, I'm knackered after last night. Need to get back on form if we're going to sort this out."

"Aye aye Boss," he said, wiping the last dregs of food off his face with his sleeve.

CHAPTER SIX

SKIN

Instead of going into town or to the station I turned off the radio and drove to the beach. I needed time to think, or at least time to not think about the dead girl. I couldn't shake her face from my head.

I got out of the car and stood at the railings looking out across the estuary. There was nothing much to see, it was dark anyway and the sea was just lolling in the moonlight.

I felt more anxious and sadder than I had since I was a teenager, when the uncertainty of what life had in store for me used to overwhelm me and force me to hide in my room for days at a time. What was happening to me? It was just a brief encounter with a sexy woman's lips, one kiss and I couldn't have done anything to stop it anyway, but it had triggered something desperate inside me. Even if it was real, it was too late, since she was already dead.

Then there was Mandy, why didn't I feel the same way about her? She was supposed to be the love of my life, yet when I imagined her side-by-side with Moira Mason she became a dull shadow. And thinking that made me feel extremely guilty.

Then, of course, my phone rang. It was Mandy. I had to answer.

"Hi Mands," I said. "I'm . . ."

"Where are you? Why aren't you responding to my messages? It's starting to get busy."

"I know, I know. Sorry. I went to see my father."

"Again?"

"It wasn't just that, I had to go to the police station."

"Why?"

"Just to go over what I told them last night. Bones was there, we had a sort of argument."

"Oh for goodness sake, when are you two going to grow

up? You can't let him affect you like this Skin."

"Yeah, I know," I mumbled.

"Are you all right?" she asked. "You sound as if you're down a drain or something."

"Yeah. I've just been thinking about that poor girl . . ."

"Well, stop it, it's got nothing to do with you, all you did was your job. She's nothing to you."

"You're right," I said.

But she wasn't right. Something had changed, I had changed, and Moira Mason had become something to me. I didn't have a clue what was happening but I knew I'd have to deal with it. She was dead and that was the end of it.

"There's a pick up on Pengelli Road, by the Backfields Estate if you're up for it, the guest house place," Mandy said. "But honestly, if you're not, we can manage."

"No," I said, "I'm fine. Who's the pickup?"

"I'm not sure, Angela, the owner, booked it."

BONES

On the way back to my flat in the Docks I called at the big Co-op supermarket and bought a large bottle of whisky. My plan was to whack a few shots back and crash out on the sofa for a couple of hours at least.

I loved the flat I lived in. I'd bought it as an investment a decade earlier, intending to let it out to holidaymakers and other visitors to Elchurch on a nightly or weekly basis. At the time everyone thought the area was going to become the new version of Cardiff Bay, and I thought I was lucky to get one of the so-called luxury apartments. It didn't turn out like that. Most of the flats were empty most of the time, until the owners gave up and either rented them out as normal tenancies or moved in themselves as I had.

Luckily, it turned out to be the perfect community for me to live in. No one bothered anyone else, you could just close the door and seal yourself in, forever if you liked, and it wasn't far from the bars and restaurants in town.

I walked up the stairs to the first floor, opened the door to my home and locked myself in. Half an hour and half a dozen large shots of whisky later I was starting to get a bit pissed and wobbly and accidentally smashed the bottle by knocking it off the kitchen unit.

Fuck. I needed more booze.

I walked from the Docks towards the town centre and instead of grabbing a replacement bottle from one of the corner shops on the way in I decided to knock the back door of Taffies Club.

Jan opened the door and eyed me up with a mixture of loathing and distrust. I wondered what her sometimes boyfriend Chunky had said to her for her to look at me like that.

I pushed past her and headed for the bar.

"Oi," she said, "we're not open yet."

"So what," I said, glowering at her.

She walked away sighing.

I helped myself to shots from the optics as she prepared the club for its busiest night of the week. After a while I got quite drunk and sat at one of the tables in the lounge with a large whisky intending it to be my last, after that I would sober up and hopefully by then I would have forgotten about, or at least come to terms with the death of Moira Mason. Damn her!

Jan came over to the table.

"Sorry, you'll have to get going now, we're opening soon."

I stared up at her. Her features were going in and out of focus and she seemed to be wobbling all over the place.

"Fuck off, leave me alone," I said. "You fucking daft tart, who do you think you are?"

"Don't you fucking talk to me like that. If you don't go now I'm calling the cops."

I laughed. "I am the cops, you silly cow."

I could feel my head falling towards the table. The next thing I remembered was someone shaking me, shoving me, punching me even.

"What the fuck?" I said staggering to my feet.

Chunky's ugly mug was looking back at me.

"Oh hiya Chunks," I said making a grab for him.

He sidestepped and I fell forward onto the floor.

"Come on Boss, you passed out," he said grabbing hold of my arm and pulling me up. "You're drunk, you need to sober up, Adams is on the warpath. He's been trying to contact you for hours."

"Fuck Adams," I said, "and fuck you too."

I lashed out at him and stumbled towards the bar.

I blacked out again.

When I woke every joint in my body felt like it needed oiling and every muscle was screaming.

Where was I?

SKIN

I parked outside the address in Pengelli Road. The small guesthouse was often used as a cheap hotel by visitors to the area. We had a good relationship with the owner Angela. We'd had some nice business from there over the years. I wondered who the passenger would be. I'd collected a few memorable fares from there in the past.

There was the Japanese businessman, or rather head of a multinational company that made electrical assemblies for vehicles. His company had just bought a local factory and his mission was to get to understand the culture from the inside. He stayed in that house for three nights and two full days. I knew because after I picked him up randomly from the train station one Sunday night, he sort of adopted me. He was a proper bundle of energy and despite his bad English and my non-existent Japanese we communicated well.

Then there was the girl from Sydney who was visiting the UK, and particularly Wales, because she had an obsession with castles and dragons. She was adept with a bow and arrow and almost made the Australian Olympic team but had gone into teaching instead.

I waited for nearly five minutes but I didn't mind, it gave

me time to reflect on the past day in a detached way. The time helped my mind to rearrange everything into some sort of understandable pattern.

I didn't notice the customer coming until the front passenger door opened suddenly. Huh, the fare was one of those types then, a bit forward, a bit cheeky. I braced myself for maybe having to deal with trouble of some kind.

The passenger's head entered the car. It was Shane, instantly recognisable from his huge frame.

"Ah," I said, "I didn't know it was you."

"And I was hoping it would be you."

"Hah, so where to then?"

"I dunno," he said. "How about we find a quiet pub somewhere, I wouldn't mind a chat, you can leave the meter running."

"Hmm, why not. There's actually a quietish pub just up the road. The Carpenters, don't know if you remember it from when you lived around here."

"Yeah," I remember. "Why not. Drive on."

BONES

Where was I?

In some dark place lying on an uncomfortable slab.

Shit! Was I dead?

There was some light seeping into the room and I could see a small window and a heavy door. Fuck! I was in a fucking cell. Me, in a fucking cell.

Jesus wept. How? Why?

Then it started to come back to me. Fucking Chunky. He'd done it before. Once, not long after I split up with Lindy, I made him come out with me and I'd got blind drunk and was apparently trying to strangle a waiter in the Asian Grill because he brought me straight rice with my curry instead of half-n-half rice and chips. I still didn't believe it but there were so-called witnesses.

I sat upright, steadied myself, pushed myself off the bed

and stood up. I was just about to scream the place down when the door opened and Chunky walked in looking sheepish and scared.

"Sorry Boss," he said, "let me explain."

"Fucking hamb . . ." I started, intending to let him have it will both barrels, but my head was screaming with pain because my brain felt like it had detached itself and was rattling around inside my skull.

I sat back down on the bed and held my head between my hands.

"Are you ok Boss," Chunky asked.

"No," was all I managed before having to dive face down and bury my face in the shitty mattress.

"Here," he said. "Take these."

I managed to twist my head around enough to see his two fat hands, one of which was holding a cup with steam leaking out of it. I assumed it was coffee. Two round white tablets were sitting in the open palm of his other hand.

"They're a mixture of paracetamol and codeine," he said. "I can get you something stronger if you like. There's plenty in the . . ."

"Shut the fuck up," I said, lunging for the coffee and tablets.

"There's two sugars in the coffee," he said.

I sipped the coffee slowly and crunched the tablets between my teeth so that they would dissolve into my bloodstream more quickly.

"They were going to arrest you," Chunky said. "I had to do something."

"Who were?"

"Couple of uniforms, one of the bar staff called them in, you scared him."

I was starting to regain control of my brain. My head was still throbbing but at least I was on the way to recovering.

"Thanks Chunks," I said quietly. "What time is it?"

"Here," Chunky said, handing me my mobile. "I found it on the back seat of my car."

I grabbed the phone and looked at the screen. It was

nearly 10 o'clock. I must have lost almost three hours. There was also a notification on the screen telling me I'd missed four calls. I checked and two of them were from Mason and the other two from Adams. Shit I was literally trapped between a rock and a hard place as they say. What the fuck, I had nothing left to lose, whatever was going to happen next I was fucked.

"I saw the missed calls, and . . ." Chunky said.

"And what?" I asked impatiently.

"So, I contacted the both of them and told them you'd totally crashed out because you'd been working non-stop since last night and hadn't had a chance to sleep, or even eat."

"Ha ha, good boy. Did they buy it?"

"Yeah, of course. I'm a good liar. You're a good teacher."

He chuckled.

"Thanks," I said.

"Adams was a bit pissed off at first but then he suggested that you clock off for the day. There was nothing new happening with the murder, so it would be better if you were fresh for tomorrow, he said. He asked me to contact you and let you know; I think he needed a break from it all himself."

"Fair enough," I said, but secretly I was already starting to plan alternative approaches to finding out who'd killed Moira and they didn't include any more sleeping on the job.

SKIN

The Carpenters was quiet, it had never really picked up since the early lockdowns. Too much hassle for most people I guessed, especially when everyone had got used to drinking at home.

"All right Fred," I said, as we approached the bar and sat on the barstools.

"Oh hi Skin, how's things?" Fred said.

"Good, yeah, good," I said. "All right here?"

"Can't grumble," he said.

"Hello Fred," Shane said. "Do you remember me?"

Fred narrowed his eyes and looked the big man up and down. He shook his head.

"Might be a better chance if you stood up," I said to Shane.

"Oi!" Fred said.

Shane laughed and stood up to his full height. "Well I haven't been in for donkey's years, so . . ."

"Hang on," Fred said, "Did you used to be . . . what was it now . . . ah, I know, Shane isn't it?"

"Yep, well done, that's who I am."

"You went away didn't you?" Fred asked. "You're a cop aren't you?"

Shane nodded. "Listen," he said, "I'd appreciate it if you didn't mention you've seen me, to anyone, especially Bones, you know him, don't you?"

Fred nodded, "Yeah."

"Or any of the local cops. Please."

"Sure," Fred said, "None of my business anyway."

"Have you seen my brother lately?" I asked.

Fred shook his head, "Can't say I have."

I didn't believe him but at least it showed that he knew how to keep it zipped.

Shane ordered a pint of cider and I asked for a pint of soda and lime cordial. It was an acceptable thing to drink when I was working, no alcohol, and it looked decent, especially with a slice of fresh lime floating in the glass with the ice cubes. Only downside was that it made me piss a lot.

We sat down at the opposite end of the room to the bar and stared back across the almost empty space at Fred as he fiddled around trying to look busy.

"Hang on," I said, "I'd better let Mandy know I'm not available."

I dialled Mandy's mobile number. She didn't answer so I left a message. *Sorry Mands, I can't take any more fares for a while, don't worry, it's all on the clock. I'll let you know when I'm available.*

"Well, what's up?" I asked Shane.

"Um, pity you're not on good terms with your brother," he

said. "It would be good to have a line to the inside. Do you think there's any chance?"

I shook my head, "Not after today."

"Why, what happened?"

"We had a fight."

"You mean you argued."

"Well yes, but it got physical."

"Seriously?"

"Yep, it wasn't pretty."

"Bummer."

"Listen," I said, "I do want to help you, I can see how important it is, but no matter how bad it gets between me and Bones I really don't want to do anything that will get him into serious trouble."

"No," Shane said. "That won't happen. He's a good cop, and underneath all that anger he's a good bloke. The powers-that-be are aware of that. The reason we want to keep it from him and everyone else in the Elchurch division is because we're not sure how deep the rot goes and a casual remark might alert the real villains."

I nodded.

"So if you can just ask around, be observant. Talk to people, I mean, not directly, but you know."

"I get it," I said. "All right, I'll keep my eyes open, and my ears. I can't promise anything . . ."

My phone pinged with a text message. I opened it. It was from Mandy asking me how long I was going to be.

"I'd better get back to work," I said. "Have we finished?"

"Oh yes, sorry, I think that's it, for now."

"I'll drop you off back in Pengelli Road," I said.

"No, it's fine, I could do with the exercise. I'll walk back to the car with you though, then I'll go for a wander."

We said goodbye to Fred and headed out to the car. I got behind the wheel, closed the door, opened the window and started the engine.

"Where will you go?" I asked.

"I'm not sure. But if I remember right, there's a lane at the side of the pub that leads to the Parade. Is Carlo's Chip Shop still there?"

"Yes, but it's not Carlo's anymore, his son Salvatore runs it now, since the old man retired a couple of years ago."

"That's great," Shane said. "I used to know Sal, he's sound. Might be good to have a catch up with him too."

"You've got my number now," I said, "and I've got yours. I'll be in touch if anything comes up."

"Great," Shane said. "Here!" He tossed an envelope past me onto the front passenger seat. "This should cover any business you've lost tonight. I've got a tidy budget for this job so might as well make the most of it."

"Don't be daft," I said. "You're a mate."

I reached over to get the envelope intending to give it back but he walked away too quickly and was gone down the lane before I had a chance to return it. I ripped the envelope open and counted the money. There were ten twenty-pound notes in there, not bad for a couple of hours work.

I switched the radio back on and checked in with Mandy, it was nearly ten o'clock and I knew it would get busy soon, as busy as it got anyway.

BONES

I said goodnight to Chunky and went back to my flat in the Docks. I had the idea that Mason knew a lot more about what had happened than he was admitting. He was a cold-hearted fucker, so I knew he was capable of anything. Could he have murdered his own daughter?

I turned everything over in my mind, trying to be methodical and detached about it, but my thoughts were constantly interrupted by Moira's lovely face with those sweet lips and deep dark eyes.

I shook myself. No, I couldn't go down that road, if I was to have any chance of finding out the truth I had to keep things professional and unemotional.

Whatever else was true I knew that Mason was keeping something back, and if he really wanted to find out who'd killed his Moira he would have to share it, with me at least, even if we kept it from the main investigation. Surely he would be reasonable when I explained everything, and if he wasn't then that might be an indication that he was guilty of something.

Thinking like that, like a police officer sifting through all the facts and then mentally testing the theories that came out of them gave me a boost. It was what I was good at. I actually enjoyed police work. The complication in this case was my personal involvement. That didn't help, but then my relationship with Mason was bound to be beneficial for the investigation in the long run, so on balance it was probably a positive thing that I was involved with his daughter.

I didn't really have any choice. I would have to go and see him again and demand answers that made sense. But first I needed to rest properly. He could wait until the morning.

CHAPTER SEVEN

SKIN

Over the next couple of hours I trawled the town and picked up enough fares to justify my existence as a cab driver but my heart wasn't in the job.

I called Mandy, she said it wasn't too busy since many of the pubs and clubs closed earlier on Saturdays and things were still quiet anyway because of the knock-on effects of the virus. I'd already earned two hundred quid from Shane so she suggested I come back to base and relax on dispatch until close of play. It was nearly midnight.

When I got in I sat down heavily on the sofa in the office with a big sigh, it had been a very strange and stressful 24 hours.

Mandy was a darling.

"I can see you're knackered," she said. "Why don't you knock off now and have an early night, well, early for you anyway. I'll look after everything, I'm still wide awake."

I sighed.

"What's up?" she asked.

"Oh, nothing really, it's been a long day, that's all."

"I don't know Skin, you've been very weird after last night, maybe it's affected you, you know, the fact that you might be the last person to have seen that girl alive, except for the killer, if that's what . . ."

"Shut up," I snapped. "You don't know anything about it."

Mandy was taken aback at my reaction. So was I.

"I'm sorry, I don't know where that came from," I said.

"Hmm, I've read about this sort of thing, it's probably some kind of PTSD, a delayed reaction at least."

"Huh? Don't be daft."

"No, it's weird, the smallest thing can set it off. You might need some kind of therapy."

"Are you serious?"

"Or, perhaps it's just tiredness, over-tiredness, nothing a good night's sleep won't cure."

"You know what, I think you're right, thanks."

I wasn't really that knackered, physically anyway, but I needed some proper rest, if only to give my head and my emotions a break. I hoped I could get to sleep.

BONES

I woke about six on Sunday morning still thinking about Moira Mason and her father. She could be crazy and scary at times but there was something about her that made me feel properly alive. I found it difficult to think of her as dead. That twat of a brother was still on my mind as well. The altercation with him had rattled me to the core and stirred up all the old feelings of disappointment and dejection I'd had to grow up with.

Skin had always been the favourite, ever since he was born when I was nearly five years old. After he came into my family's life everything changed, it was like I was no longer needed. My mother was the worst, she seemed to be constantly snapping at me, yelling and criticising until I gave up trying to get her to love me and became a sulky surly child, that's how she used to describe me anyway.

At first my father stepped in to fill the void left by my mother's lack of affection but later on, as I grew up and he started drinking a lot more . . . I shivered, I didn't want to think about all that. It was done, I'd grown up and moved on.

Maybe I should have stayed away, not taken the Elchurch post when it was offered to me. I was doing all right where I was. I made a mistake, but never mind, when this was over and Moira's murder was resolved I'd ask for a transfer. I was getting stale anyway, been in the same job in the same place for too long.

I made myself a cup of tea and ate some toast with peanut butter. Then I had a good long shower and dressed in my

Sunday best jeans and T-shirt, it was time to confront Mr Mason.

SKIN

I woke around six on Sunday morning still thinking about Moira Mason. Maybe Mandy was right, maybe I did need some sort of therapy But that was stupid, the girl was just another fare, I'd spent less than fifteen minutes in her company and for most of that time she was in the back of the cab and I was concentrating on driving.

Bones was still on my mind too, the guilt of how I'd attacked him had grown overnight. I needed to find the courage to confront him and sort it out once and for all. It wasn't fair on our father for one thing. I knew he had a soft spot for Bones, they'd been very close once.

Mandy had arranged things so that I could have the whole day off. It was never very busy on a Sunday anyway, the biggest problem was the lack of drivers prepared to give up the one day of the week they had a chance to catch up with their real lives. It wasn't easy being a jobbing cabbie, I knew all about that so didn't like to put pressure on any of them to work when I could do it myself. It also saved money in wages of course. But Mandy had had a word with Dave and he'd volunteered to cover. He was a good bloke.

I tried to relax and distract myself but it was no good, Moira's image just wouldn't leave me alone. Her physical beauty, her presence, her vibe, aura, whatever it was, had connected with something inside me that I didn't know was there. I would have to do something to put those feelings behind me if I was to have any chance of getting on with any kind of life that made sense.

Maybe it would pass naturally in a couple of days, maybe it would cripple me emotionally forever. I'd been there before, when I was just sixteen years old I fell in love with a girl from school, at least I thought it was love at the time, turned out it was all in my head, she had her eye on a so-called punk guitarist. They got married in the end. The spell lasted until I saw them together one day with a grubby infant. I still remembered the pain.

I went back to bed and dozed on and off listening to the radio. The murder made the national news. There were no further developments according to the reports. Perhaps, like any other job, the real players only worked Monday to Friday, nine to five, so it was kind of on hold for the weekend.

Despite everything else she was doing, Mandy managed to knock up a nice dhal for a late lunch. That made me feel very guilty, there I was moping around after a young woman who didn't even exist and there she was making sure I was nourished both physically and mentally.

I had to find a way to shake myself out of those doldrums, so around tea time I told Mandy I was going to visit my old man again.

"Might do you good," she said. "Does your father still drink?"

"I think he still has a glass now and again, but I'm not sure."

"Well, there's a bottle of whisky in the cupboard next to the sink," she said. "It's been there for months. You could take that and share a tot or two with him. Not too much mind. You won't have to drive, I'll get Dave to ferry you there and back whenever you're ready."

Wow, she'd thought of everything.

"That's cool, thanks," I said. "My father will like that."

I had no intention of going to see my father. But I had just decided to go out and get pissed in the hope that it would jerk me out of whatever state of mind I'd allowed myself to fall into. I justified my sneaky plans by convincing myself that I needed to get past the trauma, if that was what it was, so that my relationship with Mandy could get back on track and even improve. Perhaps after I got my head together I would ask her to marry me properly once and for all.

An hour later after I'd showered and shaved at Mandy's

insistence, I got into Dave's car clutching the whisky bottle in a manky used carrier bag, like an old-fashioned alcoholic.

"Where to boss?" Dave asked. "Your old man's is it?"

"Nah," I said. "Just drive . . . ok . . . drive towards town. Actually I want to go to the Tinworks Arts Centre. Yes, that'll do."

If I was lucky I could sit out in the garden of the Tinworks with all the smokers and drink my whisky in peace. I'd nick an empty glass first, just to make it look respectable. Fuck it, yeah, I was going to get pissed.

Dave drove in silence while I drifted off thinking about Moira Mason and what could have been.

"Are you ok Skin?" Dave asked eventually.

"What do you mean?"

"You know, after everything. Must have been a massive shock to you."

I sighed. "I suppose so, especially because . . ."

"What's that Skin? Did something happen?"

I sighed again. "It was just a kiss, but, oh I dunno."

"A-ha, crazy."

"Yes, well she kissed me when she got out of the car. I can still taste her lipstick. It's weird but I can't get her out of my head."

Dave stopped the car. We were in the car park at the back of the Tinworks.

"That'll be the shock," he said. "It'll go soon enough."

"I hope so," I said.

I got out of the car and turned back to talk to Dave.

"Don't tell Mandy where you dropped me off, she still thinks I'm going to my father's house."

Dave's eyes rolled above his mask. "OK boss," he winked.

I laughed, the cure to my misery had already kicked in.

BONES

I drove towards Mason's house. I was convinced he knew a lot more than he was letting on about his daughter's death.

Considering what he was and the sort of shady people he was involved with it was impossible to believe there was no connection between him and whoever killed Moira.

I stopped the car on the edge of the close and scoped the area. There was a patrol car parked outside Mason's mansion and a uniform was standing nearby idly playing with his phone. I should have known that a police presence at the home of the victim would still be in force, it was all very fresh after all.

Murder investigations could sometimes take years but it was proper procedure to focus as many resources as possible in the early days while everything was still fresh. You never knew what bits of information and physical evidence would be useful in the later stages.

I would have to lure Mason out of there, away from my police colleagues and away from his associates and minders. I needed to think, I needed to plan.

I checked myself. I was becoming more obsessed with Moira, dead Moira at least, shame I wasn't so fond of her when she was alive. Was there something wrong with me? Had I developed some sort of mental illness? I just couldn't get her out of my mind. Maybe she was the only chance since Lindy I'd had for some kind of happiness and peace, and I'd gone and let it all go because I was afraid of her father?

I was afraid of her father? Was I? Is that what all this was about? Fucksake, I was supposed to be a professional police detective, there was nothing I hadn't seen, no psychopath I hadn't dealt with. What the fuck was the matter with me? Scared of an ugly old twat like that!

Afraid or not, if I was to 'lure' him somewhere for questioning, interrogation more like, where would it be? There was always my flat? But then how would I get him into the building and then up the stairs and even if I could do that how would I persuade him to talk with me, to tell me his darkest secrets. No, it had to be somewhere more isolated, more remote, where the possibility of anyone else sticking their nose in was non-existent, or minimal at least.

Then I remembered about the old biscuit factory out of

town on the edge of the Northern Valleys. The owners had been importing a lot more than the ingredients for custard creams, and distributing them to customers that didn't own corner shops and supermarkets. The place had been sealed up for more than two years but the case had been finally dealt with a few months earlier and the not so jammie dodgers had been locked up for a good stretch.

Yes, if I was remembering the location and layout properly it would be perfect, not far from the main road on a quiet stretch and nestling behind a strip of evergreens, the building contained enough different spaces to ensure that at least one of them would be sufficient to keep someone isolated for long enough.

All I need to do was to figure out how to lure the old bastard to the biscuit factory and then how to keep him under control long enough to get the answers I needed.

I realised I'd have to do some preparation so turned the car around and headed for the out-of-town shopping centre where I should be able to find everything I needed.

I would need some food, or at least water, enough to last a few days perhaps? Maybe a blanket or a duvet. Was it cold enough to need a heater of some sort? Would there be a clean water supply? And what about toilet facilities?

Hold on, was I going fucking mad? Why was I thinking like that? Blankets, food, water, kidnap, what the fuck? Jesus Christ, what had I become? Was I losing it? But no, compared to all the other nonsense that passed for normal out there in the bonkers world why shouldn't the way I saw things be 'normal'?

Skin told me once, when we used to be at least civil to each other, that life is an illusion, it's a collection of experiences that we have to make sense of somehow, something like that anyway. He said that everything was just as important as everything else. I couldn't really see it myself, surely some things, some people even, are worthless, or worse than worthless, if the actions they took damaged society or too many other people.

I'm not sure I got what Skin was going on about, it all

sounded like bollocks to me, probably something to do with the yoga guru stuff he was dabbling in at the time.

Anyway, the point was that I had to prepare for any eventuality. Fair enough I needed to find a way to get Mason to take up residence in my factory, but then I would need information, more information. Most of all I needed to know more about what happened to Moira.

I had a think about it all. The conclusion I came to was that I just had to do what I had to do, whether it made sense or not. I needed to find out exactly how Moira was killed and exactly who was responsible. I already knew the answer of course, at least to the second part of the question, and the bastard who was responsible was without a doubt Mason.

So there we had it, the crime, the solution, the verdict, and last of all, the sentence. Was that up to me too? Would I have to mete out the punishment? And if so, what form would it take? Imprisonment? Forty lashes? A bullet in the head? What?

Moira, Moira, Moira, that's all I could think about, her beautiful face, her wicked smile, the bloody mess. What had happened to her had become the dominant feature of my life. What was next?

I carried on driving up to the biscuit factory and parked my car where it wouldn't be seen from the main road. It was an old building and had been vandalised since it became empty, so it didn't take long to find a door with a broken lock near the loading bay at the back. According to the debris that had been blown up against the door, no one had been through it for months. I was confident it was safe to go in and that I'd find the right part of the factory to use.

Behind the doors of the loading bay, there was a space the size of a couple of tennis courts with boxes and crates scattered all over it. These were the remnants of the containers that had once been used to pack and ship the company's products, both the crumbly creations and the harder substances. I walked further along the desolate factory floor and into a large area that once housed an array of mixing, cooking and packing machinery that had since been broken down and sold off to other factories or for scrap.

Around the walls of the manufacturing space were eight rooms of various sizes with clear perspex panels facing the shop floor. These rooms were designed to house the offices, canteens, toilets and rest rooms of the management and the workforce, though some had been re-appropriated to cut the pure product with worthless and sometimes dangerous bulking agents.

There was one particular room where the windows were covered in fake frosted glass and the inside was furnished with heavy metal desks and filing cabinets. I shoved a few things around and made a space about the size of a double bedroom enclosed by the furniture. Then I went to the car to retrieve the items I'd bought, and brought them back to my interrogation room to prepare it for its guest.

By the time I'd finished the preparations it was nearly 5 o'clock. I went back to the car and headed back to my flat in the Docks to finalise my plans.

CHAPTER EIGHT

SKIN

I didn't have the guts to drink from the whisky bottle, because I didn't want to be embarrassed if one of the staff pulled me up about it. That was a stupid attitude because although the Tinworks had a bar of its own it was still a publically subsidised arts centre and visitors often brought their own packed lunches to munch in the café-bar.

After sitting self-consciously at a small wooden table in the garden I went inside and ordered a pint of strong artisan beer. It wasn't cheap but as beers went it was pretty good.

I walked over to the end of one of the long canteen-style tables they had in there. I sat down and sipped the brew while taking in the comings and goings. I wasn't a regular in the Tinworks but did visit a few times a year, usually when Mandy dragged me to some arty film or performance, but I did know, in an acquaintance sort of way, quite a few of the people who were regulars, mostly because I had ferried them back to their lairs at the end of boozy nights. I nodded at some of them as they tripped past on their missions to and from the bar or the café, or the toilet.

One of them, a punky girl in her late twenties, plonked herself down in the seat opposite me. Her name was Raskal, or that's what she'd told me. I knew her birth name was Delia something because she'd used her debit card to pay for a fare once or twice. She was quite tall, full-figured with short spiky blonde hair.

"Hi Harry," she said. "Or do you prefer Skin?"

"Whatever suits you," I said.

"What are you up to?" she asked bluntly.

I shrugged. "Nothing," I said.

"Fancy a party?"

I hesitated. A party could mean so many things, the most

likely being a piss-up in someone's house.

"What sort of party?" I asked.

"Don't worry," she said. "It will be civilised and we are all well-behaved, well in most ways," she winked.

"Where? When?" I asked.

"At my place. Now."

"Down by the estuary?"

"No, I've moved, it's a shared house. I've known most of them since Uni. It's not far, Copper Street, do you know it?"

"Yeah," I said, "I'm a taxi driver, remember?"

She giggled. "Ha ha, I'm a proper div sometimes."

I liked her. She seemed warm-hearted and had a kind smile, besides, she was kinda cute.

"Just wondering," I asked, "What made you ask me?"

"Well, we need more people, and you looked like you needed a bit of company. But . . ."

"No, it's cool," I said. "Sounds great."

"Drink up then," she commanded. "Quick now!"

"Yes ma'am." I said, lifting the glass to my lips and chunking it down.

"We'll have to stop for more booze on the way," Raskal said, as we were leaving the Tinworks.

"Will this do?" I asked, extracting the bottle of whisky from under my coat.

She laughed. "It's a start."

We did stop off for more booze, a couple of bottles of red and a 4-pack of cider. Raskal put her arm in mine as we walked to her house through the terraces. It felt natural, but I thought of Mandy and it made me a bit uncomfortable. But then I decided that there was nothing unfaithful about being friendly with another woman, not everything was about sex.

There were about a dozen people at the house, I recognised some of them from the bars around town and from the Tinworks in particular. They were probably arty types, or musicians since most of them were more likely to be serving behind the bars than imbibing in front of them. I suppose they deserved a night off now and again. I was reluctant at first but everyone really did seem civilised and well-behaved.

BONES

I took a pizza from the freezer and slid it into the oven to cook, then I went online to see if there were any updates about the death of Moira. The news was still in Sunday mode so there were no fresh reports as far as I could tell.

I logged onto my social media accounts. I always used an alias for all of them because of my position as a police officer and my general distrust of every other person in the world. In any case I was mostly a lurker, preferring to read rather than post anything or engage with other posts, except for the odd like or share of something, usually non-controversial, just to keep up appearances.

Moira was on Facebook too, and my alter-ego had tried to make friends with her, but she was hardly active and didn't respond. I'd never mentioned it, I'd already told her, and everyone else who asked, that I wasn't signed up to any of that sort of nonsense so she wouldn't have known it was me anyway.

Someone who had accepted my friend request was Mandy. She didn't know that Jack Regan, postal worker, was actually her partner Skin's brother. It wasn't like I was deliberately stalking her or anything, I'd just stumbled upon her through other local friends and followers. But still, you never knew when such a connection could become useful.

Skin had a very minor presence on social media as far as I could tell, at least he didn't seem to make any of his posts public, but now and again his name cropped up in an online conversation involving Mandy. When I checked her profile there was nothing much going on there, but I did notice she'd been asking questions about financial advisors.

It was time. I realised I was distracting myself online. I needed to put my plans into action, now that most of the preparations were done it was time to move in on Mason. It had to start with a phone call, a bit crass but it worked, as the old saying went: KISS, *'Keep It Simple Stupid'*.

"Yes?" Bill Mason spat into the phone.

"It's me."

"I fucking know who it is, it says so on the screen. What do you want?"

"I need to talk to you. It's important – and urgent."

"If it's urgent then tell me now."

"Not a good idea, you don't know who's listening and it's best no one else gets involved. This is something you need to deal with personally."

"Fuck's sake Jones."

"Seriously," I said, "You'll want to listen to what I've got to say. It's about what happened, you know, I think I know who's responsible."

"Right, um," he hesitated. "Might be a bit difficult, there's still a cop out the front . . ."

"Well, if you can't . . ."

"No, wait, all right. Where? When?"

"Give me half an hour," I said. "There's a transport café just off that big lay-by on the road to the Northern Valleys. I'll make my way there now. Do you know it?"

"Yeah, they do a lovely sausage sandwich."

"Not by the café, it'll be closed anyway. I'll be in the car park, near the trees at the back."

"What about the cop?"

"Well you're not under house arrest are you?"

"Fuck no."

"Well just tell him to fuck off, there's nothing he can do about it."

"It will be a pleasure," he chuckled.

Daft bastard, I thought.

There was just one more item I needed before heading off to the rendezvous.

SKIN

More people arrived at the party house over the next hour or two and the stocks of alcohol increased. I should have just left and gone home for my own safety, but I'd been drinking a lot and was over my limit, my limit of common sense anyway. It got to the dangerous point where I forgot or didn't care about the risks of getting legless. I had tried to slow down the pace of my boozing, but Raskal was always there topping me up and egging me on. I didn't mind, she was brilliant company, full of fun, and besides, the attention she was giving me was flattering.

It got a bit crowded in the downstairs rooms so I didn't resist when Raskal took my hand and led me upstairs to one of the bedrooms. After we went in she pushed the door shut and produced a long fat spliff. She sat down next to me on the bed and sparked it up.

I managed two deep tokes before falling back on the bed totally stoned. Raskal flopped back next to me and kissed my cheek. I turned towards her and kissed her back on her lips. She crawled over me and rubbed her body against mine. I responded, reluctantly at first then with all the energy of a randy teenager.

I managed two deep tokes before falling back on the bed totally stoned. Raskal flopped back next to me and kissed my cheek. I turned towards her and kissed her on her lips. She crawled over me and rubbed her body against mine. I responded, reluctantly at first, then with all the energy of a randy teenager.

Despite trying to control the pace of our love-making, less than ten minutes later we were both done. She rolled off me and lay quietly staring at the ceiling for a minute before getting up and redressing.

"That was nice," she said, kissing me on the lips. "I'm off to the bog."

She didn't come back and I was too embarrassed to look for her so I crept downstairs and stumbled out through the front door. I was still drunk and stoned so decided to walk home to give me time to sober up and get straight before fronting up to Mandy.

I felt ashamed and guilty. Strangely, the guilt was because I'd betrayed Moira Mason not because I'd cheated on Mandy. I rationalised everything by telling myself that I was indeed suffering from PTSD. That helped me to feel better. I knew I was kidding myself but I'd deal with the reality later.

BONES

The gun along with the ammo was still wrapped tightly in the paper and plastic bags where I'd buried it five years earlier at the bottom of an old suitcase. I'd spent some time with the armed response team based in HQ so I knew how to handle it. It had come my way later after a successful raid on a cottage in the valleys that had been used to co-ordinate a people-smuggling operation. I'd found it under the kitchen sink during the search and tucked it into my pocket, more out of nostalgia than anything else.

I unwrapped the weapon and felt its reassuringly deadly weight in my hand. A sense of purpose came over me. Despite the obvious dangers I was about to expose myself to it was thrilling to be embarking on my little adventure. This was the kind of thing I was trained for and it was going to be a huge pleasure to finally get the upper hand with Mason.

I made sure that everything I would need was in the boot of the car and set off for the rendezvous with the bastard who was responsible for the death of the only woman who had meant anything to me since my marriage ended. Why oh why had I let them go, Moira and Lindy, and Jill to some extent.

Mason was indirectly responsible for the end of my marriage too. It wasn't long after he'd moved into the area and I was assigned to keep him under surveillance following tip-offs from the West Midlands Police. It meant I had to spend nights away from home. That led to arguments between me and Lindy and then her finding other things to keep her occupied when I wasn't there.

When I came home unexpectedly one night she was busy doing one of those other things and I lost my temper big time.

She, and the twat she was with, ended up in A & E that night. Luckily they didn't take it any further. It wasn't my fault anyway, they just panicked and fell over, but that was the end of us. It would be good to finally pay Mason back for that and for all the other grief he'd caused me in the years since.

As I was driving towards the lay-by I passed a familiar figure walking haphazardly along the pavement on the outskirts of the town centre. I slowed down and checked in the rear-view mirror as I drove past. Yes, it was that wanker brother of mine – Skin. I wondered what he'd been doing to end up walking alone along the backstreets of Elchurch on a Sunday night.

Never mind, he'd keep.

SKIN

I wasn't too drunk to notice my brother's car slowing down as it passed me. At first I thought it was one of my drivers and I put my head down and stared at my feet to stop them recognising me, I was relieved to realise it was just Bones, trawling the streets as usual in his flashy Beamer. Thank fuck he soon sped up and disappeared along the road.

I carried on in my own bubble, sobering up a little more with every step, until I arrived at the junction that would take me in one direction to my father's house and in the other to my own home. I wondered if I could redeem myself by actually going to see my dad, as I'd told Mandy I was going to do. I could have a cup of coffee there and call Dave to pick me up and take me home. Hopefully Mandy would accept the story that I'd been with my father the whole time. Then I would have time to think about what had happened with Raskal and about what was happening with my feelings for the dead Moira.

I paused and thought about my options, that way or the other way? I already knew the answer, it was too late to go anywhere but home. I started walking in that direction when another car slowed down as it was passing me. It was a shiny new hybrid in a dark red as far as I could make out under the streetlights.

The driver's door opened and a tall man got out into the road. It was Shane.

"What?" I said.

"It's a hire car," he said. "Just for the day. I've been revisiting all the old haunts, there's been lots of change, hasn't there?"

I shrugged. "Yeah," I grunted.

"Can I give you a lift?" he asked. "I wanted a word anyway."

"All right," I said.

It meant that I could adjust my story and tell Mandy I'd bumped into Shane and he'd needed a chat. There was a risk I'd have to tell her what he was asking me to do, but that was worth it if it meant I could throw her off the scent of my unfaithfulness.

"Hop in," he said. "We can go to the Carpenters if it's still open."

"Should be," I said. "What time is it?"

"Nearly ten o'clock."

"All right then, not sure if I want anything to drink though."

"Over the top already eh!" He chuckled.

I got into the car and Shane drove towards the pub.

"Been anywhere interesting?" he asked.

I smiled to myself. It had certainly been interesting.

BONES

My plan was working. The lights from the main road didn't reach the back of the car park. The café was closed and the car park was dark. I parked on the rough surface as close as I could get to the trees. I retrieved what I'd need, including the ropes and the gun, from the boot of the car and sat on the bonnet and waited.

Ten minutes later Mason's huge classic Merc drifted into the car park, its too bright headlights hurting my eyes as it approached me. The car stopped a few metres away from mine and thankfully Mason turned the engine and the lights off. The sky was clear and the area was remote so there was enough light from the stars and the almost full moon to take away the danger of total darkness.

I walked over to his car, more to check he wasn't carrying any unwanted guests than to greet him. As far as I could tell he had come alone. The driver's door opened and the ugly fucker got out.

He was full of bluster and self-importance as usual. It amused me to think that in less than a few minutes he would be trussed up and gagged in my boot and on the way to the biscuit factory.

"Well," he said, "this had better be fucking good, dragging me out here like this. And where's your fucking mask?"

"I wouldn't worry about a mask if I was were you," I said, pulling the gun from where it had been tucked in the back of my trousers and pointing it at him.

"What the fuck is that? Is it loaded?"

"Yes," I said, "now shut up and put your hands up."

"Fuck you," he said, moving threateningly towards me.

I was ready for that. The gun would still make a distinctive pop but there was no one around to hear it. I pointed the gun at the ground a few centimetres from his feet and pulled the trigger. The bullet hit a buried stone and ricocheted into the trees.

He stopped and stepped backwards.

"Don't move. Give me the car keys," I said. "Quick."

"Here," he said. "Take it easy, you'll regret this."

I took the keys from his extended hand with my free hand while training the gun at his forehead with the other.

"Now, turn around and walk back towards your car. Keep your hands where I can see them."

Suddenly he dropped to his knees, rolled over onto his back and looked up at me with a triumphant grin. There was a small gun in his hand.

I didn't hesitate, this was a deadly threat, all my instincts and my training kicked in and I shot him point blank in the centre of his forehead. His eyes opened wide in shock and surprise and I could see the moonlight reflected in them as his head fell back. He lay still. Instinctively I grabbed his gun and flung it as hard as I could into the forest. Damn stupid thing to do but it made me feel better.

Fucking hell! What had just happened? Was he dead? He must have been, no one could survive a bullet in the head. I grabbed my phone, leaned over his body and used its light to scan his face. There was no hole in his head but there was a deep red wound across his forehead. He must have moved his head to the side in the split second between realising I was pulling the trigger and the bullet's impact.

He was out cold and possibly mortally wounded. I hadn't wanted to kill him and I still didn't want him to die. I needed information more than anything, information that only a live bastard could give me.

I didn't want to take any chances so I rolled him over onto his front and tied his hands securely behind his back. When I rolled him back over again he groaned. Good, there was a chance he wasn't too badly hurt and would survive long enough to tell me what I wanted to hear.

All I needed to do was to get him to the biscuit factory and then I could take my time getting him to spill his guts. After that, well, there were several options and none of them ended well for Mason.

CHAPTER NINE

SKIN

The pub was even quieter than it had been the night before, in fact it was devoid of punters when we got there, the only person present was a dejected looking Fred doing a crossword behind the bar.

"Ah," he said, when we walked in. "I was just about to give up and close the doors."

"Where is everyone?" I asked. "It can't just be the after-effects of Covid?"

"It gets like this a lot these days," he said. "Never mind the sodding virus, when you can get a litre of whisky or three bottles of decent wine for less than fifteen quid from a supermarket what chance have we got? Add in a free television box set and we're dead in the water."

"Shame," Shane said. "There's nothing like a good boozer to oil the social wheels."

"Aye, it's all social media now though innit, and we're not allowed to oil any wheels anyway."

"Doesn't bother me too much," I said. "Except how it affects business of course. I've never been much of a party animal."

"What can I get you boys," Fred asked.

"A nice cold cola will do me," I said.

"Same for me," Shane said, "but stick a double rum in it."

Fred laughed. "Coming up."

We sat far enough away from the bar so that Fred couldn't overhear us. He was a good bloke but there was no need for him to get involved in anything we had to say.

"Anything in particular you wanted to talk about?" I asked.

"Yes, well, you know the girl who was found dead was Bill Mason's daughter. He's someone we're very interested in as part of our investigations, so I wanted to ask you more about what happened last Friday night. If you can tell me anything else about what she said, how she was, that sort of thing, it would be very helpful."

"At the time she was just another fare, I don't know much more than that."

"Even the tiniest detail can turn out to be significant. Do you mind telling me everything you remember please?"

"I've already told the local police everything – there's not a lot to say. But let me think."

Shane nodded. "Take your time."

I took a swig of the cola, my head had started to hurt and I needed the caffeine.

"It was about midnight, I'd had a long day so decided to take just one more fare before heading home for the night. She was standing on the pavement outside Taffies club. I pulled up nearby and she just opened the back door and hopped in."

"Had she come out of the club?"

"I don't know sorry, she wasn't by the main entrance, maybe twenty or thirty metres down the road, there's a decent Indian restaurant opposite there. The Raj Mahal, they do a really good aubergine masala."

"Nice."

"Anyway, it turned out to be quite a lucky fare, her destination wasn't far from where I live . . . sorry, that's a bit stupid isn't it."

"Why?"

"I mean, it wasn't lucky, not for her anyway."

"Did something happen on the way?"

"No, I mean it was probably the last journey she took, well the last but one anyway."

"I see. So did you chat at all, on the drive?"

"Sort of, nothing memorable though, but we talked a bit more when we got to her place. She asked me to wait with her, as if she was plucking up the courage to go into the house."

"Just checking, that would be her father's house?"

"I guess so, that's what she told me anyway."

"What sort of state was she in, you know, did she seem upset or anything?"

"Not upset no, but she was agitated, anxious about something, I thought she was nervous about going into the house, I thought maybe she'd argued with her parents. And she looked tired, yes tired, from what I saw of her."

"Did she tell you anything in particular?"

"Not really, we talked about her living in Manchester – and London."

"Did she mention anywhere else?"

"Not that I can remember."

"What about Bristol, did she say anything about Bristol?"

"Ah, yes, that's right, she did say something, I can't remember what, but I don't think it was anything important."

"Anything else?"

"She said she had a boyfriend. I remember that because she said his surname was Jones, same as me. And no, she didn't mention his first name."

"And that's it?"

I hesitated as I remembered the taste of her lips – strawberry and pernod.

He raised his eyebrows. "What?"

"Um, there was one other thing, it can't be relevant though."

He continued to stare at me, I could see why he was a cop.

"Um, we kissed . . . well, she kissed me. I didn't have time to do anything about it. It was more a friendly . . ."

"Peck on the cheek?"

"No, it was a proper kiss – on the lips, and she said she liked me."

Shane smiled. "And did you like her?"

I could feel myself going red. I drained the last of the cola.

"It wasn't really like that – it was just a moment, she was gone before I knew it."

"OK. Did you see her go into the house?"

"No, she was still standing on the pavement when I drove

away."

"Did you see anyone else after that?"

"No, I went straight home."

"No one?"

"Not really, but there was a big black MPV, nearly ran me off the road. And Bones of course, he drove past, but then that's run of the mill these days."

"What do you mean?"

"He's just always driving about that's all, our paths often cross. I saw him earlier as a matter of fact, not long before you picked me up."

"Oh yeah."

"Yes, he drove past me as I was walking out of town. Don't think he saw me though."

Shane sat back.

"Thanks," he said. "That's all very helpful, if you think of anything else . . ."

"Sure," I said. "I'd better go, Mandy will be wondering where I am."

"I'll give you a lift."

"No, it's fine, it's not too far now and I need the exercise."

BONES

Mason wasn't fatally wounded but he was concussed and confused enough to cooperate with me when I led him to the boot of his own car and pushed him in. I tied his feet together, gagged him, and closed the lid.

I flashed my phone's torch on again and checked the area to make sure there was no obvious evidence of what had happened. I found the spent bullet casings and put them in my pocket, planning to toss them out of the car window in some remote spot on the way to the factory.

I drove my own car away from the scene to the other end of the car park behind the café building, I wasn't sure how long it was going to be before I could pick it up again. I would have to get rid of, or at least hide, Mason's car somewhere after making sure he was safe in his makeshift cell and somehow get back to pick my own car up. I wasn't sure how I was going to do that but was confident I would find a non-incriminating method.

I walked back across the loosely packed gravel of the car park, got into Mason's Merc and drove out, away from the café, back to the main road and towards the factory. The roads were quiet apart from the odd vehicle and I knew that there were no active traffic cameras and no CCTV along the route. You learned a lot from the mistakes of villains when you'd been a cop for as long as I had.

When we got to the factory, I parked the car near the door I'd used earlier and opened the boot. Mason was still groggy, just about semi-conscious, but I managed to help him out of the car and in through the door of the factory without too much resistance from him, but he was a big fucker and heavy, and almost a dead weight.

There was a discarded trolley near the entrance on the inside of the despatch bay. I pushed the bastard onto that. He struggled to sit up for a few seconds then fell back and passed out. Handy.

After I secured him in position in the prison I'd prepared, I slapped him awake. He was still gagged but his eyes screamed hatred at me. I knew then that I was definitely going to pay a high price if I ever let him go, so decided that that was never going to happen so I'd have to finish him off when the time came. I'd never killed anyone before although I'd come close when I was a firearms officer, but I was determined that Big Bill Mason was going to die and that I was going to be the one that made sure it happened.

I needed him alive for the time being and I needed him to cooperate with me so I'd have to pretend that there was a chance I'd set him free if he told me what I wanted to know.

"Sorry about that," I said. "I had no choice. I don't want to hurt you," I lied, "so if you help me out I'll let you go. Now, try to keep calm, and I'll remove the gag so you can drink some water, you're going to need to. Don't make too much noise or I'll have to replace it and tie it even more tightly."

I moved my hand towards his mouth and tugged the gag down. He immediately started spluttering and coughing. I tipped some water from the bottle into his mouth and he spluttered some more.

"You're a fucking dead man," he croaked predictably.

"Now now," I said, "didn't you hear what I said? Be a good boy and before you know it you'll be back in your filthy kennel."

"What the fuck do you want?" he asked.

"The truth, that's all," I said.

"What truth?"

"About Moira. What happened to her? Why did you kill her?"

"Are you fucking crazy," he spluttered. "Me? Kill my own daughter? What do you think I am?"

"I know what you are."

Mason tried to spit some words out but started coughing uncontrollably. I drew back and waited for him to stop. He got visibly weaker and eventually his eyes rolled upwards as his head fell back. His couldn't seem to breathe properly. Christ, was he going to die? That wasn't what I wanted, I needed him to stay alive and compos mentis enough to give me what I wanted – after that of course, well, it wouldn't matter.

I tipped more water over his head and face and some of it got into his mouth. He reacted to that with a more violent coughing fit but at least it seemed to bring him back from the brink. He lay back quivering and wheezing and his eyes closed. He was either dying or falling asleep. I retrieved a towel from the box of stuff I'd brought and wiped his face dry.

The blood from the wound on his head was coagulating but it didn't look very pretty and I didn't know if the impact of the bullet had done any damage to his brain. I would have to at least dress the wound in some way. I'd have to go and get some medical supplies.

I rearranged his body into what I hoped was a more comfortable position. I couldn't risk reapplying the gag in case he couldn't breathe. There was a good chance he would die anyway, not that that would be the worst thing to happen, but if I could keep him alive for just a little while longer and find out what happened to Moira it would be a bonus.

I threw a blanket over him and went outside to his car intending to drive to get supplies to dress his wounds. I sat behind the wheel to think and to catch my breath, my plans were unravelling but there was still hope. Where would I go to get the antiseptic creams, the bandages and the painkillers I'd need? It was late on a Sunday, even the 24 hour supermarkets would be closed and I couldn't take the risk of visiting a smaller establishment at that time of night, there would be CCTV and they'd remember me.

There was no choice, I'd have to go back to my own flat, there should be enough of the right supplies in my bathroom cabinet.

I decided to exchange Mason's Merc for my own car, at least until I'd retrieved what I wanted from my place, so I drove back to the café to get it. If I parked my own car near my flat no one would notice it because they were used to it being there.

I pulled into the car park behind the café.

My BMW was gone.

CHAPTER TEN

SKIN

I walked the rest of the way home in a bit of a daze, trying to get my story straight. I was hoping that Mandy was in a good mood because I was feeling very shaky after overdoing the booze and the weed and what it had led to with Raskal.

Mandy was not in a good mood. I opened the front door and walked along the passage to the kitchen at the back of the house. It was a large kitchen that led to the taxi office, a re-appropriated utility room, equipped with a fairly decent set up including a bespoke dispatch system that boasted such features as automatic texting based on the geo-location of the cars. It was more than we needed for our small operation but we'd bought it anticipating faster growth than we'd actually achieved.

Things were tight in the business but I was confident that with determination and hard work we would soon reach the point where we'd actually be making more money than we would do if we were to pack it all in and get proper jobs. We were still paying for the hardware and the software but once that was done it would only cost a relatively small amount every year for software updates and the occasional upgrade or replacement of faulty equipment.

The overheads were sometimes hard to predict but the maintenance and repair costs of the vehicles were linked to the amount of mileage they did, so of course, as long as you kept a reasonable level of activity they paid their own way.

As I entered the kitchen from the passage Mandy was standing in the middle of the room facing me. She looked agitated and was holding a mobile phone.

"Where have you been?" she asked, looking at me suspiciously.

"You know where I've been."

"Do I?"

"Yes. Why? What's the matter?"

"There's nothing the matter with me."

"That makes two of us then," I said, trying to make light of her obvious anger but dreading where it was leading to.

"Dave told me where he dropped you off," she said.

"Ah, I was going to say . . ."

I was feeling a bit wobbly so sat down at the table and put my head in my hands.

"Have you been drinking?" she asked.

"Um, yes. So what? Anyway, you gave me the whisky."

I was beginning to get tired of the blunt way she was interrogating me, and, I suppose, I was fronting it out, since attack is the best form of defence as the saying goes.

Mandy glared at me. I stood up and moved towards her in an attempt to defuse her anger.

"Sorry, I . . ." I started.

"I don't want to talk to you now," she said. "I know what you're like after a few pints. We'll discuss it in the morning. I'm off to bed. You do what you like, but Dave is still out there, driving around, doing what you should be doing. So you'll have to man dispatch."

I couldn't be bothered to argue with her, besides it suited me that she didn't want to talk to me then. It would give me a chance to come up with a plausible story.

"Good night," she said, before brushing past me and heading off out of the kitchen and towards the stairs to the bedrooms.

I went into the office and used the system to check where Dave was. It looked like he was at a standstill outside the railway station. It was usually a good place to park up and wait for a call or to pick up the odd passenger, even on a Sunday night.

I phoned Dave's mobile.

"Skin," he said, when he answered. "Where are you? Do you want me to pick you up."

"No Dave. I don't want picking up, I'm home. But I do want to know why you let me down."

"Ah," he said. "Yes, sorry about that, it wasn't my fault."

"I asked you not to tell Mandy," I said.

"She already knew you didn't go to see your old man," he said. "She threatened to sack me if I didn't tell her where I dropped you off."

"Why didn't you warn me?"

"I tried to phone you but it went straight to answerphone."

"Bollocks," I said.

"Yes, straight up," he said. "Mandy had been trying to phone you too."

"Hang on."

I pulled my phone from my pocket. The screen was blank and there was a large crack in the middle of it. Shit, I must have damaged it earlier when I was rolling around with Raskal.

"Sorry Dave," I said. "My phone's dead. Hang on."

I pressed the power switch and the phone beeped into life.

"Thank fuck for that," I said. "It's working, sort of."

"All right," he grunted. "Can I knock off now?"

"You may as well," I said, looking at the monitor screen, doesn't look like there's anything booked for the rest of the night."

"OK boss," he said.

"Hang on, before you go, did Mandy say anything else, you know, like how did she know that I wasn't in my Dad's?"

"No sorry."

"Thanks Dave," see you tomorrow.

I moved the phone from my ear and was just about to disconnect the call when I thought I heard Dave saying something. I brought the phone back to my ear.

"What was that Dave?"

"Nothing really, just that earlier on, Mandy sent me to pick a fare up from the service station on the motorway. When I arrived there was a woman waiting in the car park. She came over to the car and opened the front passenger door. Then when she sat down, she looked at me and suddenly decided she didn't need a cab after all."

"Weird," I said.

"Yeah, well it happens in this game."

"True."

"But that's not it. When I told Mandy, she said that the woman asked her if it was the same company that Harold Jones worked for. Mandy seemed a bit worried about that."

"Weirder. What was she like, this woman?"

"I didn't see much of her but she was youngish, pretty, dark hair. Sorry, that's all I know."

"Ah well, just one of those things I suppose."

"Yes boss, ta-ra."

I disconnected the call and sat back in the chair. It was a bit puzzling, although you often do get fares asking for particular drivers, though that was mostly older people, because they liked a familiar face behind the wheel.

Perhaps that's why Mandy was so annoyed with me, she'd got hold of the wrong end of the stick and thought I was up to something. I was of course, or had been at least, but that was with the definitely blonde Raskal. I shrugged it off. I was sure we'd sort it out in the morning.

I turned the system off and went to sleep on the sofa in the front room. I fell asleep very quickly and besides getting up once in the night to empty my bladder after the booze, had a restful night.

I woke just before six and made a cup of instant coffee on my way to the office. I switched everything back on again and waited for another Monday to begin.

I heard Mandy moving about in the bathroom and a few minutes later coming down the stairs. I went into the kitchen and was putting the kettle on as she came in the door.

"Coffee?" I asked, turning around to greet her. "Good morn . . . what?"

She was fully dressed in outdoor clothes and was holding a small suitcase.

She shook her head. "No Skin, I don't want any coffee. Just get one of the drivers to come and take me to the station."

"What? Why?"

"I've decided to go to my mother's for a few days. I need to think."

"Think? About what?"

"About whether I want this relationship to continue."

"But . . ."

"Never mind that now, just get me a cab please."

I moved towards her – she backed away.

"Now," she commanded.

"OK."

I checked to see if any of our drivers were active. There was no one available.

"Sorry," I said.

"No problem," she said. "I'll call another firm, Cassie's Cars maybe."

"If you have to go then let me take you."

She shook her head. "Nope. I'm fine. I'll start walking and ring Cassie on the way, might even get a bus."

She turned her back on me.

"How long will you be away?" I asked.

"Don't know," she shrugged, and she was gone.

BONES

Fuck fuck fuck!

What the fuck was I going to do? Where was my car? Hang on, I had to check myself, did I really leave my car there or was I deluding myself or even having some sort of mental breakdown?

No, I was sure, I had parked my car in that spot behind the café and it was hardly much more than an hour earlier. What had happened to it? Most likely some chancer had nicked it but I had to consider other possibilities? Maybe one of Mason's associates or heavies had followed him there. Maybe he was being investigated by some crime agency and I wasn't aware of it, but then why would they take my car?

Nah, the only plausible explanation was that some scrote had nicked it, it was one of those cars that attracted the attention of wide boys and posers alike. I had debated with myself for a long time before buying it, it really was too flashy and recognisable for a police detective, even Chunky had been surprised when I turned up with it.

The car was a dark blue BMW 7 Series, cost over seventy grand new but I'd bought it cash when it was three years old, low mileage, good nick, for less than twenty-five from Byron Perego, a low level villain from the edge of the Backfields Estate who'd got in too much debt and wanted a quick exit. What the fuck, I'd thought in the end, I didn't have any kids and hardly any mortgage, I had to spend my money on something.

Maybe having my car stolen would be a blessing in disguise. Despite my precautions it could have been picked up by a camera or spotted by a passing copper. At least I'd be able to say it was nicked from the docks area where it was usually parked.

I checked around the car park and the front of the transport café just in case I'd missed anything earlier but there was no sign of anything incriminating and there were no cameras anywhere near.

First thing I had to do was to get back to my flat and sort myself out and the only way I could do that would be to drive Mason's Merc, it was even flashier than the BMW but I didn't have any choice. There was an old boatshed half a mile from the docks alongside a silted-up tidal channel. That area had been waiting for decades for redevelopment and as far as I knew nobody bothered with it anymore. I'd shove the Merc in there and deal with it in a few days when things calmed down a bit.

Shit, I was in a proper mess and was beginning to regret the madness of my plan to sort Mason out. I'd been reckless and stupid but it was too late to worry about all that, I just had to make the best out of a bad job as they say.

Just over thirty minutes later I closed the door of my flat behind me and sighed with relief. I didn't think anyone had spotted me coming in from the boatyard and if they had, well it was where I lived so it wouldn't even register.

I was grubby and very tired but still buzzing with the excitement of what I'd done. I realised I needed to ground myself before I could think properly so went straight to the bathroom and had a hot shower. Afterwards I put most of my clothes in a bin-bag ready for me to dump in the communal rubbish skip that would be collected in the morning. Then I wolfed down a bowl of cereal before crashing out on top of my bed, intending to catch a power nap to clear my head.

I was woken by the ringing of my phone. I rolled over and retrieved it from the bedside cabinet, it took me a second to focus on the screen. It was Chunky and it was nearly 6 am. Fuck!

I grunted into the phone.

"Boss," Chunky said. "Is that you?"

"Of course it fucking is, what do you want?"

"Were you asleep," he asked.

"What's with the twenty questions?"

"Sorry Boss, have you been there all night?"

"What the fuck do you want?"

"It's your car, it's been found abandoned, on the side of the road a couple of miles outside town, looks like it's had a scrape."

I was fully awake. My first feeling was panic. I took a deep breath. "Are you sure? My car is outside, where I usually park it."

"I haven't seen it myself, but the description and the number plate match. You'd better check Boss."

"Fuck!" I said, continuing with the act. "OK, hang on, I should be able to see it from the kitchen window."

I actually walked over to the window and looked out. There was an empty gap where my car was usually parked – of course.

"Bollocks," I said, "you're right, it's gone. Is it still where it was found?"

"Should be."

"Are you in the station?"

"Yes Boss."

"What the fuck are you doing in at this time anyway?" I asked.

"Ah, well, Adams asked me to come in, there's been some developments . . ."

"Adams? What developments? Why didn't he talk to me?"

"I dunno Boss, he asked me to keep it to myself."

I was puzzled and angry. What was Adams playing at?

"Why are you telling me now then?"

"How about I come and pick you up, then we can go and look at your car and talk on the way. He's breathing down my neck here."

"Just tell me you prick."

Chunky sighed and whispered into the phone, "It's Bill Mason, he's disappeared."

"Fuck," I said, trying to sound surprised. "You'd better get down here now then."

I filled my pockets with the meds and bandages I'd need for Mason and went outside to wait for Chunky. A few minutes later he pulled up in his manky old motor. He loved the car, it was just as chunky as he was, and almost as battered. He thought he was fucking Columbo or something.

"Hiya Boss," he said as I got in. "How's it hanging today?"

"Never mind about that, what the fuck is going on with Adams? Why didn't he call me?"

"I dunno. I did ask him, sort of anyway."

"What do you mean sort of?"

Chunky shrugged, "I just asked him where you were."

"What did he say?"

"None of my business, he said."

"Fucker, where is he now?"

"He went home for a shower just as I was leaving. He's doing a briefing about the Mason girl at eight o'clock this morning."

"Better get a move on then," I said.

I used the ten minute journey to where the BMW had been abandoned to try to get more information from Chunky, thinking he might be able to shed more light on why I had been excluded. Chunky was no help, although he did say that Adams seemed to be distracted, like he was looking over his shoulder all the time. Adams didn't like me, that much was obvious, but why he didn't like me was not at all clear. During that few minutes I also came up with a plan to get back to the biscuit factory and check on Mason. I hoped he wasn't dead.

Some considerate uniform had put half-a-dozen traffic cones around my car but there was no other sign of any police activity. I don't suppose an abandoned vehicle was on top of their priority list even if it was a flash Beamer and belonged to a colleague. I was happy about that, it meant they weren't giving it much attention, so I'd have a chance to cover any tracks I might have left.

The nearside front headlamp was smashed in and the tyre looked a bit flat. I looked further down the road and a concrete bollard had been freshly bent over. They'd somehow managed to overcome the security features of the car but there didn't seem to be any other damage. I tried the ignition and everything sparked up ok.

"You'd better fuck off back to base," I said to Chunky. "I'll sort the tyre out and follow you later."

"Let me help you," he said. "There's plenty of time."

"No, fuck off. Keep an eye on Adams for me. I'll probably be a while because I want to road test the car to make sure it's all OK."

"Righto Boss."

After Chunky left I checked the tyre, it needed a bit of air but should be ok to drive. I tidied up the headlamp glass, then I got in and started the engine. Yes it was still good to go. It would cost me a few quid in repairs but it had worked out perfectly in the end. Sometimes car-nicking scrotes were useful.

I headed off to the biscuit factory.

CHAPTER ELEVEN

SKIN

After Mandy left I went into the office and sat in front of the computer trying to make sense of what had happened. I couldn't take it in properly, the truth was I didn't have a clue what was going on, we'd been together forever and I was a bit lost without her.

Her parents lived in Bristol so we hardly ever saw them and I'd never really communicated with them anyway since they didn't approve of me, believing I was holding their daughter back from her planned career as a teacher.

The switch was quiet. After an hour of staring at the screen and trying to figure out what had led our relationship to fall apart so quickly, I sent a text to Mandy asking if she was ok. She didn't reply so I logged on to Facebook, which I normally avoided, so that I could check for any clues about where she was going or what she was doing.

I starting typing her name into the search box but after I typed the M of her name I found myself completing my search with Moira Mason instead of Mandy Dando. Why couldn't I get her out of my mind?

It took a while but I found a profile that must have been Moira's, though there was hardly any public information available. I clicked through her history of profile pictures and found a four-year-old snap taken on what looked like Brighton beach though there was no description. I clicked on the photo, enlarged it and spent too many seconds staring wistfully into her deep dark eyes. I came to my senses and closed the browser.

I shook myself and went to make a coffee. I had a busy day ahead, especially without Mandy and I needed to put all that Moira nonsense aside and get on with it.

There was so little work coming in that I checked online to make sure there hadn't been another total lockdown or sudden economic collapse. There hadn't of course but it was a bit weird.

I phoned Dave to ask if the other drivers were quiet. He didn't answer. I texted Mandy to ask her if she knew of any reason why there were no bookings for that morning. She didn't answer either.

I tried to connect to the dispatch software but a message came up telling me the account had been suspended and to contact the suppliers. My mobile rang, I looked at the screen. It was Ravi, one of my regular drivers.

"What's going on Skin?" he asked snappily.

"What do you mean?"

"Why aren't there any pick-ups this morning?"

"Yeah sorry, I just noticed. Looks like the system is down. I'll check and get back to you."

"Yeah sure," Ravi said, he didn't sound convinced. "Just give me a shout when you're ready."

Ravi owned his own car and I knew he occasionally took work from other firms, so he wasn't totally dependent on us. He was a good driver though, and a good bloke, so I didn't want to piss him off, or worse lose him.

I got a text from Dave saying he was out the front of the house and would I come out to talk to him.

Dave had parked the car in the drive. I was puzzled.

"What's going on Dave?" I asked.

"Sorry Skin, I'm packing it in. I've got another job and they want me to start straightaway."

He handed me the car keys I took them automatically.

"You didn't say anything."

"I have spoken to Mandy about it a couple of times, she told me to go for it."

I was totally confused. What the fuck was going on?

"Uh?" I said.

"Just the way it is," he shrugged. "Better money, less hours, more security. I've got to think of my own family."

"But things were just starting to pick up again . . ."

"Don't kid yourself Skin. It's been going downhill for ages, we never recovered after the pandemic . . ."

"Yeah, yeah," I said. "The bloody pandemic, I know."

He shrugged.

I realised he was right. I'd been in denial but we'd invested in a couple of new cars, and the IT equipment, just before the virus hit, so it was obvious we were going to be badly affected, especially with all the money we'd borrowed. On top of that the mortgage on the house was still quite big. It wouldn't take much to tip things over the edge. We were actually in a lot of debt. If things had gone to plan that wouldn't have been a problem because the income from the business would have paid the loans off in no time. Yes, it was time to bite the bullet and contract back to just me and my car, at least then I wouldn't have to waste my own time with too much paperwork and all the management bollocks.

"Skin?" Dave said. "Are you all right?"

"What, sorry, yes, I just drifted off. You're right, it's not working out at the moment, I can't stop you. Good luck with it all. I'll settle up with you as soon as I can."

"Thanks Skin, good luck yourself."

Dave started walking away.

"Hold on I said, let me give you a ride, for old times' sake."

He laughed. "It's fine, I'm getting a lift from the top of the street."

That made me feel even more useless.

BONES

When I got to the biscuit factory and went into the room where I'd left Big Bill tied up there was no sign of him.

I panicked, he couldn't possibly have escaped. Perhaps someone else had helped him? Perhaps I should have gagged him after all? I felt a presence behind me and whipped around expecting the worst.

The bastard had somehow rolled across the room and was

squashed under a desk. He was facing away from me and was very still. I moved slowly towards him and pushed his body with my foot. There was no response.

I leant down and moved closer. I put my hand out and over and touched his forehead, it was warm. Suddenly the body moved, his head spun around and he clamped his teeth on my fingers. I yanked my hand away and out of his mouth but not before he'd bitten almost down to the bone.

I shrieked in pain and stepped back. His eyes were staring at me like a demonic cat stalking a rat.

He tried to speak but only incomprehensible sounds came from his mouth along with his spit and the blood from my damaged fingers. Fuck, I should have tied him to something solid instead of just leaving him on the floor.

Lesson learned I retrieved a length of rope from where I'd left it earlier and tied his ankles and his wrists to the legs of the heavy metal table, making sure his forehead was easily accessible.

Thankfully, the wound hadn't developed into anything too serious, the scabs that had formed naturally were doing a good job of keeping it clean. On the negative side he was trying to talk but was still not coherent. If he was brain damaged he wouldn't be much use to me but at least he'd be out of action, probably permanently, and I might not have to actually kill him after all.

I cleaned him up as best I could, considering he was still resisting as much as he was able. Then I soaked a towel in water and squeezed it until it dripped into his mouth. There was no way he'd be able to eat in that position but it had been less than twelve hours since I shot him so he should survive for a while longer without food.

I stood up.

"I've got things to do now," I said, not knowing if he was able to understand what I was saying, "so I'm going to leave you again."

His body writhed and lifted towards me, his eyes still full of hate.

"Dead man," he said, his voice barely audible.

I was relieved, maybe there was a chance he would be well enough to co-operate after all, but that would have to wait, I needed to get back to the station and get up to date on whatever Adams was doing.

I felt quite good on the drive back, it looked like the nightmare that had begun when Mason tried to shoot me was over. I'd managed to get that situation under control through a mixture of determination and luck. I hoped I'd be just as lucky with the rest of it and find out the truth about Moira's death. Although I'd been a sod to her when she was alive I was determined to honour her in her death.

By the time I got back to the station Adams's briefing was well underway. I hadn't been invited but walked straight into the room anyway. Adams, who was standing at the front stopped talking and stared at me. The other heads in the room, including Chunky's, turned around and stared too.

Adams addressed the room, "Excuse me," he said. "I need a word with DI Jones."

He walked across towards me, "Hello Barry," he said. "Do you mind coming outside for a private chat."

I shrugged and followed him into the corridor. We stopped a few metres away from the briefing room.

Adams took a breath, "Sorry to be the bearer of bad news but concerns have arisen about your involvement in the Moira Mason case, because of your recent relationship with her. Do you agree?"

There was no point denying it, it was a clear conflict of interest and was common knowledge by then anyway.

"Yes," I nodded, "but it has been over for some time."

"Nevertheless, it's not appropriate for you to be involved in the investigation."

"I guess so," I said. I was cornered, there was no other response I could give.

"Thanks, I'm glad you're happy with that."

"I'm not happy. I was very fond of Moira and to be honest all this has rattled me a bit."

By admitting that I was badly affected by Moira's murder

I was doing myself a favour because then there would be some explanation for my behaviour, and it might throw my colleagues off the scent of what I'd done to her father. And, I really was rattled, if only I'd realised how much she meant to me while we were still seeing each other.

"Well thanks for accepting it then."

"Yeah," I said. "It's ok. I guess I'd better find something else to focus on. Do you know if anything's going?"

"Not a lot," I'm afraid. "There is that spate of far right graffiti, it had quietened down but it seems to be flaring up again."

"Oh yeah."

"Yes, a couple of incidents yesterday. By the Co-op in the North of the Backfields."

"Sounds interesting."

Adams raised his eyebrows.

"Well ok, interesting in a way," I said. "It'll keep me off the street at least."

"Don't you mean on the streets?"

Jesus, he was trying to be funny. I forced a chuckle of false amusement.

"I'll take it," I said. "But what about Chunky, is he still going to work with you?"

"Well, yes, we're a bit short-handed, and he knows his way around. So it's probably best."

And it was probably best, that way I'd have a sympathetic supporter on the inside. A couple of pints is all it took for Chunky to start spilling his guts.

SKIN

I stood on the pavement staring at Dave as he walked up the street and out of sight. I had to face facts, I was on my own – for the time being at least. I vowed to myself that I would start again, from scratch if I had to, this wasn't going to beat me. Then I thought about Mandy, I couldn't do it without her. What if she didn't come back? Jesus, what chain of events had I started when I lied to her, got pissed, and shagged Raskal? I wasn't built for all that cheating stuff.

Back in the office I made a cup of tea and looked through the drawers and filing cabinets for clues as to what might have gone wrong so quickly.

I found letters and final demands from the usual suspects and a disconnection notice for the landline and "associated services". There was also some heavy-duty correspondence from the bank regarding both the business and the personal accounts, asking me to contact the branch to arrange a meeting as soon as possible, it was dated two weeks earlier. I'd been aware that our cashflow was shaky but hadn't understood just how bad it was. It looked like Mandy had been keeping things from me for some time.

Stupidly, it kind of made me feel better about my infidelity, since Mandy's crimes were possibly just as bad, or even worse in some ways.

I slumped, suddenly exhausted. I shuffled into the living-room and flopped face down on the sofa.

I was woken by the sound of a text arriving on my mobile. I looked at the screen, I'd been asleep for more than an hour. The text was from Mandy. I opened it.

'Sorry Harry. I've sent you an email explaining it all. I can't cope right now. I'll be in touch when I'm ready. Please do what you have to do.'

I texted her back telling her it would be all right but we needed to talk. She didn't answer. The email function on my phone had never worked so I would have to take my laptop to an internet café to be able to read what Mandy had sent.

BONES

That stupid fucker Adams was too dense to realise I had no intention of wasting my time investigating a splattering of graffiti on The Backfields, even if it was swastikas and racism from a deluded moron. The estate had been part of my patch for more than a decade and before that I already knew the area intimately enough from my crazy teenage years. There were a lot worse things going on behind those grubby flowery curtains than a bit of spray paint. Anyway I was already almost one hundred percent certain that I knew who was behind it, but the Davies twins, Daisy and Dylan, could wait until I was ready to deal with them. They weren't exactly harmless but they were useless.

I made a token visit to the estate and talked to a couple of lowlifes who were hanging around in the little children's play area around the corner from the Co-op. I told them to get the hell away from the swings or I'd bust them for being perverts. They looked very scared and I even felt a little sorry for them, they were hardly more than kids themselves and had no doubt grown up using the same play facilities they'd been abusing.

After they went I sat in my car to think about what I was going to do next. The graffiti incident was way below my pay grade, but I didn't mind. The only attention it needed was for me to continue the pretence of working on it, and then, when it was necessary, move in on the Davies twins. In the meantime I would keep tabs on the murder investigation and make sure that Big Bill Mason stayed alive long enough to get what I wanted from him.

While I was sitting in my car, I noticed a familiar figure wobbling past on a too small bike, a common occurrence on the Backfields and in similar environments where scrotes roamed too freely. If something wasn't screwed to the ground the bastards would nick it. They especially liked stealing bicycles and took great pleasure in taking those bikes that were meant for young children.

As the bike-nicking twat wobbled past I saw that it was indeed Jackie Mann. I wondered if he had any more information for me, but he'd keep.

After that I drove back to my flat to sort out a plan and get on with it. First thing I did was to phone Will at the Riverside garage, he was always ready to accommodate the servicing and repairs on whatever vehicle I was running, even when I needed him immediately. I knew that the reason he was so keen to keep me on his side was because of his little sideline of growing weed in his attic. He knew that I knew about it but we never openly acknowledged it, it was important to keep the spell going.

"Of course," Will said. "Bring it over whenever you like, even if I haven't got the parts I'll get you on the road legally in a jiffy."

Will's workshop was in a back street not far from town, so after I dropped the car off I made my way to the shopping centre to pick up some fresh pastries to tempt Mason with, I knew he had a sweet tooth and would be starving by the time I got back to him.

Will had told me to come back in about an hour, so after picking up the sugary bread I wandered around town checking out the talent, except there was no talent, not on show anyway, in fact there was hardly anyone on show at all. I guessed that most tidy people were hiding out at home or else wandering around at the out-of-town shopping estates, since the decrepit streets of the town centre had long been abandoned to car-less pensioners, hopeless alcoholics, and drug addicts.

To be fair there were some attempts to revitalise the place, amongst the charity shops and the pawnbrokers a few new enterprises were trying to get established. There was one place in particular that I liked to visit whenever I found myself in town. It was a kind of café, mixed with a sort of charity shop with local art pinned to its white walls. In another life I might have been an artist, I was pretty good with a pencil at school, but was never encouraged or supported by my clueless parents.

There was one painting on the walls of the art café that I always paused to look at. It was an abstract I suppose, smothered with deep colours and flowing shapes that combined to create a sort of peaceful vibe. It was a little big for my walls but cheap enough at two hundred quid. I could have made space and could easily afford it but I couldn't bring myself to buy it because I didn't know enough about art and didn't want to make a fool of myself.

As I was leaving the café I was shocked to see someone who I hadn't seen for years coming in, and the last time we'd spoken it hadn't exactly been on friendly terms. I recognised him immediately, he had such a distinctive look. We used to be good mates, close even, but he'd turned into a gigantic wanker, like a switch had been turned on, or off, in his personality.

He saw me at the same time as I saw him and we both had pretty much the same reaction of surprise and 'how the fuck do I deal with this bastard'.

Shane broke the silence. "Um . . . er, Bones," he said.

I couldn't help myself, "Yep, that's me Shane, but it's DI Barry Jones to you. What the fuck are you doing back in Elchurch?"

"Ah, you know, friends, family."

"You don't have any friends here, nor any family left as far as I know."

"Ah well, lots of connections."

"Huh!"

"Fancy a catch up? A coffee or something?" he asked.

"Are you serious?"

"Yeah, well, time passes, we all change, we move on."

"After what you did?" I was genuinely stunned by his suggestion that we could just sit down like old pals and laugh about our past.

"Sorry," he said. "I didn't realise . . ."

"You didn't realise what? That you were, still are, a cunt?"

"Um . . . can't we talk?"

"Yes, as it happens I do have something to say to you."

His face lit up with the beginnings of a smile.

"Fuck off," I said.

I pushed past him and strode off along the street in the direction of Will's workshop. If it hadn't been a public place I would have strangled the bastard.

CHAPTER TWELVE

SKIN

I went to the Tinworks in the end, it had free and usually reliable wi-fi. I nearly didn't go there because I was a bit worried that I might bump into Raskal but part of me welcomed that idea so I went anyway.

The place was more than half empty, but the space that was being used was, as usual, bristling with Apple Macbooks as the arty-farties pretended they were working on important musical or artistic projects, when all they were really doing was stalking their friends' friends on Facebook or searching for images of labradoodles.

I got myself a simple filter coffee and sat down against the side wall with my laptop. I liked that position, I could see all the corners of the large space and make stories up in my head about the characters who weaved their ways through it.

I put extra sugar in the coffee to give me strength then I booted up the computer and opened the email app.

There it was in black and white.

Subject: *Sorry*

Message:

Hi Skin, sorry about what's happened. It's not all your fault. I've been all over the place for months and you've been so busy and I've just felt so alone, having to deal with my own issues and keep the business going. We've both made mistakes, my biggest one was not telling you earlier just how bad our financial situation was.

It's too late now that it's all come to a head. I wanted to talk to you yesterday but you disappeared and when you came back, your lies were the final straw.

Anyway, I can't do anything more about it for the time being. I need to sort my own head out. I don't know what happens next but I want you to know that I did love you, and still do, but there's no trust between us anymore and like I said it's not all your fault.

I'll be in touch when I can.

Mandy xx

I looked up from the screen and scanned the room. No one else seemed to have noticed but my whole world had just fallen off a cliff. I wasn't sure what her *'own issues'* were but she was right about the lack of trust, she was right not to trust me and, I suppose, I shouldn't have trusted her to look after the admin and the finances.

I was ashamed that the first thing I thought about was my encounter with Moira Mason. Those few moments were the start of something I couldn't explain, the start of something that could never be, not in this universe anyway.

Never mind, I'd just have to face up to things and find a new direction in my life. I'd carry on driving for a while, just to bring in some income while I decided what to do. Hopefully I would be able to hang on to the house, though, of course, if our split became permanent, Mandy would have to have her share of any equity that might have built up since we'd bought it on a joint mortgage, although there was a possibility that any equity would be wiped out by the as yet unknown amount of accumulated debt.

BONES

Will was in a chatty mood when I went to pick my car up. He'd heard about the murder and that the victim was called Moira Mason. Usually, I would have made some excuse to bat his questions away, there was no reason I should tell him anything, but because of the way I'd been sidelined by Adams, I thought fuck it, I might as well give Will something to talk about.

"Aye," I said. "Big Bill Mason's daughter, bit of a shock to be honest. She was a nice girl too. We're looking into the possibility that it was related to his, let's say, less than honest activities."

"Ah, yes. I've heard a lot about Big Bill," he said. "Bit of a tough guy by all accounts."

"Yep," I sighed. "Trouble is, and keep this under your hat, don't mention my name at least – he's disappeared, so it makes you think."

His eyes widened. "That's a bit suss don't you think?"

"Not for me to say, we're still investigating."

"Good luck with that," he said.

"Thanks, how much do I owe you?"

"Nothing Mr Jones, I haven't done much, just patched things up for now, you're going to have to bring it in for a proper job when you can."

"Cool," I said. "Watch how you go now."

Will laughed.

I drove back to the station to see if I could pick up any more info. Chunky was hanging about in reception chatting up Ana, one of the civilian support staff, and stuffing his face with a bacon buttie by the look of it.

"Oh, hello Boss," he said, spraying crumbs of greasy bread over his shirt. "How's it hanging?"

"All right yeah," I said. "All good."

I noticed Ana edging away from the fat fuck.

"Come on Chunks," I said.

Ana looked relieved as he followed me along the corridor and into a side office.

"I'm going to need your help," I said. "I'm sure Adams is up to something, I wouldn't be surprised if he's Mason's bitch."

"Straight up?"

"Yes, well, I can't be sure yet, that's why I want you to keep an eye on things here, let me know if you notice anything dodgy going on, even if it doesn't look dodgy it might be useful if you know what I mean."

Chunky took a bite out of the sandwich and nodded.

"Will you do that for me then?"

He crammed the rest of the buttie in his fat gob and spluttered, "Goes without saying Boss, you know me."

"Yes, I do," I said, trying to convey the vague threat that I really did know things about him that he'd prefer to keep out of the public domain. "I know I can trust you."

I wasn't really sure if I could trust him at all. It had never taken much for me to get him involved in activities that were anything but straight, so I had no doubt that he'd be just as compliant for anyone else. I was sort of fond of him but really he was just a useful idiot.

"Only thing is," he said, "Adams is keeping me cooped up here, he wants me to liaise with everyone else, so I won't be out and about."

"Actually, that's perfect," I said. "That's a very important position to be in, you'll be at the centre of operations in a way, like the fat controller," I laughed.

Chunky laughed too. "That's funny Boss."

"Yes Chunks," I said. "Very useful. Well done."

"Aw thanks Boss," he beamed, gulping down the last shreds of his piggie sandwich.

After I left the station, I drove back to the Backfields. On the surface it was a perfectly legitimate use of my time since I was supposed to be investigating the graffiti incident.

It was time to give Jackie Mann another tug.

SKIN

I decided to leave the Tinworks, not because I had anywhere else to go but because I was beginning to feel self-conscious taking up a whole table to myself and the place was getting a little busier as it came closer to lunchtime. I closed my laptop and put it in its bag.

As I was standing up, my mobile phone rang. It was an unfamiliar number.

"Hello," I said.

"Is that the taxi guy?" a quiet voice mumbled, it was probably a woman. I could barely make out the words.

"Yes, I guess," I said. "But can you speak up, it's a bad line."

"Are you available now?"

I paused, was I available? What the hell. "Yes," I said.

"Can you pick me up from outside Taffies club."

"All right, give me a few minutes, I'm not far away but will have to get back to my car."

"Thank you," the voice said softly.

"Hang on, what's your name?"

There was no reply, she had already hung up.

I grabbed the laptop bag and went out to my car and put it in the boot. I tugged the driver's door open. As I was sitting down in the driver's seat I heard a familiar voice. I turned and looked up.

"Hey Skin, what's happening dude?"

It was Raskal. To my surprise I was genuinely happy to hear her cheeky tones.

"Howdy pardner," I said, trying to keep the friendly style going, god knows I'd had enough animosity recently.

"Steady on old chap," she said.

"What? Oh shit, I didn't mean pardner as in partner . . ."

She punched me in the arm and laughed. "Only joking," she said.

"Ha, not a lot happening," I said.

"You look tired," she said, leaning down and staring into my eyes.

I almost kissed her but reckoned that would be pushing it. She was a friendly person and we'd had sex less than twenty-four hours earlier but we weren't that familiar.

"Yeah, it's been one of those days," I said with a sigh.

"Do you want to talk about it?" she asked with a cheeky

shrug. "There's nobody at home in my place at the mo."

I was tempted. "Sorry, not now," I said, "I've got a pick-up."

"Fair enough, it's your job. Maybe later?"

I nodded. "Yeah maybe."

"Have you got my number?"

"I'm not sure, probably."

"I'll ring you now and you can add me if I'm not already in your contacts."

"Go on then."

She retrieved her phone from somewhere. Of course it was an iPhone, those creative types always had iPhones to go with their MacBooks.

"What's your number?"

I told her my number. She dialled it. My phone rang. She rang off.

"Thanks."

"Maybe later then," she said.

She leant down again and kissed me on the lips. It felt nice but the feeling didn't compare to the kiss Moira Mason had given me.

After Raskal walked away I closed the door, started the engine, and drove across town to Taffies club, hoping the delay with Raskal hadn't pissed my fare off too much. There was no sign of anyone waiting outside the club, so I got out of the car and walked up the pavement a bit, then down the lane, to look around the back. Still no sign of anyone, maybe she'd gotten pissed off and called another cab because I'd taken too long to get there.

Ah well, it was just one of those occupational hazards. I scrolled to the number that had booked me earlier and dialled it. It went straight to answerphone. I didn't bother leaving a message.

I got back in the car and headed home. On the drive, I couldn't get Moira Mason out of my head. I'd just stopped for the phantom pick-up in almost the exact spot I'd picked her up on Friday night. Maybe I'd invented the call, maybe I was having delusions. Fuck, maybe I would need some kind of psychiatric help. I even thought I could smell that smell again, strawberry and Pernod.

I shook myself and drove on.

BONES

I was about to give up looking for Jackie Mann. I realised I was using my search for him to distract me from going back to face Mason. I had no idea what the next step would be with that one. The truth was that I'd been very stupid, I'd got myself worked up into a frenzy like a crazy dog after a bitch on heat, and about someone who didn't even exist anymore. If I'd used my head, I would have come up with something much more intelligent. The anger inside me had got me into trouble more than once and when it came there was nothing rational about it.

I shook myself, there was no point thinking like that. It was what it was, I just had to deal with it. I put the car into gear and pointed it towards the main road that led out of town, past the Backfields and under the motorway to the valleys beyond. Just one more slow drive along Meadow Road on the way just in case the toerag was loitering with intent.

I spotted someone who looked like it could be him ducking down an alley that led into the heart of the estate. I wasn't sure, because whoever it was I'd seen, was dressed in black, with a hoodie pulled up over their head.

I stopped the car near the entrance to the alley, got out and followed the ninja. I lost sight of them as the alley twisted and turned. When I emerged at the other end there was no sign of anyone at all. I thought that was a bit suspicious since unless, they'd belted it they should still be in sight.

I paused on the pavement and scanned the street. There was a thick unkempt privet hedge spilling over the low wall of the house to my left. I heard it rustle and snapped my head round to look, a bird or a cat maybe? I moved towards the hedge and suddenly the ninja figure stood up behind it, then ran towards the gate and onto the pavement a couple of metres from where I was standing.

There was no doubt that it was Jackie Mann. He froze. Because of my police training I reacted instinctively and charged at him without hesitation, smashing into him and sending him flying back into the garden. He fell on his back struggling for breath.

As I followed him into the garden, the curtains in the front window of the house twitched. I waved at the occupant, pulled my police ID card out and held it towards them.

I stood over the wannabe ninja. He was still struggling for breath. He was reaching into his pocket. I moved closer.

"Stop that," I commanded. "Put your hands where I can see them."

"Asthma," he hissed.

I nodded. He withdrew an asthma pump from his pocket and I waited to catch my own breath while he used it.

"Up you get," I tugged at his arm.

He struggled to his feet.

"Now where's my cuffs?" I said out loud.

"Am I under arrest?" he asked.

"Maybe. Why, what have you done?"

"Nothing. I haven't done nothing."

"I know that you haven't done nothing you prick, but you have done something, you're always doing something. Now tell me what you know about Mason's operation."

"I can't," he said. "They'll kill me."

"What? What the fuck are you on about? Come on, I'm taking you in, you'll go down for this."

"For what?"

"For the drugs, for those wraps of coke you've got in your pocket."

"What wraps? I haven't got any wraps."

"You will have," I said, "by the time I get you to the station."

"Bastard cop," he spat at me.

I lunged forward, put him in an armlock and marched him out of the garden and back up the alley. As we went through the gate I turned around smiling and waved at the twitching curtains.

I stopped halfway up the alley and released the armlock.

"Now, come on, tell me what's going on. Who will kill you?"

He cleared his throat and spat the resulting phlegm straight into my face, it landed on my cheek. I reacted immediately and pushed him to the floor realising that he wasn't going to talk, not then anyway.

I suppose I must have lost it because I proper laid into him with my bare fists and my steel-toecaps.

When I'd finished I yanked his head up and unloaded a mouthful of gob onto his battered face. Then I let his head drop onto the tarmac of the alley.

"I'll be back," I said, chuckling at my own joke.

SKIN

I parked outside my house, opened the door and got out of the car. I had a feeling something wasn't right, like I'd forgotten something. Never mind, I locked the car with the remote, walked up the path and opened the front door.

Ah, I had forgotten something, it was the laptop stuff in the boot. I zapped the key to open the car, walked back to the boot and flipped it open. The car moved unexpectedly, the rear door flew open and a slight figure in a long dark hooded coat flashed up the path and into the house through the open door.

Shit! I must have had a stowaway, I hadn't bothered to lock the car when I'd gone around the back of Taffies to look for my fare. Whoever it was, there was a chance they were dangerous, so I walked hesitantly along the path and into the house.

I heard a noise coming from the kitchen. I still had my laptop case in my hand so held it above my head and moved slowly along the passage.

The kitchen door had swung shut, as it was meant to do. I pushed it open with my foot and moved cautiously inside.

The figure in black was standing in the doorway of the taxi office facing away from me.

They turned around.

What the actual fuck!?

BONES

Mason was silent and still when I got back to the factory. At first I thought he was dead, but I wasn't too bothered about that possibility even if it meant that Moira's murder would be harder, if not impossible, to solve.

I nudged his prone body with my foot and stepped back. He groaned and rolled over towards me. He did look pretty bad, with residues of his own blood and spit, mixed with filthy debris from the factory floor. His lips were dry and cracked and his eyes were dull and almost lifeless.

"Help me," he hissed in a weak voice.

I retrieved a bottle of water and a tissue and dabbed his mouth.

"Are you ready to talk?" I asked.

He nodded.

I kept his hands and ankles tied together but I untied his arms and legs. He was virtually a dead weight but I shoved and dragged him until I managed to sit him up with his back against a filing cabinet.

I showed him the painkillers I'd brought and put two of them on his tongue, he was too weak to resist. I helped him to drink some water, both for his thirst and to help him swallow the tablets.

"Right," I said. "They know you've gone missing and they believe that you have gone on the run because you murdered your daughter," I lied.

He shook his head. "No, never. Not me."

"It's just a coincidence then? That the last time she was seen alive it was on the pavement outside your house."

"Not me," he shook his head. "I'm not fucking stupid."

He was getting some of his mojo back, I'd have to watch myself.

"I'm hungry," he said.

"So?" I shrugged.

"Is that your plan? Let me starve to death?"

"All I want is the truth."

"I don't know what happened to Moira. She was my little girl, whoever did it will die. That is the fucking truth."

He glared at me, then his face crumpled, he looked defeated. I almost felt sorry for the old bastard.

"I'll pay you to find out who it was, never mind your pathetic police pennies, I'll give you ten years' worth of that, and more, as much as you want."

"Give it a rest Bill," I said. "I know what you're like."

"Whatever I am, my word is gospel."

"Ha ha, who do you think you are, Jesus Christ?"

But he was right. If I knew anything about Big Bill Mason I knew that he was a man of his word. I decided that I believed him. He had nothing to do with the death of his 'little girl'. I'd been reckless, more than reckless. I think I'd become sort of possessed.

"I loved her," he said. "She was the world to me."

My will crumpled as quickly as Mason's face had. What had I done? How had it come to this?

"I loved her too," I said, but I wasn't sure that I did.

I sat on the floor opposite him with my back against another filing cabinet.

"I'm sorry," I said.

"All right," he said. "I believe you, I believe that you loved her and I believe you're sorry that you . . . you tricked me. I get it. I would have done the same if I was you. But now . . ."

"Now what?"

"Let me go, I won't hurt you. We can work together."

I didn't trust him about that. What had happened was such a bad thing that I was sure he was capable of anything, including breaking his word. But I was finished. I had pushed things too far, and a part of me didn't care anymore. I was struggling to overcome the urge to let the old bastard loose, whatever happened after that would be a relief, even if he did kill me.

"Let me think," I said.

CHAPTER THIRTEEN

SKIN

Was I looking at a ghost?

I lowered my arm and my laptop, then stepped forward, thinking I was hallucinating or dreaming. She pulled the hood down.

"Fuck!" I gasped. "Who? How? It can't be."

That smile. Those lips. Strawberry and Pernod!

"Hello again Harry."

My legs weakened and I dropped to my knees.

"Yes," she said, "it's me."

"You're dead."

She put the palm of her hand on her chest to check for signs of life. She shook her head.

"No, I'm not," she laughed.

She stepped forward and caressed my face. Her touch was as real as it got. I stood up and stared, unable to speak or move. She kissed me on the lips. My head spun.

"Does that prove it?" she asked.

"So who . . .?"

"Patience," she said. "You'd better put the kettle on."

BONES

Mason was too smooth, too forgiving, and he was giving me the creeps. Maybe I should have let him die, maybe there was still time, but he was too weak and too tired to be an immediate threat, so I let my guard down.

I loosened the ropes on his hands and ankles and let him fill his stomach with some of the food and water I'd brought. He ate like an animal, a greedy dog.

"Take it easy," I said.

He ignored me while he filled his stomach. Then he belched and sat back.

"Where's my car?" he asked.

"It's safe."

"So, what next?"

I had nothing left to say, I'd been focusing on getting the truth out of him and now that I'd succeeded there was nowhere else to go.

"Well?" he said. "This is a waste of time. You should be out there, talking to your grasses, finding clues, whatever it is you people do."

I shrugged.

"For fuck's sake," he said. "Get out there and find the psycho scumbag that took our girl away."

Did he say 'our girl'? Wow. Did that mean that he had accepted me as someone who had loved his daughter as much as he seemed to have, and did it mean that we would march on together, both with the same aim? Or was he fucking with my mind?

I weighed it up. Both of those possible scenarios could be true, I just didn't know. I couldn't think. I had to break the deadlock.

"Right," I said emphatically.

I stood up, took a breath, walked over to where he was sitting and removed the bonds from his wrists and ankles completely. While I was untying the ropes he sat patiently. When I'd finished he stood up slowly and stretched his limbs. It took a while before he was able to stand up and move properly. He was obviously in a lot of pain.

"Thanks," he said. "I'm ready."

"Now what?" I asked.

"Take me to my car. After that you can do what you like."

"What about Moira?"

"She's dead," he said.

"That doesn't mean . . ."

"Don't you think I fucking know that? But I need to think, and plan, and talk to people. Even I would be a better cop than you for fuck's sake."

"I think I need to rest," I said. "I'm not thinking straight."

"I told you, do what the fuck you want. If you come up with anything relevant let me know. Now come on, let's get the fuck out of here."

SKIN

Moira didn't tell me much at first, just that the girl who was found dead under the motorway wasn't her, but that she knew who it was and had some ideas about what had happened.

"But your father thinks you're dead," I argued. "You should let him know you're ok at least."

She looked away and started sobbing.

"Sorry, I can't talk yet," she said, "I'm so tired."

"Fair enough," I said. "Take your time. Freshen up a bit, have a bath if you like."

"That sounds great. I knew you were a good man. Is it ok if I have a rest first?"

She slept for an hour on the sofa in the front room and spent another half an hour in the bathroom. When she came back downstairs she was wearing Mandy's dressing-gown, the huge red towelling one with the hood. It looked even bigger on Moira than it did on Mandy. She looked so innocent and vulnerable but seemed comfortable.

"I promise you," Moira said. "It does make sense. I will explain. But I need your help."

We were sitting at the kitchen table drinking coffee. It was mid-afternoon.

"Are you hungry?" I asked.

"A bit," she said, "but I don't think I can eat."

"Don't you think it's a bit weird," I said, "that they think the dead woman is you?"

"I suppose so," she shrugged. "I don't know, perhaps they just assumed. She is about the same size as me and has a similar hairstyle."

"So . . ." I said.

"Please, I'm not ready to talk about all that yet."

She sighed heavily, it was as if she was filled with black fog.

"Are you ok?" I asked. "Can I get you something?"

She stared at me from across the table and smiled with her beautiful eyes as well as with her luscious mouth. I was transfixed.

"Can we do something a bit more exciting than this? I'm getting bored," she said with a flirty glance.

I didn't want to misinterpret the signals and anyway I wasn't in any mood for any kind of intimacy, it had been a strange few days and I needed to get my bearings.

"Um, we could go for a spin," I suggested. "It's nice down by the water park, even at this time of year."

"Yeah, why not. Can we take a picnic?"

"Um, I'm not sure what's here."

"A sandwich will do," she said. "Come on, it will be fun."

She was acting as if we'd known each other forever. I couldn't work out whether it was a brother and sister kind of relationship or if we were lovers. Although I was almost certain that I was getting to love her more in some way with every passing minute. It was scary.

"Look, I'm sorry," I said. "This is all a bit much to take in. I can't pretend to know what's going on. Someone is dead, we can't just ignore that and carry on as if everything is normal."

She looked down as I was speaking. When she looked up again her eyes were red and filled with tears.

"I know," she said tearfully.

"If you told me more about it then maybe I could help, or at least it would help you to talk it through. What do you think?"

She started sobbing, she was trying to speak but the words wouldn't come out coherently. I immediately felt like a complete bully. I couldn't bear to have caused that much pain to another human being, especially one that I loved.

Shit! Did I really love her? Can love develop so suddenly?

I stood up, walked around the table and sat down next to her. I put my arms around her and hugged her.

"Ssh," I whispered. "It's going to be all right."

She snuggled into me and the sobbing gradually subsided.

"Sorry," she said. "I will talk to you. It's . . ."

The sobs returned. I stroked her hair and hugged her closer.

"It's all right," I said. "There's plenty of time."

She pulled her face away and looked back at me, her beautiful eyes glistening with tears.

"I love you Harry," she said.

A wonderful sense of bliss surged through my body like the kick of an expensive drug. I was addicted, it was already too late.

"I love you too Moira," I said.

"There's something you need to know," she said, looking down as if she was afraid or ashamed.

"What?" I asked, fearing some terrible revelation about her health or something.

"I am not Moira," she whispered.

BONES

When we got outside the biscuit factory it became obvious just how much Mason had been affected by what I'd subjected him to. He was a shambles physically and a wreck mentally. His body was shaking as if it was going to splinter into bits at any moment. It scared me to see how close I had come to killing him off.

I drove him to the old boatshed in the docks in almost total silence because I was too afraid to engage with him and because he needed all the energy he had just to stop from disintegrating. On the plus side he'd discovered just how dangerous I was, and how vulnerable he was, so I hoped that would end his attempts to intimidate and control me.

"There's no need for anyone else to know about what you

did. It wouldn't do either of us any good. Understand?" he said menacingly.

"Yes, no good would come of it at all. It will be our secret," I said, trying to convey as much threat as he had.

I watched him as he accelerated away from the docks area towards the road that led out of town and back to his house. He was going to have to do some explaining to his comrades in arms and to Adams about his sudden disappearance but after what he'd said to me I knew that explanation would not include the truth.

I drove the short distance back to my flat, parked in my usual space and went into the building. I was shattered and needed to rest but also needed to know if there were any developments in the Moira Mason case.

I sent a text to Chunky asking him to call me when he could. He replied to say he was in yet another briefing and would meet me in an hour in Taffies club. He told me to come round to the rear entrance when I got there and Jan would let me in.

I had a shower, mainly to get the smell of Big Bill off me, and then I took a twenty-minute nap hoping to reset my brain before heading up to town and Taffies Club.

When I got to the club I tapped on the back door and it was opened almost immediately by Chunky, who grabbed my sleeve and ushered me in. I followed him along the passage to the bar. There were no punters there at that time of day, so I sat down at a table near the bar while Chunky sorted us both out with a double brandy each.

"You're going to need this," he said.

"What's going on?" I was puzzled but not too concerned.

"Adams is gunning for you," Chunky said. "He thinks you know more than you're saying about the murder. You're going to be suspended – as soon as he gets the formalities done."

"Fucking Adams," I knocked the brandy back in one glug.

"Well, at least you won't have to investigate the graffiti

incidents," he chuckled.

"Fucksake Chunks," I said. "It's not funny, you're talking about my livelihood, my life."

"Sorry Boss, I didn't mean . . ."

"Never mind that, it's not your fault. Is there anything else going on?"

"Yes, someone's made a complaint about you."

"Fuck! Who?"

"Someone on the Backfields estate. Something about you attacking some bloke."

"Bollocks!"

"Who was it Boss?"

"Just that fucking lowlife Jackie Mann."

"It was some woman who complained, I think."

"Yeah yeah, I know. At least Jackie himself won't take it any further, I think he knows what's best for him."

"Aye Boss, and there's something else you might be interested in."

"Oh yeah?"

"Well, just before I left the office, a call came in from the officer watching Mason's house. He's come back apparently, didn't want to talk about where he'd been."

I tried not to show any reaction to that piece of news, maybe I underplayed it a bit but I reckoned that was better than too much false shock or surprise.

"Probably best not knowing with a dirty bastard like that," I joked.

"So what are you going to do about the suspension?"

"Not much I can do. Anyway, I've got nothing to hide, just been doing my job innit Chunks? I'm sure it will get cleared up soon enough."

"True, true," Chunky said. "Anyway, I'd better get back. I'm looking into Moira Mason's past, her social media, stuff like that, so if you've left any dodgy comments . . ."

"You? They've asked you to do that?"

"Yeah, well, they're short-staffed in that department apparently."

"Thanks for all this. You're a good friend. I won't forget

that when all this is over."

"You'd do the same for me."

"Aye Chunks," I said, but knew I wouldn't.

Was I supposed to feel guilty about that?

CHAPTER FOURTEEN

SKIN

I stood up and moved away from the person who I thought I'd fallen in love with. Who was she? I sat back down on a stool at the other side of the table and put my head in my hands. We were both silent for ten seconds or so. I looked up at her, still gobsmacked. She smiled at me. It felt like I was bathing in a flood of warm bright light.

"What do you mean?" I managed to say. "What about the photo in the paper?"

"That wasn't me, that was my sister."

"Sister?"

"Yes, my twin, we are . . . were, almost identical."

"So she was Moira?"

"Yes."

"So who are you?"

"Mel."

"Mel?"

"Short for Melinda"

"So, was it you in my cab?"

"Yes."

"I don't get it."

"I will explain everything. I promise. But I'm in trouble, big trouble."

"Why? Was the murder anything to do with you?"

"Sort of."

"Sort of?"

"Yes, my father killed her because he thought she was me."

"Fucking hell," I said. "Why would he do that?"

"She was always the favourite, when we were growing up. I don't know why. I always thought there was something rotten in me. I was a bad person, I felt dirty."

"Wow!" I said. Why are you telling me?"

"It's obvious isn't it? I love you. I want to be with you. That's why I've been waiting, hiding here in Elchurch in a B&B. I didn't know what else to do. When he finds out that he got rid of the wrong daughter . . . well he won't make the same mistake again. I wish I'd stayed at home and never set foot in this town."

"What do you mean stayed at home? Don't you live with your father?"

"No, he split up with my mother when I . . . we were eleven years old. I went with her, he didn't want me. I hadn't seen him or Moira since, not until last week."

"This is a lot to take in," I said. Do you want a drink, or a cup of tea?"

"I don't think there's time. I'm very scared of him, he's a powerful man. Please come with me, you told me you loved me and I've got no one else."

"What about your mother?"

"We don't get on, not since my stepfather died, she blamed me."

"Why?"

"He killed himself after I told her what he was doing."

She hesitated, couldn't find any more words.

"What did he do?" I asked gently, feeling my way.

She took a deep breath. "I was only fourteen when it started. I couldn't hold it in any longer, but she wouldn't accept it. I left her after the funeral, got a flat of my own, I was seventeen by then. I've been on my own ever since . . ."

Her body shook and she started sobbing again, huge gut-wrenching sobs of a kind that dredged up all the nightmares I'd ever had. I moved back towards her and took her in my arms.

"Come here," I said. "You're not on your own now. Don't talk anymore, it can wait. How do you think I can help?"

"Come with me. I need to think, to get away. It's too dangerous to stay here, and he will come after me when he realises his mistake. Before that happens I need to find a way to get the truth out. To let the world know what a monster my so-called father is. Please help me."

"Getting away might be difficult. I have a business to run. I've got commitments. I don't know."

Her face dropped into the saddest expression I'd ever seen, as if she had completely given in and was just waiting for the fatal blow. What was I thinking? My business was fucked. My relationship was fucked. My brother hated me and vice versa. The only other person in my life who meant anything to me was my father. I couldn't leave him. Could I?

I had to make a positive decision for myself, for Mel and for our future. After all the mess was sorted out we would find a way to be happy together. There was no need to think about it any longer. I didn't have any choice at all. Life could be tough and I just had to deal with it.

"All right yes, I'm sure we can do it," I said. "After all, it won't be forever, just until we figure out . . ."

Mel threw her arms around my neck and hugged me so hard I could hardly breathe. I prised her off me gently.

"Steady on," I said. "Or I won't make it to the car."

Mel looked up at me, her eyes were still red but there was the spark of a new light growing in them.

"We'll need to get a few things sorted before we can go," I said. "There's no need to panic, best to take our time and get it right."

"I do love you," she said.

BONES

I went home and tidied up a bit then got the call an hour later. I decided to walk to the meeting so that I could prepare my story on the way.

Adams was busy when I arrived at the station, or pretending to be busy more like. I knew his type too well. Totally clueless. When I was a fresh green PC a sergeant had told me that there were two types of cops: good cops and bullshit cops. Good cops got the job done, gathered the evidence, collected intelligence and all that, but most importantly they got results by knowing just how far they could push things with suspects. Bullshit cops lived by one rule only and that was *'bullshit baffles brains'*.

It was a saying the sergeant had picked up in the RAF or somewhere. At the time I'd hoped that the saying itself was bullshit, just something he used to help us learn, I didn't want to believe that the defence and security of our country was in the hands of bullshitters. Since then experience had taught me more or less the same thing. I couldn't stand bullshit but I knew how to get the job done and I knew that sometimes, when the stability of society was threatened or people's lives were at risk then smacking a toerag in the mouth to get the truth out of them was the right thing to do.

I paced up and down the corridor waiting for Adams to call me into his office. I was screaming with frustration inside but just had to put up with it even though it made me feel like a naughty boy waiting outside the head teacher's office.

When he eventually called me in, he was surprisingly polite and understanding.

"So," he said. "You've got nothing to worry about, but we can't risk a third party using the fact that you were having a relationship with the victim as a weapon against you, or us."

"Fair enough," I said.

"Yes, so it's best all round if you take a little break. Don't go anywhere though. We might need to talk to you again, just for clarification perhaps."

"Yes," I said. "I know the drill."

"Well ok then. I'll be in touch. Use the time to relax if you can, though of course this can't be easy for you. You will probably be referred for counselling, is that ok with you?"

"I guess so," I said.

Despite the easy ride Adams had given me I was feeling down. My life was pretty crap in many ways, always had been really and I didn't know if I could carry on without considering some major changes, like, did I really want to continue doing the job? Maybe it was just Moira's death affecting me? Maybe I just needed a break, or maybe I should take up the offer of counselling, if only to get someone to talk to. I'd always believed that I didn't want, or need, any friends as such but I realised I was very lonely really. Truth was I didn't have a clue about much at all.

On my way back to the flat I made a detour to the Tinworks to get myself a pint. While I was there I got talking to a woman I knew through my ex Lindy, she was a cousin of some sort. Her name was Vicky and she was probably in her late twenties.

I'd come across her now and again since I'd split up with Lindy, she'd become some kind of musician but still worked behind the bar at the arts centre to earn her rent money. I liked her, but not really in a sexual way even though she was cute, and she was one of the very few people who seemed to get where I was coming from, and I got the impression that she liked me too.

Vicky came to sit across the table from me.

"Howdy Mr Bones," she said. "What's the score?"

"Ah!" I said, "Ten-nil to them at the moment."

"That's good then," she said with a cheeky grin.

"How come?"

"The only way is up innit."

I laughed. "You know what, you're right. Thanks."

"No need for thanks," she smiled, "just doing mah job man. But there is something you might be able to help me with."

"I'll have a go."

"Hang on, I'll get you another one of those," she said, pointing at my pint glass that was nearly empty. "I might join you, I'm on a break."

I didn't really want another alcoholic drink but didn't want to reject her offer. "Maybe a half?" I said. "It's a bit gassy for this time of day. Anyway, let me get the drinks."

"No need, call it a sample," Vicky winked at me, "I'll just nip over."

While I was waiting, I checked my phone for messages. Radio silence – kind of nice in a way.

She came back and plonked two half pint glasses of beer on the table.

"I lobbed in a tot of vodka," she whispered. "Perks of the job innit."

I smiled, how could I refuse?

"So, how can I help?" I asked.

"Well, I've got this Facebook friend," she paused. "Well, she's not really a friend, in fact I've never met her. But she contacted me a few months ago, saw that I was a member of a group for ex-pupils of Elchurch High."

She took a sip of her drink.

"Oh yeah."

"She wanted to know if I was in the same class as, you know, the girl who was found, you know, up by the motorway."

"Moira Mason?"

"Yes."

"And were you?"

"No, she was quite a bit younger than me, but I did sort of know her."

"Is that what you told the woman on Facebook?"

"Yes. Then she asked me loads more questions, like if I knew what she was doing now, where she lived, that sort of thing. I thought it was all a bit stalky, if you know what I mean."

"Yes, sounds like it was."

"So I asked her why she wanted to know. She was a bit vague, said something about family tree research and that it wasn't that important."

"Did you give her any information?"

"Only what I knew, which wasn't a lot. That I thought Moira was still living with her father Bill Mason. I knew about that because a mutual friend used to know her well, she told me about Moira's father once, he sounds like a very dodgy character."

"What's the name of this Facebook friend, the one asking all the questions?"

"Alice something. Hang on, let me check."

Vicky pulled her phone out of her jeans pocket and unlocked it. She tapped at the screen.

"Right, here it is, let me have a look at my friends list, I'll do a search, there's a lot of them. Here we go. Hmm, that's weird, she's gone."

"Can you remember what she looked like?"

"No, sorry, she didn't post very much and as far as I can remember there were no close-ups. Come to think of it perhaps she wasn't who she said she was anyway, could have been anyone, a man, a catfish. A name means nothing online."

"True," I said. Although, I thought, it could actually mean something, if only a place to start from. What alias someone chose could sometimes say a lot about them.

"Anyway, who cares about gender nowadays?" Vicky said.

I shrugged. "Depends who you talk to. So, what about the messages, have you still got them?"

"I suppose so, let me have a look."

"No, don't bother now. It's probably just a coincidence. I'll get back to you if it turns out to be relevant. In the meantime, it's best to keep it to yourself. If they contact you again please let me know."

"Sure," she said.

Truth was that I wanted to keep the information she had given me to myself, just until I found out more. There was something not quite right about what Vicky had told me and if there was some vague person known as Alice who'd been pathologically interested in Moira not long before her death then I needed to know why.

"Now, what are you doing tonight?" Vicky asked.

"Um, nothing, I don't think. I'm actually taking some time off at the moment."

"We're having a bit of a get together tonight back at mine. One of my housemates is thirty today, god help us. I know you're a cop and all that, but even you must have a social life and you look like you need cheering up."

"Um, I'm not sure. What sort of a get together is it?"

"The usual, you know, couple of drinks and . . ."

"Drugs," I said with a stern look.

"Oh shit," she said. "Forget I asked."

I laughed. "Only joking, that sort of thing doesn't bother me, as long as nobody's growing opium poppies in the attic that is."

"It's nothing special, there's six of us living there and there's something going on nearly every day, we've got a lot of friends between us, real life friends that is, not Fakebook friends."

I chuckled. "I'm not sure. Thanks for the invite though."

"Well if you do decide to come it's anytime after half six at 61 Copper Street, not far from here. Do you know it?"

"Well yes, it pays to know your way around in my job."

"Thanks for the chat then," Vicky said. "I'd better get back to work. Might see you later?"

Vicky went back behind the bar and I finished my drink. Afterwards I walked home and tried to piece together all the information I had about the murder. It wasn't easy since Moira's image was always present in the front of my mind.

When I got in I decided to go online and do a bit of stalking myself. Maybe I would have more luck than Vicky in tracking down the mysterious Alice.

SKIN

Mel brewed us both a cup of fresh coffee while I was gathering the few items I thought might come in useful for travelling, including spare t-shirts and underwear. We packed the car boot together then sat down in the kitchen to drink the coffee and plan our next move.

"What about you," I asked. "Where's your stuff?"

"I've got a bag in the B&B," she said, "and I need to settle up with them. But, I'm sorry, I don't have any money left."

"Ah, don't worry about that, I'll get some cash on the way."

"Thanks, that would be cool. I will pay you back."

"No probs," I said. "You're going to need something to wear, just until you can pick your own stuff up. I can get something from Mandy's wardrobe if that's ok."

"I feel so guilty already, but I suppose there's no other

choice. Something simple will do, a long t-shirt perhaps, I can put my coat on over it. If there's one there?"

"Yes, probably, I'll go and get something in a minute."

"Thanks."

"I want to pay a visit to my father on the way too, he's not very well, and I don't know when I'll see him again."

"Sorry. Are you sure about this?" she asked, her face creasing with anxiety.

"Absolutely," I said. "It seems right, it is right. I want to be with you."

She smiled and the light returned to her face. I just wanted to protect her.

We stopped outside the Co-op on the Backfields and I went in while Mel waited in the car, with her head and most of her face covered by an old beanie hat I'd grabbed from the bedroom. I bought a bagful of travel essentials, like bottles of water and snacks and withdrew a few quid from the cash machine outside the shop.

After that I drove across the estate to where my father lived. I parked in a quiet cul-de-sac around the corner from his house. Mel stayed in the car again. I told her to keep the door locked and to phone me if anyone bothered her, knowing that there were a few characters prowling those streets who would see a young woman as an easy target for a scam or something even worse.

I knocked and waited for half a minute before turning the handle, the door was unlocked. When I walked into the living room my old man was sleeping in his favourite armchair. He opened his eyes.

"Ah Harry, I knew it was you," he said sleepily.

"And I knew you'd say that," I laughed.

I sat down in the other chair and looked around the room at the overflowing mess of his life that was littering all the surfaces.

"To what do I owe the honour?" he asked.

"Well, I did tell you I'd be popping in, but I'm sorry, I can't stay long. I've got to go away for a few days."

"Don't worry about me. Holiday is it?"

"No, it's work," I said. "I'm driving someone around for a bit." I realised that my excuse was too feeble so I added, "He's a musician going to do some recording, his usual driver got laid up at the last minute."

"It's not the virus is it?"

"Nah," I had to think quickly, "he twisted his ankle or something."

"Where are you going?"

"Not sure exactly where yet . . . but it's around the Brighton area."

"Sounds interesting. Who is he? "Anyone I'd know about."

"Um, not really," I said. "A sort of folk singer, up and coming, but not well known yet."

"Hope it goes well," he said. "Bring me a stick of rock back."

"I will," I said.

He tried to stand up but fell back onto the seat struggling for breath.

"Let me help you," I said.

He waved me away. "I'll be all right in a minute," he gasped.

"Damn long Covid," he said, "on top of everything else."

"You don't look too good," I said. "I'll cancel the booking."

"Don't you dare."

"But . . ."

"That would make me feel worse. I'll be fine, I've got my helper Carol coming in every day, she's due soon. She'll sort me out, she's an angel."

I made him a cup of tea and we chatted pointlessly for a few minutes.

"I've got to go," I said.

My phone went. I looked at the screen. It was Mandy. I looked up at him unable to say anything.

"Well answer it then," he said. "It might be important."

"It's Mandy," I said.

"Well it is important then isn't it?"

"Yes, you're right," I said.

I answered the phone. "Hi Mandy."

"Can you talk?"

"Hang on," I said. "I'm with my dad."

I lowered the phone and turned to my father. "Sorry dad," I said, "I'd better get going. Is that all right with you?"

"Yes, of course, say hello to Mandy for me."

"Thanks," I said. "I'll see you in a few days."

I put the phone back against my ear as I walked out of the house. I stopped on the pavement outside.

"Sorry Mandy, are you still there?"

"Yes."

"Dad says hello," I said.

"Say hello from me," she said.

"I will. Anyway what did you want, I thought you were going to your parents' house."

"I'm there," she said. "I wanted to apologise for my behaviour. I'm sorry, I've been under so much stress, I didn't know how to handle it."

"It's ok, if that's the way you feel."

"But I don't really feel like that. I'm so sorry Skin. You're a good man. I've let you down."

"It's not your fault," I said. "I should have paid more attention to things."

"Anyway . . ." Mandy paused to take a breath. "It's good news. Very good news."

I waited.

"Skin? Are you still there?

"Yes, what's going on?"

"My parents are going to help us, financially. They've been thinking about it for ages apparently. Now that they've retired and on good pensions, they've got a lot of spare cash doing nothing. They are going to give me a lump sum."

I was speechless.

"Fifty thousand," she said.

"Wow, that's crazy."

"I know. It's great isn't it?"

"I suppose so. What's the catch though?"

"No catch."

"Wow, I don't know what to say."

"Anyway, I'm coming home tomorrow. That's ok isn't it? I'm sorry about everything."

My phone was beeping, I pulled it away from my ear and looked at the screen. There was a call waiting from Mel.

"Um, sorry," I said, "I've got a call waiting, probably a pick up."

"You'd better take it. We can talk later."

"Yes," I said, relieved that I would have time to take it all in and decide how to react.

"I'll ring you later," she said. "And Skin, I do love you, I really do."

Shit! I disconnected, unable to respond in any way.

I took the call from Mel in a daze. "What's up?" I asked.

She didn't answer but I heard her shouting at someone. "I'm on the phone to the police," she yelled, "they're on the way."

I put the phone in my pocket and ran around the corner to where I'd parked the car.

BONES

Using my alter-ego, Jack Regan, I found Vicky's profile on Facebook and looked through her friends' list for anyone called Alice. Vicky had a lot of friends, over a thousand, and two of them were called Alice and one was called Alys. All of the Alices had what seemed to be genuine profiles and lots of posts going back years so it was easy to rule them out.

Next, I revisited Moira's profile to check for anything new. It hadn't been frozen but there had been no activity for a few months apart from a recent flurry of shocked condolences posted around the time Moira's name was first published.

Unlike Vicky, Moira had very few friends, just twenty-five in fact and she'd had very little public interaction with any of them. At a glance they looked like people, mostly women, of around the same age as her, people she'd known in school or college I guessed. I would probably have to come back and check them out at some point, if all other avenues finished in dead ends.

I carried on searching, on the social media sites and in general searches, for Alice and for Moira Mason, and while I was at it I also searched for her father. Nothing remotely relevant was coming up until I found a reference to Bill Mason from almost fifteen years earlier. He was mentioned in a report in a Manchester newspaper about an incident at a nightclub where a number of people had been injured by an attacker. The article said that Mason was a businessman and a part owner of the club.

That was news to me even though it was old news, but then I'd never before thought about looking for information about Bill Mason in that way. I remembered that he came to my attention not long after the publication date of that article in Manchester. Yes, I was as certain as I could be that it was the same person as the Bill Mason I'd come to know and hate. He'd moved into the Elchurch area not long after that incident and probably as a result of it.

I couldn't find any more out about what had happened from a public search, partly because it was a long time ago in internet terms and partly because I was getting tired of it all and needed a break. I remembered about the party in Vicky's house. It might do me good to let my hair down for a few hours, put things back into perspective, get Moira out of my head.

I sniffed under my arms, not too bad, anyway I wasn't going on the pull so it would do.

I decided to walk through town to get to Copper Street, it was still quite early and I could do with the exercise. I thought I might get a cab back after the party, as long as it wasn't that wanker of a brother's manky cowboy outfit of course.

There weren't many people about and it was a nice evening for a walk so I tried to convince myself that I was enjoying myself along the way. Truth was I still couldn't get that daft girl out of my head and every step I took was a struggle against myself to stop, turn around, go home and bury myself under a quilt.

But on I had to go, otherwise I would probably have lost my mind. It was no good giving in to that sort of thing.

I was ambling along one of the back streets not far from the Tinworks. All those streets round there held a lot of memories for me. Behind every other door there was a story I'd been involved with in one way or another. I knew the area so well because that was where I'd spent much of my time as a teenager escaping from the Backfields Estate where I'd grown up, and later as a young police officer ferreting out the petty criminals and scrotes who tended to go to ground there.

Since that time the area had become more gentrified as more people associated with the arts centre moved in. Of course there was just as much misery and bad behaviour going on behind those Ikea blinds as there had been behind the tatty curtains that were there before them.

I had the feeling that there was someone else around who was interested in what I was doing. I wasn't being paranoid, I trusted those kind of feelings, they had helped me out a hell of a lot in the past, kept me alive even.

All my senses were on high alert, but because it was getting dark, it was my hearing that kicked in first. When I heard the footsteps behind me it was already too late as I felt the hood being pushed over my head and the rope winding round my body.

I was being kidnapped.

CHAPTER FIFTEEN

SKIN

When I turned the corner into the cul-de-sac there was a figure that looked like a man dressed in black. He was pushing the bonnet of my car up and down aggressively. I ran straight at him, grabbed the hood of the black top he was wearing and yanked him away. He fell back onto me and we both ended up rolling on the tarmac.

I jumped to my feet and stood over him. He was laughing like a maniac and frothing at the mouth. I thought I'd seriously injured him so stood back. I moved towards the car to check if Mel was all right. She nodded at me through the windscreen, then her eyes opened wide with horror and she pointed frantically to whatever was behind me.

I turned around quickly and the crazed attacker was almost on top of me. I managed to dodge sideways and he slammed into the car and fell down again. I knelt over him as he was threshing about on his back and pinned his arms to the ground. He was weakening but still had a manic look in his eyes.

"What the fuck are you on?" I asked. "Why are you attacking my car? Don't you know there's someone sitting in it? Calm fucking down, or I'll call the cops."

I could see him moving his closed lips and realised he was collecting a mouthful of gob, so when he moved his head back and then forward to unleash the disgusting substance I was ready and easily moved my own head to avoid it.

I needed to minimise any damage the man could cause in his demented state, so my survival instinct kicked in and I pushed myself up to my feet and laid into him with my steel toecaps until he was gasping for breath.

I moved quickly towards the car. Mel leaned over from the passenger seat to open the driver's door. Just as I was getting into the car I looked around to check what state the attacker was in. He was lying on his side, his head bleeding with multiple wounds and he was grinning like a frenzied fighting dog.

"I fucking know who you are Mr Jones," he said. "And I know who that bint in the car is. I'm sure Big Bill would be happy to get to know you too."

Big Bill? Of course he meant Big Bill Mason, fuck, the old bastard was probably onto us. I finished getting into the car and closed the door.

Mel was shaking with fear.

"What did he say?" she asked.

"I'll tell you later. We've got to get the fuck out of here."

As we zoomed out of the cul-de-sac and into the guts of the estate Mel tugged my arm.

"What about the B&B?" she asked. "My stuff is still there.

BONES

It was obvious I was in the back of a van. The feel of the cold metal floor and the noise and smell of the diesel engine were the giveaways. Whoever had kidnapped me stunk of stale tobacco and piss so I guessed they were some kind of low-life bob-a-job thugs hired by someone further up the chain of cuntiness. It had to be Mason behind it, it would be too much of a coincidence if it was someone else given what had happened over the previous couple of days.

They tied me up more tightly as the van was moving. Not one of them said a word but there were a lot of grunts. The van swerved and slowed down before stopping suddenly. At least two sets of arms yanked me out and across what felt like a gravelly drive through a door and into a room with a cold concrete floor.

I heard the footsteps of the people who had dragged me disappearing back outside. The door slammed shut and I was left lying on the concrete in the dark for what seemed like several minutes but was probably only a few seconds. Two sets of other, softer, footsteps came towards me and stopped near my head.

"Get that fucking hood off him," an angry voice said, it belonged to who I was expecting to be responsible for my predicament – Bill Mason.

The hood was yanked away and a large boot pushed me over onto my back so that I was looking up straight into the masked face of the man who I'd almost killed.

"Put him against the wall," Mason said to his companion, one of his regular heavies.

I'd never actually been told the bloke's name and I'd never heard his voice, but I did know who he was because I'd researched him at some point like I had with all known associates of Big Bill. Through searching the police databases and making a phone call or two I'd discovered that he was a hard boy from Coventry called Colin, he'd been arrested a couple of times for suspected assault but never charged.

I was manhandled roughly and pushed back against a breeze block wall. Mason sat down on a cheap plastic chair about two metres in front of the wall and stared at me. I was concerned I would suffer some permanent damage because bits of me were rapidly going numb.

"The ropes are too tight," I said. "I can't feel my fingers."

Mason sighed. "Loosen them," he said to the non-speaking bastard. "Then leave us."

The man did as he was told. After he left the room and closed the door Mason paced around smoking and shaking his head.

"I really don't know what to do with you," he said.

"Let me go, I can help you," I said.

"Help me to do what? Can you chop yourself into little pieces and chuck them in the docks for the eels to eat?"

I lowered my head.

"Sorry," I said, "but I really can help you."

While I was speaking my mind was racing through every detail of the events of the last few days and assessing all the information relating to Mason and his daughter that I already knew. I remembered my earlier chat with Vicky when she'd told me about her shady Facebook friend.

"I've got a lead," I said, "a suspect."

"Don't give me none of that bullshit son, I heard you were off the case."

"I've got contacts on the inside," I said. "Besides, no one else knows what I know."

"Stop talking rubbish."

"I'm still investigating her but I'm sure she was directly involved."

"What do you mean her? Who's she?"

"A woman was trying to track Moira down."

"A woman?"

"Yes. Look, I know we've had our differences . . ."

"Differences?" he almost exploded with rage. "You fucking tied me up and fucked me up big time. And you've probably given me the coronavirus you . . ."

I could see he was making a huge effort to bring himself back under control, I almost felt sorry for the big bastard.

"We have to try and forget all that for now, if we're going to find out what happened to Moira."

"Stop saying her fucking name like that."

"Look, let me go. I'll do some more digging, then I'll tell you everything I know and everything I find out. Like I said I've got contacts in the force and everywhere else."

He stopped shaking, and stared at me with a cold calculating gaze.

"This is the deal," he said. "You don't say a fucking word to any fucker, any fucker at all, about what you did to me. If I find out that you've told anyone else, then there'll be nothing left to lose for me. Do you know what I mean?"

I did know what he meant. He could be a vicious merciless bastard, especially when his pride was threatened.

"I do," I said.

"And if you fuck me around, same thing applies. Get it?"

"Yes," I said lowering my head in submission.

"Don't forget what we've talked about."

I don't think he was too sure but he had nothing else.

He walked over to the door and called out. Mr Muscle appeared in the doorway.

"Let him loose, he's learned his lesson," Mason said. "Give him a lift back to town."

Mason walked straight outside without looking back.

SKIN

I stopped the car in a side street on the way out from the Backfields Estate to tell Mel that her father either knew what we were up to, or would know very soon because the ninja scumbag had recognised us.

"How? Who is he?"

"I'm not sure," I said, "but I meet a lot of people in my game, maybe he's an ex-driver? And because you look so like your sister, he may have thought you were her."

She trembled. "I'm scared," she said. "I can't stop thinking about her. I'll be all right in a minute. I need to get my stuff."

It was tempting to suggest to Mel that we abandon the idea of going back to the B&B to settle up with the owner and pick her bag up, but that could be counterproductive because there's nothing like abandoned luggage and unpaid hotel bills to draw attention to yourself.

"We'd better go get it now," I said.

I drove the car to the guesthouse and parked on the road nearby.

"I'll wait in the car this time," I said to Mel.

"Yeah, well look out for madmen in black hoodies," she said laughing, as she got out of the car.

I was surprised that she seemed to be recovering from the violent attack on the Backfields so soon and so easily, especially considering how hysterical her reaction had been when it was happening. But then I'd seen how fragile she was when I'd reminded her about her sister

The street used to be one of the best in town, lined with mature trees, large semis and detached houses, surrounded by well-tended gardens. It had started to go downhill a couple of decades earlier when buy-to-let landlords had taken advantage of the low property prices and the departure of the aging population either to the grave or into care. Many of the houses had been converted into flats and bedsits and others into small hotels and bed and breakfast establishments.

The street was one of those that led to the docks area which was where my brother lived, so I'd parked discreetly in a shaded spot between a huge camper van and a dilapidated Volvo estate on the off-chance that Bones might just happen to spot me while driving past on his way to harass some poor sod for possessing a speck of weed.

I sat in the car for about ten minutes getting increasingly anxious that I might be looking suspicious and could be challenged by a concerned resident. At one point a passing bus was held up for a few seconds right alongside my car. I had the feeling of being watched so looked up at the windows of the passenger compartment. I couldn't be sure if it was her but there was a person who looked very much like Raskal looking back down in my direction. I looked away quickly hoping she hadn't seen me, the last thing I needed was any kind of witness to our hasty departure.

When Mel returned she threw a holdall onto the back seat and then sat next to me in the front of the car.

"Fire the bitch up!" she said with a fake American accent.

"Uh?"

"It's from a film silly. Let's fly away Batman."

I started the engine.

"What film?"

"Doesn't matter now, it was supposed to be humorous."

"Ha ha," I said.

"Very funny," she said.

"Where to?" I asked.

"I don't know."

"Nor me. How about we head east?"

"Which way is that?"

"In the general direction of London," I said.

"Sounds good to me. Step on it."

I didn't really want to go anywhere near London. What I was hoping for was simply to get away from the chaos my life had become. Perhaps hole up somewhere off the beaten track for a day or two, let things, including Mel, calm down a bit.

Then maybe we could talk properly, get to know each other a lot more. I had to believe in love at first sight because it had just happened to me, and it was as real as anything could be, but life was about a lot more than love.

We drove out of town and then along the motorway for about half an hour. I was starting to feel like we hadn't thought it through properly, that maybe we needed to pause and talk about what our options were.

"I'm not sure this is a good idea," I said to Mel, who was sitting happily beside me humming some chirpy tune that I'd heard before but didn't know the name of.

"What do you mean?"

"You know, racing away like this without a plan."

"But we had to."

"I know," I said, "but we're far enough away now. The immediate danger is gone."

"What do you think we should do, where should we go?"

"Haven't got a clue. That's why I think we should stop somewhere and think about it all. There's quite a few nice little towns along the coast, it's not far, we could drive down there. Then . . ."

"Ooh, I love the seaside. Let's do it."

I took the next exit off the motorway and headed south.

BONES

As the silent Colin drove the vehicle back towards Elchurch town centre I stared out of the window. I could see that we were coming from a small industrial estate at the edges of the Western Valleys. What I didn't understand was why Mason was being so reckless by allowing me to know the location. That sort of information could become very useful in any future investigation into his operations.

The van stopped almost exactly where I'd been dragged into it. Quiet Colin left the engine running and looked pointedly at me. I opened the door, got out, closed it again and stood on the pavement watching the taillights of the van as it zipped up the street and out of sight.

I felt surprisingly relaxed. Maybe it was because things could have got a lot worse with the old fucker. At least I had a chance to pull things back under control. I wondered if it was too late to go to Vicky's party, after all, she was one of the people I would have to talk to about the unknown Facebook friend. As well as that, and despite looking like a shambolic mess after rolling around on the floor of a van, I was in the mood where I thought I might get lucky, or at least find someone interesting to talk to for an hour or two.

'Yeah, fuck it,' I thought.

It wasn't too late when I got to the house in Copper Street, but the party was already getting a bit rowdy and that wasn't a good thing. I hoped the party wouldn't get noisier because that would risk the police getting called and me being found in an embarrassing situation.

Christ, if I thought like that all the time I'd be better off banged up anyway.

The front door was unlocked so I went straight in. It was a big house for the location. There were two big rooms on the ground floor. At the front of the house was a double sized lounge where the front room and the middle room had been knocked into one and at the rear there was a large kitchen diner with a door that led outside onto a patio area.

There were people in all of the rooms and outside. They were a very arty and swotty looking bunch but down to earth enough going by their loud voices and general loutishness. I'd never been to university, never wanted it, never really had the opportunity either and of course no support from my parents, but shit, I didn't care and I wouldn't have fitted in anyway. I wouldn't have been able to keep my mouth shut about all the pretentious crap those sort of people liked to spout.

Despite my low opinion of the twats in the house, I could cope with people like them for a few hours at the odd social occasion, and who knew, it could be fun and I might pull after all.

I didn't have any booze because to be honest I was still very rattled by what had happened to me at Mason's hands, and still afraid that the worst was yet to come, so I hadn't even thought about bringing any. But, what the hell, fuck it.

I found some fancily-labelled bottles of strong cider in the fridge, the sort of stuff the dossers on the streets used to drink from two-litre plastic bottles. It was just as deadly at nearly nine percent proof but repackaged in coloured glass and stuck with metallic labels so that it looked like a solid premium drink, fit for aspiring creative writing teachers, songwriters and theatre directors, the sort of people who's second home was the Tinworks Arts Centre.

I drank the first bottle as I walked around among the pratts and by the time I finished it my mood had improved, and I even started to think they weren't so bad after all. I opened a second bottle and headed back to the front part of the house, I'd noticed a couple of young women there who I recognised from the bar at the Tinworks and had often exchanged a little bit of banter with. Maybe it was time to get to know them better?

As I moved towards them they shifted up on the sofa, I assumed it was to make room for me, I didn't care if it wasn't anyway, it was a party, people were going to talk to you.

As it happened, they were both very polite and respectful, but I got the impression that it was because, to them, I was an older man, even though I wasn't even thirty-nine years old. Luckily Vicky came into the room at that point. When she saw me she came across and stood over me swaying a bit, she was already drunker than I was.

"Hey Bones," she said. "You came."

I stood up. "Yep, and I'll behave, I promise." Jeez, the drink was turning me into some kind of nice-guy wuss, what the fuck was that all about?

Vicky laughed, "I hope you're not going to behave too

much, if you know what I mean."

Shit, she was already coming on to me. No I wasn't ready to pull at all. I still couldn't stop thinking about Moira. What the fuck was I thinking, coming to a fucking party?

"Um, I'll probably not stay long though. I'm feeling a bit rough to be honest. Could do with an early night, I'm knackered."

"I know something that will wake you up," she said with a wink.

She put her hand in her pocket and pulled out a tiny transparent plastic sealable bag crammed with what looked like white powder.

"Coke?" I asked.

"Yes sir! How about it?"

"I can't be seen," I said.

"No probs, follow me."

Vicky tugged my arm and led me out of the room and upstairs to a small bedroom next to the bathroom. She closed the door behind us and then went over to the single bed and sat on the edge of the mattress.

"This isn't my room," she said. "One of the postgrads lives in it, but he's hardly ever here, always away teaching or researching somewhere."

She dragged the small bedside cabinet towards her and cleared its surface. Then she tipped a small mound of the coke on it and pushed it into a line with her finger. She sucked the residual specks of cocaine off the end of her finger then nodded at me.

"Go ahead," she said.

I wouldn't normally have sniffed up a line of untested white powder from someone who was more or less a stranger to me but there was something about Vicky that made me trust her, that and the couple of bottles of strong cider had put me in a 'fuck-it-why-not' mood.

I leaned down over the coke, closed my right nostril with my index finger and sucked it up my left nostril. There was an immediate hit, it was good, top notch. I wondered how a poor bar worker could afford to buy drugs of such quality, and who from, but it wasn't the time to pursue that line of thinking. I would keep that information in reserve.

We went back downstairs and continued drinking and socialising. I knew I was in danger of behaving like a total tosser like I had done in similar circumstances, so had to make a conscious effort to control myself, but it was still fun.

Vicky's housemate, a young woman called Raskal, joined us on the second visit to the bedroom. She knew that I was Skin's brother, not that it was any kind of secret, and she told me that he had been in that same house just a couple of days earlier.

"Who was he with?" I asked casually.

"Me," she said. "We know each other quite well."

"How was he?" I asked.

"Yeah, all right, but when I thought I saw him again, he blanked me. I'm not sure if it was him though, I was going past on a bus at the time, on the way to the out-of-town shopping centre.

"How do mean he blanked you."

"The bus was passing a parked car and got held up for a second. I looked down and there he was sitting in the driver's seat. He looked up towards where I was sitting. At least I thought it was him, but when I waved, he just looked away."

"Perhaps you were mistaken or he didn't see you through the glass," I said.

"Yeah, I guess so, and the car window was closed."

It was my turn to do another line. Vicky had set it up ready. I leaned down and sniffed. Wow! Just then the door to the bedroom was pushed open from the outside and a big bloke poked his head around the door frame.

Fuck me, it was Shane.

CHAPTER SIXTEEN

SKIN

We parked near the seafront. Because of the time of year there weren't many tourists or day-trippers; most of the people wandering around seemed to be posh pensioners and most of them were being dragged along by determined-looking dogs on thin leather leads.

We sat on a bench overlooking the waters of the channel. Mel snuggled up to me. It felt comfortable and thrilling at the same time. I started to imagine a future with her. We would be best friends as well as passionate lovers. We'd live in a house in between the sea and the mountains. We might have kids or we might open a guest house, or do both.

"What are you thinking about?" she asked.

"Nothing much," I said. "Just enjoying the air and the view, and of course the company."

"Me too," she sighed contentedly.

We sat like that for about twenty minutes but the cold and the damp started getting to us so we got up, walked down to the beach and strolled arm-in-arm at the edge of the rising tide. Given the time of year, everything was grey, but it was also full of light. God! I had never thought like that before, was I turning into a fucking poet or something.

This could only end in grief. I shook that thought away; after all, everything ends in grief, it's just a question of where and when. But there and then were not the where and when of the end of our relationship. We'd come such a long way in so short a time that I was determined to make it work. It wouldn't be worth the cost otherwise.

The cold pushed us from the beach in less than half an hour and we went back into the town to find somewhere warmer and drier to hang out while we decided where to go next.

We poked around in the charity shops and sat down for coffee in an almost deserted but friendly Italian café. As we sipped our Americanos we stared out of the window at the locals passing along the pavements outside – lugging their bags and dragging or pushing their shopping trolleys.

"Wherever we end up," Mel said, "I don't want it to be a place like this, it's too miserable and old."

"Aye," I said. "Probably be better in the summer though."

"Well then, we can come back for our holidays sometimes."

I realised I was staring at her. I never wanted to forget that moment, it was like a beautiful dream yet it was real.

"Can I take a pic of you?" I asked, picking my phone up from the table.

Mel smiled. "Give it to me."

She took the phone from my hand, moved over to my side of the table, sat down next to me and took a selfie of the two of us that also captured the shuffling locals in the grey street outside. A perfect memento.

After we left the café we bought a doughnut each from a baker's shop and walked back towards where we'd parked the car. It was already dark. I'd had such a wonderful time in her company that I didn't want to break the spell and I didn't fancy driving in the damp and dark to god-knows-where anyway.

"Fancy a drink?" I asked. "I still haven't got a clue about where we're going."

"I don't care where we go," Mel said.

"Nor me really," I said, "but I'm a taxi driver and I need a destination."

She laughed. "Let's get that drink, then we'll decide."

We walked back into the town centre again and found a large pub that was almost deserted. We sat down at a corner table.

"What do you fancy?" I asked.

"Besides you, you mean," she laughed with a distinct twinkle in her eye.

"Ha!" I said, not really knowing how to react.

I was actually embarrassed. I'd never been spoken to like

that by anyone before, not even Mandy. It did get me thinking about how and when and if we would get it together sexually. I was surprisingly anxious about that prospect.

"Just a half a cider for me," Mel said, "I feel like something refreshing."

I looked around the room as I waited for somebody to serve me at the bar. It was furnished with faded plush seats and the walls were decorated in heavy-duty flock wallpaper that still carried the nicotine stains from the days when smoking in such places was legal. Everything looked tired and smelled of stale beer.

A tall middle-aged man appeared behind the bar and smiled at me.

"Good evening sir, what can I get you?" he asked.

"A pint and a half of that cider please," I said, pointing at the pump labelled premium Hereford cider.

"Good choice," he said.

"Quiet here," I said, as he was filling the glasses.

"Yeah, it's been a bad year," he said. "Still I don't mind. We'll make up for it next summer with all the stags and hens."

"Oh," I said. "Is it your pub?"

"I'm the manager," he said. "It's owned by the brewery. They bought it nearly five years ago now, been promising to do it up ever since."

"It's nice though," I said.

"Are you staying in town?" he asked.

He pushed the drinks across the bar towards me.

"Not really, I said, just passing through."

"Seven pounds twenty please," he said.

I gave him one of the three twenty-pound notes we had left in cash after paying Mel's B&B bill.

"Ta," he said. "By the way, if you do decide to hang around, we have plenty of rooms available upstairs."

"Thanks," I said as he handed me the change. "I'll bear that in mind."

"I can do you a great deal too," he said.

It was so comfortable and we felt so at home in the pub that we lingered longer than we should have, and in the process spent far too much on booze. Mel upped her game and was knocking back large gin and tonics at seven quid a pop by the end.

"I'm hungry," she said.

"God, yes, I'd forgotten about food. I'll ask the manager if they've got anything."

"Get me another one of these," she said tipsily, holding her empty glass out.

"Yes ma'am," I joked.

"And you can't drive in that state – ask the man if we can have a room," she giggled.

At the bar, the manager was a little more than tipsy.

"How can ie alp yoo shir?" he asked

"We were just wondering if you have any food?"

"Nuts," he shook himself. "Sorry, I man we go nuts. Ishts too late."

I wasn't sure if it was his or my drunkenness but I couldn't understand what he was saying. I guessed it was too late for food.

"Nicsh tekway in shtreet," he mumbled.

"Thanks. By the way, are those rooms still available?"

"Rooms?"

"Bedrooms."

"Ah, yesh." He turned around and retrieved a set of keys from a hook on the wall behind the bar.

"Thanks," I said. "How much?"

He waved me away. "You can shot it out in morning"

"All right then," I said. "Ta."

"Where's mah drink?" Mel asked when I got back to the table.

"Oops, I forgot," I said.

"I'm hungry," she said.

"There's nothing here," I said. "But I think there's a takeaway nearby."

"Come on then cowboy, gee up," she said, getting to her feet and falling into me.

I caught her to stop her falling. She looked up at me with drunken eyes.

"My hero," she said, and planted a full-on sloppy kiss on my lips.

God, she still tasted of strawberry and Pernod.

"Now," I said, "we have to make an effort to keep upright if we're going to last the night. And, look what I've got."

I dangled the keys in front of her eyes.

"You got us a room?"

"Yep."

"Cool, let's go get some grub."

BONES

When he saw the look in my eyes Shane looked just as surprised as I felt. How the fuck did he happen to be there the same time as me? Why was he in Elchurch at all?

"Bones!" he gasped.

He stood still as a statue for a few seconds before hurriedly pulling himself back out of the doorway. I was still fired up after what Mason had done to me, and looking for an outlet for all that anger I suppose, because my body launched itself towards Shane and out of the bedroom door without any conscious intention from me.

When I got to the top of the stairs Shane was just reaching the bottom, he must have moved fast. I leapt down after him two steps at a time so that by the time I was at the bottom, he was still fumbling with the front door.

I made a grab for his collar just as he managed to open the door and pushed him outside into the damp street. He slipped on the wet pavement and still without any conscious intention my body threw itself on top of him.

I forced him to turn over onto his back and look me in the eyes. I could see that same pathetic scared look I'd seen when he realised I knew what he was all those years ago, after what he'd done, dirty stinking cheat.

"Sorry Bones, I'm sorry."

A small audience of about half a dozen partygoers had gathered outside the front door of the house. A couple of them were smoking joints and most of them had glasses of wine or beer in their hands. It looked like we had just become the entertainment for the evening. I would have to get a grip on myself.

I stood up. Shane tried to stand up too but I shoved him back onto the pavement and walked away along the street, every nerve in my body bristling. It was probably the coke.

I turned down a side street and sat on a low wall to get myself together. I couldn't catch my breath properly and my heart was pumping like crazy. I felt myself slipping off the wall, then someone's arms grabbed me and yanked me back onto it.

"Take it easy, sit down," it was Shane's voice.

That was enough to bring me round. I realised what had happened because it had happened before. I'd had the beginnings of a panic attack, contributed to, and probably started by, the cocaine. Oh, why would I never learn, I was getting too old for that shit.

"It's time to sort this," Shane's voice again.

"Fuck off!"

It was never what you thought it was," he said. "We were mostly just friends apart from that one time, and that was . ."

"Fuck off, we've been through this years ago. Just fuck off will you."

I pushed myself off the wall and stood up. My nerves were still jangling so I couldn't face a fight with Shane. I just wanted to get away, get home to my bed, and sleep that stinking day off.

"She was already seeing someone else," he said, "I was just a . . . I don't know what I was . . . she used to be my best friend."

"What do you mean seeing someone else?"

"I didn't want to tell you, it had been going on for months. You were working all hours. We used to talk a lot. She confided in me about the other person she was seeing. I begged her to stop. I didn't want you to get hurt."

"Shut the fuck up, what sort of crap are you talking. You were protecting me? From what? Who did you think I was?"

"I didn't even know who I was at the time. I'm sorry."

"Did you love her?"

"No."

I turned away from him. He'd ruined my life, and even if what he was saying was true, that she was seeing another person at the time, he should have told me, we were best mates, at least that's what I thought then.

"I loved you," Shane said quietly.

"Huh! I loved you too, as a friend."

"I don't mean like that."

"What the fuck are you talking about?"

"I'm gay, I was in denial."

"Well fuck me!"

Shane smirked at me. I realised what I'd just said and there was nowhere else to go. I started laughing until I was almost hysterical. I forced myself to control my breathing, I didn't want the panic to come back, I couldn't cope with too much more of that.

"Gay?" I said, when I'd regained my composure enough to speak. "What the fuck's the matter with you? Why were you hiding it? No one gives a shit about that any longer."

"It's nothing to do with anyone else, I don't know, maybe it was my upbringing or something, my father was a tosser, as you know. He was very homophobic."

"So, who was it that Lindy was screwing? Besides you that is."

"It really was a one-off, we were both . . ."

"Blah blah, yes, who was it?"

"Just some bloke from work, it didn't last."

"What bloke?" I asked.

I used to know a lot of Lindy's work colleagues, since she worked for a PR firm and they were always putting on social occasions. I was often invited to make up the numbers. Maybe I had come across this bloke – whoever he was.

"Ben something or other I think, though I can't be sure," Shane said.

I wanted to get angry at Ben whoever he was, but I realised that I didn't give a short fuck about him, or about Lindy, or about what had happened back then. I realised that the thing that had hurt me the most was Shane's betrayal. He was my best friend at the time. I'd never had a close friend since then and it was unlikely I'd ever have one again.

"Are you all right?" Shane asked.

"Yes, you know what, I'm good mate. I really am."

"That's great to hear. You had me worried, when I saw you using that . . . stuff, and you look like you've been in the wars."

"Aye, well life is a battle, especially in the game we're in," I said

"I wanted to talk to you about that, if you're up for it. I know things have gone crazy for you. I'm sorry about what happened to Moira Mason."

"What do you know about that?" I asked.

Part of my brain was telling me to tell him to fuck off and mind his own business, but most of it was eager to learn what he had to say. The old cop instinct kicking in I guessed.

"Not much more than what's public," he said, "but I do know a fair bit about her father and his operation. That's why I'm here."

"Talk away then," I said.

"Not here," he said. "I'm staying in Pengelli Road, there's a pub near there, the Carpenters, do you know it?"

I laughed. "Too well," I said.

"Somewhere else then. And by the way, do you know anyone you can trust? I'm going to need some help. We're going to need some help."

"You can't trust anyone," I said, looking straight at him. "But maybe there is one person, Chunky, he works with me. And there's a club in town, he's always there sniffing around the manager Jan. We can probably use a room there; it will be quiet tonight."

"Ideal," Shane said. "Let's go."

SKIN

I made a big effort to keep myself upright as we walked to the takeaway that the pub manager had recommended. To be fair, Mel made almost as much effort as I did and only fell down once. Luckily she got away with no visible injury. I helped her to her feet and she held on to me the rest of the way. We stopped outside and read from the menu pasted to the window.

"A biriani for me I think," I said, "though I do like chips with my curry."

"Onion bhajees," Mel said.

"Is that all?"

"And veg samosas." She paused, "And pappadoms and chutneys."

We went into the shop and ordered the food.

"Twenty pounds fifty," the young man behind the counter said, with a polite smile.

I pulled my debit card out and waved it at him.

"Oh sorry," he said, "the machine's playing up, I think it's the internet connection again."

"Hang on, I've got some cash."

I pulled what cash I had left out of my pocket and put it on the counter. There was only eleven pounds and some change.

"Bummer," I said. "Have you got any cash Mel?"

She shook her head, then regretted it. "Ouch!" she said.

"Is there a cashpoint nearby," I asked.

"Yes, just down the street, on the right."

"Ta. You wait here," I said to Mel, who sat down gratefully on a bench designed for such occasions.

The damp and cold night air started to hit me as soon as I got outside. I didn't mind, it was helping me to sober up a bit and I didn't want to make a twat of myself on my first night with my new love. God, was it real?

I put my card in the machine and asked for fifty quid. It refused to give me any cash? I checked the balance '£28.90'. What the fuck? Then I realised, of course, the bank, Mandy and all that. Shit. I took twenty-five out and went back to the takeaway.

Mel was out cold lying on the bench. The food was ready. I paid the man, took the bag of food and nudged Mel awake. I was going to have to sort our finances out, but hell, that would have to wait until the cold light of the next day.

We managed to find our way back to the pub and followed the signs pointing up a wide staircase to the few guest rooms. Ours was more of a suite than a room, with a large sleeping area and a king-size bed, plus a separate lounge with sofas, dining table and a huge television.

We put the television on and Mel flicked through the channels while I unpacked the food. We sat down to eat with an ancient episode of Kojak providing the mood music.

"This is a weird programme," Mel said as she was stuffing her face with onion bhajees.

"Yeah," I said. "Quite good though, they don't make them like that anymore."

"How old are you?" she laughed.

We shared all the food but Mel ate a lot more than I did, she attacked it and stuffed it down like a hungry, and angry, tiger. God she had some energy. If we hadn't been so drunk I might have made a move. I almost did.

Then suddenly, she got up from the table and walked into the bedroom. I finished the last scrap of a samosa I was eating and followed her in. By the time I got in there she was face down on the bed sleeping like the drunk she was.

I smiled and lay done next to her in a similar position. I closed my eyes, and I was gone.

BONES

I was sitting with Shane in the office of Taffies club while we were waiting for Chunky to arrive. I'd phoned the fat bastard before we'd left the terraced streets near the Tinworks. He hadn't answered but had sent me a text to say he was still in work and needed to talk to me. I'd texted him back asking him if he'd meet me in the club. Jan had been surprisingly good-humoured with me when we'd turned up, not her usual style. Who knew, perhaps Chunky had proposed.

A text arrived from the fat man. *'Sure Boss, just leaving, see you there in five mins.'*

"He's on his way," I said to Shane. "Now, what's really going on? Why are you here?"

"I'd rather wait for your colleague to get here, saves having to say the same thing twice."

"Don't worry about it," I said. "He won't care about the details, won't even take them in. But, he's a good cop, and loyal."

"Fair enough. So, I'm here because of my local connections. I work with the Jamaican Police but I'm seconded to an international team who investigate global crime."

"Sounds heavy," I said.

"Can be," Shane said. "Anyway, your Big Bill Mason, is actually a bit bigger than you might have suspected, but he's still small fry in the overall operation. Or I should say operations. Wherever there's an easy buck to be made they're involved. Drugs, guns, human trafficking, child prostitution, contract killing, politics, and big business of course. And that's not all, you don't want to know how low they can go."

"You've come a long way since you were a young plod catching lowlifes nicking fags from the newsagents. Haven't you?"

"Ah, they're all the same. Stealing booze, selling smack to kids, or guns to Mexican cartels, what's the difference?"

"I suppose you're right," I said. "When I think about some of the murders, rapes and abuse that I've had to investigate, even here in Elchurch, it . . . well you know what it does."

"I do," Shane nodded. "Now listen, what I'm hoping is to get as much as I can on Mason, find out his secrets, then turn him. From my preliminary investigations he has a lot of skeletons in a lot of cupboards. He wouldn't last five minutes if he got locked up."

"Are you going to let him go afterwards?"

"That's the plan," Shane said, "but we don't except him to go very far, if you know what I mean. He has a lot of enemies out there, and he'll have even more when this goes down."

"Phew, good luck," I said. "Where do I come into it – and Chunks?"

Just as I mentioned his name the office door opened and the fat fucker came in.

"Hi Boss," he said to me. He spotted Shane and nodded at him. "Hello."

"This is Shane," I said, "an old friend of mine, we started in the job together."

"Nice to meet you, Barry has said a lot of good things about you," Shane said.

Chunky nodded, he seemed a bit nervous.

"He's all right Chunks," I said. "He's just been telling me about something he's working on, undercover. He wants our help. Don't mention it to Adams or anyone else, got to keep it to ourselves, for now at least. Is that all right?"

"You know me Boss."

"I do Chunky, and I know what a good job you do, despite all the bollocks from people like Adams."

"Bollocks is right Boss."

"Can I call you Chunky?" Shane asked.

"Well yes, that's my name. Since I was a kid anyway."

"So, yes Chunky. As I was telling Barry . . ."

"Hang on," I said. "If you can call him Chunky, you can call me Bones."

Both men laughed.

"I think we could make a great team," Shane said.

"You can fill me in later," Chunky said. "I'm busting for a piss, and starving, and thirsty, Adams is a boring bastard."

Shane shrugged.

"See you in the bar in a bit then," I said.

Chunky left the room in a rush.

"I see what you mean about him," Shane said. "Seems like a great bloke though."

"Yes he is. Now what's the plan?"

CHAPTER SEVENTEEN

SKIN

I woke up in the dark. My mouth was dry and the inside of my head was raw. The loud vibrating sound had become constant, like I was trapped inside a huge cement mixer. I sat up. The noise was not in my head, there really was some hellish machine nearby.

Mel stirred next to me and rolled off the bed onto her feet. She rushed into the bathroom and knelt over the toilet bowl.

I put my feet on the floor and walked over to her. She was kneeling on the floor retching into the bowl.

"You all right?" I asked.

She puked, again, and again, and again. Then she stood up and turned to face me.

"That's better," she was smiling.

I laughed.

"What about you?" she asked. "You drunk as much as I did."

"Not quite, but I haven't slept much."

"Aw, poor baby."

"It's not funny, can't you hear it?"

"What?"

"That noise, like a big engine ticking over."

"Hang on." She paused to listen. "Oh yes, must be a lorry in the street, deliveries perhaps?"

It's too late for that, or early."

"What time is it?"

I picked my phone up from the bedside table. "It's only half past one."

I walked over to the window and opened it a little. The noise got louder.

"I'll go and have a look around," I said.

"I'll come with you," Mel said. "I need some air."

We went out into the corridor and found an open fire door that led to a platform with wide metal stairs leading down to an outside area. Three middle-aged men were busy drinking, around a table in the open air. The manager of the pub was standing up holding court, swaying as he spoke and smoked.

The mysterious noise seemed to be coming from behind the stairs. We edged down and into the courtyard. The men stopped talking and looked over at us. I looked around under the platform and realised that the source of the noise was a huge compressor of the sort that is used to keep commercial freezers and fridges cold.

I was a bit hesitant to tackle the manager considering he was pissed and had three pissed companions to back him up, but puffed myself up anyway and marched up to them. I stared at the manager and held my posture.

"Can you do anything about that compressor over there? It's keeping us awake."

One of the other men looked up at us then turned his attention to the manager. "I told you to fucking deal with it," he said.

The manager put on a crumpled, defeated expression and nodded.

"I will sort it out," he said.

"Thanks," I said, deciding to leave it at that. I didn't want to draw too much attention to myself.

By then Mel was standing next to me her arm in mine. She tugged me away. We went back up the stairs into the corridor and back to our room.

"What a wanker," she said. "But you were great, although you know he's not going to do anything about it, don't you?"

I looked across at her, she moved towards me and kissed me passionately. I responded and we fell back on the bed tangled together. Suddenly she pushed me away. I was horrified with myself, it looked like I'd pushed things too far too early. I stood up and looked away.

"Really sorry," I said. "I didn't mean to . . ."

"Shut up you idiot. I love you Harry, but . . ."

"It's too soon," I said.

"No, I stink of puke, I need a shower. We need a shower," she said, emphasising the 'we'.

I laughed.

BONES

Shane sat down again and sighed.

"The truth is, I'm making it up as I go along," he said. "Perhaps you can help me to come up with something that would work."

"I'll try."

"By the way, I've also been speaking to your brother, after I bumped into him in the town centre the other day. He said he'd help me too."

"Fuck's sake, why didn't you tell me this before? I can't stand the bastard, and the feeling's mutual."

"Sorry," he said.

I should have told Shane to fuck off there and then. That would have been the end of it once and for all, but I thought about Moira. Whatever she was, however fucked up she was, it wasn't her fault. Mason had it coming and if the only way I could deliver it to him was by cooperating with my old friend then that's what I would have to do.

I sighed. "I'd also like to know more about what Mason's role is in this criminal organisation. I've had to deal with him for a long time now, he's always been a slippery bastard, but I've never thought of him as anything other than a local villain."

"He's a lot more than that, he's a crucial connection in a long chain of abuse and suffering that affects just about every country in the world."

Fuck, had I got it wrong again? Not just about the depths of absolute evil that Mason was up to his neck in, but my decision long ago to paddy up to the fucker so that I could use him to keep scumbags off the streets of Elchurch. I realised that of course, he'd been using me as much as he used every other person that happened to come his way. I was actually a victim, never mind a police officer. The petty criminals he fed me were just titbits to keep me under control.

I'd been used, there was no doubt about that. The question that remained was how much did he have on me? Had he recorded every conversation we'd had? Had he set me up in ways that I'd never even thought about? Maybe even Moira had been a part of his web of criminality and corruption. Fuck, what was the point of thinking like that. Things were what they were and I'd done what I'd done, it didn't mean I couldn't bring the bastard down. The rest was irrelevant.

Then I realised that if he was as ruthless as Shane was implying then he was never going to forget what I had done by kidnapping him, and he was not going to let it go. I was indeed a dead man.

In a way that thought made it easier, whatever life I had left I would dedicate to nailing Mason good and proper, and if I was very lucky I'd survive.

"You all right Bones," Shane asked.

"Yeah, just thinking, that's all."

"So," Shane said, "the deal is that Mason's involvement is mostly associated with the human trafficking element plus he runs a lucrative sideline in immigration services if you know what I mean."

"You'd better explain," I said. "Just so that I can get it right.

"Well, he arranges the logistics at both ends, liaising with contacts in parts of the world where people are desperate. He gets them into the pipeline at that end and then when they emerge at this end he's waiting for them."

"What about the immigration services, what do you mean by that?"

"He's behind several companies that offer advice and services to people who need visas. A lot of that is legit, well, enough of it to keep it looking kosher at least. But he also offers extra services to those who can pay, fake passports and other documents like employment contracts, marriage certificates and so on. He has contacts inside just about every government agency. His MO is quite simple, just throw cash at it, and he gets that cash from whoever will pay. He's not fussy who his clients are or what they've done."

"You seem to have a lot of information already. Why do you need me?"

"We don't have a lot of physical evidence, they are a very sophisticated outfit and cover their tracks well. We know the evidence is somewhere, they must keep some records, there's just too many people involved to keep it in their heads, we just need to get at that evidence, and we need something to help us do that."

"Like what?"

"Some sort of confession would be a good start, an admission from him about something specific. Then we could use that to instigate a complete forensic investigation of his operations and find the physical evidence, even electronic evidence would help. We know you've got close personal connections to him, so."

"So what? Do you want me to wear some kind of wire, ply him with alcohol and get him to brag about his global criminal activities and connections?"

"As unlikely as it sounds then yes, that's all we need, something like that."

"Where does my brother come into it?"

"I'm not sure, the only thing we know is that he was there, that night, when Mason's daughter was murdered. Perhaps he saw or suspects something that would lead us to Mason in a different way. The end result would be the same, and we might be able to find out who killed her and why."

I slumped in my chair. A feeling of great sadness swept through me and reminded me of everything I'd lost when Moira died. I could have made more effort to keep her close to me when she was alive, but she was dead, and so if I could somehow help to find the killer it would go some way to putting her to rest.

"All right," I said. "So now we really do need a plan."

"It's late," he said. "We won't be able to do anything if we're too tired. Best get some kip and we'll meet again in the morning. What do you think?"

"Yes, you're right, I am knackered, it's been a long day. Give me your number," I said. "I'll ring you first thing."

SKIN

I'd never been so nervous at the prospect of sex with a beautiful woman, not even before my first time, though then of course I was a teenager and she was a girl of the same age as me. That time it had been more weird than good, we weren't in love and she was way out of my league in social terms, the daughter of a headmaster and an MP, she was staying locally during the holidays at the house of a friend from the private school she went to. She was sexy and beautiful and I'd never forget her, but afterwards I felt like I'd been used. All I'd been was a bit of rough for the posh girl.

Maybe that's why I'd fallen for Mandy, something to do with pride, not wanting to be used. After all Mandy was beautiful physically and she was a lovely person as well, I just knew she would treat me with respect.

Mel was like a combination of both of them, and though she was mostly unknown to me I was drawn to her like a moth to a flame. Deep down I knew I'd get burned but I couldn't resist the promise of her soft body against mine no matter how much I tried to rationalise it. Besides that, I believed I really had fallen in love with her and love is the true purpose of life, isn't it?

We both kept our underwear on as we stepped into the shower. Already I was responding, shaking with anticipation at the sight of her perfect body.

As the water flowed over us she put her arms around my neck and pressed her body against mine while kissing me with a pure sexual passion that I'd never experienced before. I responded and pushed myself against her.

"Wow," she said, pulling away. "I really want you, but first we need to wash and the best way to do that is to get naked."

She let herself slip down to her knees and tugged my underwear off on the way. I almost exploded there and then, but she pulled away stood up and turned her back on me.

"Your turn," she said.

I undid her bra and pulled it away from her. She turned back to face me and pushed herself against me. She grabbed the shampoo bottle and tipped some on her hands before rubbing them on my hair as the water from the shower cascaded over us. I followed and did the same to her, rubbing and kissing every inch of her body, all the time sending messages to my body to hold back, not yet, not yet.

Finally Mel tugged my arm.

"Come on, I can't wait any longer," she gasped.

She grabbed my hand, led me out of the bathroom and fell back onto the king size bed. I lay down top of her.

Afterwards, we both lay panting for a minute or two then she turned to face me and kissed me on the cheek.

"That was amazing," she said. "We'll have to do it again."

"Now?" I asked.

"Don't be daft, she said, but give me five minutes."

"Oh," I said.

"No, only joking," she laughed. "Sleep is what I need now."

We both went to the bathroom again, separately, and washed away the sweat and the sex. Mel rinsed our underwear under the shower and put them on a radiator to dry. Then she found two white dressing gowns in the wardrobe. We put them on and lay back down on top of the bed. The low rumble of the compressor outside was still there but it wasn't bothering me at all.

"So, where to tomorrow Captain Jones," Mel asked.

"Um, I'm not sure, it depends," I said.

"Well yes, everything depends," she said.

"We're broke," I said. I'd been wanting to say something since I withdrew what we had left from the cashpoint.

"How come?"

"My bank account is empty, we've only got about fifteen quid in cash left and I can't get any more."

"Ssh," she said, "let's not spoil it all, we've got each other. We'll sort it out in the morning. Go to sleep now."

I took her in my arms and kissed her forehead. "Good night," I said.

BONES

When I got back to my flat I felt very sad that I'd wasted all those years hating my best friend. I thought about my relationship with my brother and started to get the same feeling about that too. I promised myself that I would make an effort, control my emotions and talk to him properly.

I was too wired to call it a night so sat down in front of the television and flicked through the channels. As usual there wasn't anything of interest to me. I was going stir crazy so after a while I thought I'd go for a walk into town. There'd be nothing open at that time on a weeknight but I might pop into the station to see if there was any gossip I could use.

The streets were dark, damp and quiet, it was going on for two in the morning and I guessed the few officers on duty would be huddled in the office drinking tea and eating bacon sandwiches while trying to avoid the admin. It can get so boring on those shifts sometimes that people often chatted shit about things they probably shouldn't. If I was lucky, I might pick something up, perhaps about Adams. I really didn't trust the bastard.

Thank fuck. As it happened the duty sergeant that night was Elena Jackson, she wasn't really a friend since I had no friends, but she was an old colleague and we understood each other. We'd both started in the job around the same time and had often collaborated on cases where our interests had overlapped.

She was alone in her office, staring intently at an open folder. She looked up when I walked in and smiled at me.

"I didn't know you were around tonight," she said. "How's it going? Are you ok?"

I sat down opposite her.

"Hi Elena," I said. "Thanks yes, I'm all right."

"That's good to hear, I know how fond you were of her."

"I was, but it was more or less over anyway."

"You're not going to fool me Barry. I know you, remember. And I know how much of an effect this must have had."

"Anyway," I said, "I'm a bit out of the loop on all that."

"I heard," Elena said.

"I was stupid to get involved with her in the first place. I knew whose daughter she was. I knew she'd be trouble, but," I sighed.

"There doesn't seem to have been much progress," Elena said. "Though it's early days I suppose."

"Are there any decent theories about who the killer is?" I asked.

"I don't think so. There is a bit of chatter about her father, he disappeared for a day or so apparently. Though I can't imagine he would do that to his own daughter."

"I can," I said.

"I know what you think of him," Elena said.

"Have you heard anything else? Especially about him, Bill Mason?" I asked.

I knew I was pushing my luck by focusing on Mason but it was worth the risk and Elena had never let me down in all the years I'd known her so I trusted her to keep her mouth shut.

"Well, his name does come up quite often. Not that he's ever been pulled in, it's mainly because of the people he seems to associate with more than any other reason."

"Yeah," I know. "He's very clever, knows just how far to push things, and when to back off. He's a crafty bastard."

"Ah yes but he's lost his daughter and he's still a human being," she said.

"Are you sure?"

Elena shook her head in disapproval but she was smiling.

I left the station and walked slowly back in the direction of my flat. Elena probably didn't know it but she had given me what I needed, a way to get much deeper into Big Bill Mason's operation and a path that would hopefully lead to a major impact on the global criminal network that Shane was investigating. Along the way I would find out the truth about Moira's death. Despite my earlier feelings I believed that Mason was definitely involved in some way, even if he was not directly responsible.

My plan was coming together in my head, it was going to take a bit more thought but I already had the basics, Shane had said he needed physical evidence, something that would then facilitate a much deeper investigation.

Both Shane and Elena had mentioned Mason's associates and that's where I believed the weakness in his armour was. Everyone who knows anyone else knows something about them, that something could seem to be insignificant or irrelevant but if you put all those little bits of knowledge and insight together it would build up into a bigger picture, or at least provide a pointer to something that could provide the catalyst for Shane and his outfit to take action and move in on Mason and his more powerful associates all over the world. So I would just talk to as many people as I could who had some connection to him. Something relevant was bound to come out of it.

Of course there was a danger he'd get wind of me poking my nose into his business. I was sure he already had his spider senses on high alert and would feel even the smallest disturbance in his operation from every thread of his web. I'd have to be ultra alert and careful.

As I was walking along the road to the beach I noticed a taxi stopping outside one of the many guest houses and small B&B's that had developed along its length.

The driver got out of the cab, opened the boot and took out a wheeled suitcase. A passenger got out and paid him before walking down into the guesthouse. As the driver was getting back into the car I drew level with him. I looked over. I recognised him from somewhere. He became aware of me staring at him and looked up at me.

"Oh hello," he said. "You're Skin's brother aren't you? The cop, sorry police officer."

"Whatever," I said. "I suppose you know him from the

taxis?"

"Aye, I'm Dave," I work with him, well used to work with him to tell the truth, He sort of gave me the sack to be honest."

"Oh! Not a very nice thing to do."

"He didn't have any choice, he's in the shit, financially, anyway I've got plenty of work, as much as I want anyway."

"Haven't we all."

"Have you got anything to do with that murder? You know, Bill Mason's daughter."

"Yes," I said. "What do you know about it?"

"Not much," Dave said. "But I know she had a ride with Skin on the night she died. That's common knowledge around the place. He seemed quite upset about it."

"Yes, I know I have talked to him about it. Did you hear any more yourself?"

"Not really. I expect he told you about the kiss?"

I didn't know anything about a kiss but if I admitted that to Dave he might clam up. I braced myself for too much information, I wasn't sure if I'd be able to handle any intimate details.

"He said something," I said, thinking on my feet. "The detail is all recorded but there was so much going on that night. Do you think the kiss might be significant?"

"I don't think so, from what he told me she was in a very flirty mood and just kissed him on the lips without asking. I don't think he minded at the time, he was flattered. He told me she was very beautiful."

I nodded, "Yes she was," I paused, remembering her smile, and those lips.

"Is that all?" Dave asked.

"Sorry, yes, I'm in cop mode, just one more thing. How much do you know about Bill Mason?"

"Only what's public knowledge. You know, he's someone you don't want to get mixed up with, nothing specific really. There was one of the drivers, must have been about five years ago, his name was Abdul, nice bloke, he didn't like Mason at all, kept telling everyone to stay clear. Not many people knew what he was talking about at the time. I suppose he just picked up on something."

"Does Abdul still work on the cabs in Elchurch?"

"Nah, I think he went away to see his family, haven't seen him since."

"When was that?"

"Um, three or four years ago probably."

"OK ta, and thanks for the chat. I'd better get going, it's late."

"No worries," Dave said. "Anytime."

"Can I contact you again if I need to clarify anything?" I asked.

"Sure," he said. "Hang on."

He leant back into the car and came out with a business card in his hand.

"Here you are," he said. "They're a bit rough, but they'll do for now. I printed them myself just this morning."

"Thanks," I said. "And can you contact me if you think of anything relevant, no matter how insignificant it might seem?"

"Sure," he said. "What's your number?"

"I can never remember and I haven't got a card on me now, but hang on, I'll ring you so you know it's me."

After I rang him, I saved his number in my contacts and gave him his card back.

"Zero waste for the environment," I said.

Dave laughed.

As I carried on walking back home, I was choking with a mixture of anger and grief. I would find my brother after I'd had a good sleep, confront him about that kiss, and ask him why he hadn't told me about it.

I wasn't used to feeling like that – all hurt and upset. It puzzled me. I didn't want to think of myself as someone who got hurt so easily. I'd dealt with far too many victims and did not want to end up as one. Maybe it was because of something in my childhood, some trauma or other, but then, show me a human being who hasn't had bad experiences.

Yes, we were all damaged, and in a way that's why I loved being a cop. Yeah, I knew that a lot of cops did more harm than good, too many probably, but there were some, and I liked to think I was one of them, who's only mission was to catch the real bad guys.

Then I thought about Jackie Mann and wondered whether my treatment of him was justified, since he was a victim too. It was a tough question and I promised myself that I would think very carefully about all that.

I shook myself. Jeez, I'd be opening a soup kitchen next.

CHAPTER EIGHTEEN

SKIN

I was woken suddenly by the sound of something in the corridor. I sat up in bed and watched the door as it swung inwards. I had the brief stupid thought that it was the drunken manager coming to have a go at us for disturbing his little get together, so I nudged at Mel who I thought was lying beside me.

She wasn't there. Shit! But then the door opened and she came in. She was still wearing the white towelling dressing-gown.

Mel closed the door carefully.

"Boo," I said, as she turned around.

"Shit!" she said holding her hand to her heart. "You scared me."

"Yeah, well you scared me too, creeping in like that."

"Sorry."

"Where have you been? Has anything happened?"

"No. Calm down, I just needed some cool air, it's a bit warm in here."

"Ah ok, you're right. Shall we open a window?"

"You can't do that with that compressor thingie outside."

"True. Are you ok now?"

"Yes," she yawned. "What time is it? No, hang on."

Mel picked her phone up from where she'd left it on the coffee table in the lounge area and waved her hand over it.

"Actually," she said. "It's nearly six o'clock. There's nobody else about as far as I could see."

"No wonder," I said. "Did you see the state of that lot outside last night, or should I say earlier this morning."

I yawned I could really do with another couple of hours sleep.

"Come on," she said.

Mel walked over to the main light switch and flicked it on.

"What are you doing? Come back to bed," I said. "We should get a couple of hours more sleep. We're going to need to be alert for when we have to face the fact that we can't pay for this room."

"Let's leg it now then?"

"What do you mean?"

"Yes yes," she said. "I love it. Come on, let's get the fuck out of here. Now!"

"Hang on. What if they call the cops?"

Mel laughed. "Don't be daft, they won't remember us, they won't even remember who they are themselves. And, even if they do call the police I'll tell them he tried to rape me."

Fuck! That was quite a shock. I couldn't understand why anyone could think about themselves in that way. She could see my surprise.

"Ha, just joking," she said. "But you know what I mean."

"I suppose so," I said.

"Anyway we don't have any other choice Skin."

I had to accept that she was right. It was the perfect time to make a quick getaway, and there was a possibility that the landlord wouldn't bother with the cops, even if he could remember us.

"Fair enough then," I said. "Come on. Grab your things, get dressed."

"There's no time for that," she said. "Just chuck everything in the bags and get going. We'll sort it out later."

I stood staring at her open-mouthed.

"Come on then," she held her hand out towards me.

She looked so cute and happy, with an excited childlike expression and dressed in that white towelling dressing gown that was much too big for her. I couldn't resist.

I took her hand. Mel yanked me off the bed and dashed around the room, collecting the few bits and bobs we had unpacked.

Less than ten minutes later we were running through the streets of the town wearing only the white robes from the hotel. Ten minutes after that we were bombing it along the main road in the direction of the motorway.

I was shaking because my nerves were shot. I couldn't believe what we'd just done. Surely we wouldn't get away with it? Mel, on the other hand was shaking with laughter and trying to speak but could hardly get the words out.

"Are you all right?" I asked. "Do you want to stop?"

She shook her head vigorously. "Oh no, never stop, I've never had so much fun in my life. Thank you Skin. And put your foot down."

I didn't put my foot down because that would have risked getting pulled over. There wasn't a lot of traffic but I knew it would start getting busier as people began their journeys to work. I still didn't have a clue where to go though.

"Have you had any thoughts about where to head for next?" I asked.

"We've seen the sea," she said. "So, how about we head for the hills?"

"Sounds about right," I said. "We'll go over the motorway and up the valleys."

"Great. Let's go for it."

We drove the next few miles, and crossed the motorway into the valleys in silence, perhaps allowing ourselves time to process what we were doing and where we were going. I couldn't see an ending myself and that scared me. At heart I was not a risk taker and liked an ordered life.

I broke the silence first.

"Maybe we should stop and think for a bit?" I suggested. "We don't have much fuel, so we don't want to waste it until we know where we're going."

She wasn't listening, she was too busy looking back over her shoulder at the road behind us.

"Stop!" she said suddenly.

"What?" I said.

"Just stop, quick."

I pulled up at the side of the road, as close to the stony scrubland as I could. I turned to Mel.

"We can't stop here," I said.

"No, turn around, go back. There's a lay-by, we just passed it."

"All right, but why the urgency?"

"I'm busting," she said. "I need to pee."

"Ah, ok."

I did a risky three-point turn, drove back the way we'd come and pulled into the lay-by; it was deep and surrounded by bushes so I was able to park almost out of sight of the road. Mel leapt out of the car and ran towards the undergrowth. I got out and stood gazing over the landscape, taking deep breaths of the almost unpolluted air.

I drifted off, thinking about the last few days. I couldn't decide if I was a complete idiot and heading into something that was bound to go tits up, or if I was finally discovering who I was and how I wanted to live. Truth was, I didn't feel any control over any part of my life anymore and I was terrified.

I shook myself and looked around. It was a beautiful place and I had never felt so alive. What was I thinking?

I got back in the car and waited for Mel. My eyes closed themselves, god I was tired.

Mel got in next to me and her head lolled onto my shoulder.

"We'd better get on with it," I said. "You'd better move your head, or I won't be able to drive."

"Do we have to?" she mumbled. "I'm so tired."

"Me too," I said, "how about we recline the seats and have a nap."

"Hmm, yes," Mel said.

We were still wearing the bathrobes we'd taken from the hotel, so we wrapped them around ourselves, wound the seats back and snuggled up.

Mel reached across and grabbed my hand.

"I love you," she said.

"I love you too," I said without thinking, I was too tired to argue with myself.

We woke up more than three hours later. We were both cold and grumpy.

"This is no good," I said. "We can't go on much longer. We'll go and talk to the police, get some protection from your father."

"Ha, they're all in the same gang. No, what we need to do is to get as far away as possible."

"Sorry Mel, we've got to be realistic," I said. "Like I told you earlier, we're low on fuel and we're not going to get very far on a few quid."

Mel laughed. "Never mind, we'll find a petrol station, fill up, and then do another runner."

"Nah," I said. "Those places are smothered in CCTV and the cops would be on us in minutes."

"Oh no, we're stuffed," she said in mock horror. "Hang on, I've got an idea."

"Uh?"

"Patience," she said. "We've got to sort our shit out and get properly dressed first."

I obeyed. After we'd rearranged ourselves in silence I turned the engine on and waited.

She remained silent.

"Well, if you're not going to say anything, I'd better switch the engine off to save petrol."

"Don't do that, there's no need," she said.

"What?"

"Wait there a minute."

Mel got out of the car and opened the rear door. She rummaged around in the stuff we had chucked on the back seat then came back inside and sat down with her hand behind her back and a triumphant grin.

"Voila," she said, pulling her hand out with a flourish.

She was holding a large white envelope. She threw it onto my lap.

"Open it," she said. "Look inside."

I opened the flap of the envelope and peeked in.

"What the fuck," I said. "Where did that come from?"

"I nicked it," she said proudly. "When you were sleeping. I crept downstairs and into the office. The manager guy was comatose on a seat in the bar. Stupid bastard had left the safe open."

"Jeez," I said. "How much is there?"

"I don't know, I haven't counted it."

I pulled the wad of notes out and stared at it. It wasn't very thick.

"It's not that much," I said.

"How much?"

"Couple of hundred, something like that."

"Cool, it's a start. We can buy plenty of petrol with that, and I'm getting hungry."

"They'll definitely call the cops now," I said.

"So what?"

Who the hell was Mel? And what was I doing racing around the valleys with her like Bonnie and Clyde. I shivered remembering how that story had ended. I wondered how ours would.

BONES

I woke at eight after a short but deep sleep and went straight into the shower to set myself up for the day. I'd always found that a shower worked better than a good breakfast to get me going in the morning. I could understand that some people needed the reassurance of a full stomach but I didn't see the point in me stressing about food when the way I lived I could fill my belly within a couple of minutes of feeling hungry simply by popping into a corner shop or a supermarket and grabbing a sandwich or a bar of chocolate. It wasn't like I was going to starve, at least not while I was earning a good wage in Elchurch in the twenty-first century.

In the end I did have a cup of tea and some toast with peanut butter while I sat down with a notebook and planned the day ahead. I never got too hung up about it but I found that making a list was a good place to start and if I lost my way during the day then I could find my way back by referring to the list.

My list started:

Talk to:
Skin
Dave again (Why?)
Chunky
Elena (possibly)
Fucking Adams (if I could stomach it)
Fred in the Carpenters
Jackie-fucking-Mann
Vicky
Raskal (probably)
Mandy (not sure about this?)
A fucking therapist (Joking)

and finally
Big Bastard Bill Mason

Then I would study and collate all the bits of info and look for connections, before hooking up with Shane again.

I looked at the list. Which person should I tackle first? I decided to begin with a couple of the more straightforward targets, start in first gear so to speak, it would establish the pattern for the day and psych me up to deal with the awkward bastards later.

I paused to think about what I was doing and the way I was thinking. I wasn't really in control of any of it. It was like all my training and all my years of experience were combining with my instinct to drive me to a solution. God, I was on fire.

So who would be the easiest? There were complications with most of them but Chunky and Dave seemed like the least stressful options. I phoned Chunky first. He didn't answer and I didn't leave a message. I would try him again later but I wouldn't answer if he phoned me back before I was ready because I needed to be in control of my own schedule.

It had to be Dave then. I wasn't sure how busy he'd be and didn't want to have to negotiate in a telephone call, so I texted him and asked him to meet me in an hour in the Tinworks, it would be just about ten o'clock by then and he shouldn't be too busy. If I got there earlier I could get some decent coffee from the café-bar and drink it while I was waiting. Maybe I'd bump into one or more of the other people on my list.

The Tinworks was a twenty minute walk from my flat so I tidied up a bit, had a piss and set off. I got a reply from Dave as I was coming into town, it read 'ok, see you then'.

It always upset me to see how run down the town centre had become because most of the commercial and public investment over the past couple of decades had been channelled instead to the out of town retail parks. On top of that of course, more and more people were buying their shit online and the pubs in the town centre were on their last legs because of the cheap booze available in every supermarket and corner shop.

Still, that was change I suppose, and I was probably getting wound up because I was just about old enough to remember a bit about what it used to be like.

Fuck! Why was I thinking like that? Was I really getting that old? I was less than two years away from forty, and then sixty was the new forty so they said so I'd better get a grip and stop thinking like an old fart. Change happened and I just had to deal with it like everyone else.

I got to the Tinworks just after half nine. The available space was already filling up, mostly with groups of mothers with toddlers and an assortment of arty types tapping away on their Macbooks and drinking fancy coffee.

I sat at the end of one of the long canteen tables near reception and ordered an Americano. It was a good position to survey the whole place from, so Dave would easily spot me when he came in, and as a bonus I'd get to observe the comings and goings of the clientele. You never knew when the tiniest titbit of information would come in useful.

I checked my phone for any messages or calls from

Chunky but there weren't any. I connected to the wi-fi and checked my personal email. It had become too much of a habit but I was getting bored.

My inbox was full of the usual junk email but there was one from Chunky with the subject *Lost my Phone*. Silly fucker was always doing that, but he'd never actually lost it, just forgotten where he'd put it. The text of the email read, *'Lost my phone again if you don't hear from me meet me at taffies lunchtime one o'clock'.*

I knew he'd probably text me in the next half hour to tell me he'd found his phone but answered his email anyway and told him I'd see him then. That meant that after talking to Dave I'd have more than two hours to fill so could fit in a chat with one or two of the others at least. I consulted my list. Vicky and Raskal were the obvious choices since even if I didn't see them in the Tinworks I could always pop around to their house in Copper Street, it wasn't far. At least one of them should be in.

Dave turned up at about five to ten. I needn't have worried about his ability to find me in the big hall-like space because he spotted me before I spotted him. I should have thought, he was a cab driver after all and used to picking people up in busy locations.

He sat opposite me at the canteen style table, I'd just finished my coffee. I stood up and pointed at my empty cup.

"I'm going to order another one of these," I said. "What can I get you?"

"A cup of tea ta. Nothing special, just normal tea please."

"Milk?"

"Yes, but can you make it soya milk? Just a splash ta."

While I was sitting back down at the table after ordering the beverages at the counter, I noticed Vicky coming in from the car park end and walking towards the staff entrance to the kitchens.

"Vicky," I called, perhaps a bit too loudly.

She stopped and looked around, a smile came to her face, she was actually quite good looking and I wondered why I hadn't thought of her like that before.

"Hi Barry Bones," she said as she approached me. "Great to see you here again, were you looking for me?"

"Sort of," I said. "I do want a little chat. Do you think you'll be able to talk, say in half an hour or so, maybe a bit later. I'm in a meeting until then."

"Probably," she said. "I'm supposed to be working but they're quite flexible here. They have to be with all the flakes who work here."

"That's great thanks. I'll still be here, even if Dave has gone by then."

I nodded at Dave who was looking at Vicky with a smile on his face.

"Ah," it's you, she said to Dave. "How's it going?"

"Good thanks, despite all the covid shit."

Vicky rolled her eyes and turned to me. "See you in a bit then. By the way, how are you? After all that commotion last night, I missed most of it."

"I'm fine," I said. "It wasn't a big deal."

"In a bit then," Vicky said, and went back to the kitchen.

Dave was looking at his phone intently.

"All right?" I asked.

"Yeah, sorry, I just had a text from Mandy. She's coming back, says she's got it all sorted and wants me to go back and work for them."

"That was quick," I said. "Will you?"

"I'm not sure. I'll think about it."

Someone had put the beverages on the table. Dave picked his cup up and took a sip.

"Ta, that's perfect," he said.

I nodded. "Sorry to bother you again, but when I spoke to you last night, it was late and I was tired, it was a long day."

"You did look a bit out of it to be honest."

"Yes. Anyway there was one thing you mentioned, it didn't go in properly. Just wondered if you could tell me again."

"Sure," Dave said. "Not a problem. But can I ask you something first?"

"Go on."

"Why did you want to meet me here? Why not at the police station? I'm not bothered really, just want everything to be as clear as possible."

"Ah! To tell the truth, I'm not officially working on the case, but I used to know the victim, and want to do the best for her. I mean the only reason I was taken off the case is because I knew her."

"Thanks. I already suspected that, there's been a bit of gossip. I just wanted to check. I'm happy to talk to you, in fact I'd rather talk to you than any of the others."

My instinct to tell more or less the truth had paid off.

"Can I ask you why you feel like that?" I asked

"I just don't trust them, Inspector Adams in particular. I've heard a few things about him."

"Go on."

"He's let some people off the hook, so they say, and stitched up others. Just something someone once said."

"Who was that?"

"You remember I told you about Abdul, used to be a driver?

"Yes, he wasn't a big fan of Mason."

"That's right. Well he felt the same about Adams."

"Thanks Dave, interesting."

"What was it you wanted to ask me?" Dave asked.

"Funnily enough, it was about Abdul. I was wondering if you could tell me anything more specific, like how did he know so much about Mason?"

"Sorry, can't help you there. But there is someone who might be able to, his cousin Imran, used to be a taxi driver around about the same time."

"Used to be?"

"Yes, he works in the Raj Mahal now, part owner I think."

"That is very helpful, thanks Dave."

"You're welcome."

"Can I ask you to keep this to yourself for a bit longer?"

"Of course."

I added another name to my list – Imran.

CHAPTER NINETEEN

SKIN

We drove for a few more miles. After the madness of the last few hours I began to relax in Mel's company and appreciate her beautiful presence next to me. She seemed very happy and chilled out and I pushed my reservations to the back of my mind. It all began to feel right again and my anxiety decreased. We stopped at a roadside petrol station and while I was filling the car Mel went in to buy some crisps and fizzy drinks to keep us going until we found somewhere to eat a proper meal.

I only put twenty quid's worth of fuel in the car just in case we had to abandon it at some point. I went inside to pay. Mel was talking to the bloke behind the perspex window on the counter. He seemed to be enjoying her company and had a big grin on his face. She turned to me as I approached.

"Tom was just telling me about a lovely little pub about five miles from here," she said.

"Oh yeah," I said, grimacing inside, knowing that he wasn't going to forget us after her obvious flirting.

I nodded at Tom. He looked like the sort of bloke who played prop forward for the local rugby team, thick-set with a friendly grin and not much sign of intelligent life. Shit, I realised why I was thinking like that, I was jealous.

I pulled myself together. "Hello Tom," I said. "Anything there you'd recommend?"

He shrugged his shoulders, "I'll eat anything me," he said.

Perhaps I hadn't been wrong about his intelligence level after all.

"Twenty-six pounds with the petrol please," he said.

Mel handed him thirty quid in notes.

"What's it called?" I asked.

"What's what called?" Tom said.

"Don't worry," Mel said. "I know all about it. Tom has been a great help."

She winked at the poor man who was still fumbling with the till.

"Keep the change," she said, blowing him a kiss.

"You're a naughty girl," I said as we got back in the car.

"Oh I don't know, he was a hunk don't you think?"

I shook my head. "I hope he was worth that four quid tip you gave him.

She opened her coat and there was a litre bottle of vodka stashed under her arm.

"Oh, I think it was worth it."

I'd no idea how she'd managed to get hold of that, and thought it better not to ask. I laughed, she was a hell of a character, but I wasn't sure if I could keep up with her for much longer.

BONES

After Dave left I sat alone for a few minutes and checked my messages and my emails again. There was nothing new so I had to assume that Chunky was still phoneless and that I'd be seeing him at one o'clock.

While I was waiting for Vicky I entertained myself by checking out everyone who was hanging about or working in the Tinworks. I found myself making little stories up about them, giving them imaginary lives. What the hell was happening to me? I was turning into one of them arty-farty types, making up stories. What next? I laughed at myself, I'd have to boycott the place before it was too late.

I was hoping that by asking Vicky to talk again about her mysterious Facebook friend she would remember more details that might lead me to work out if there was any connection between so-called Alice and what had happened to Moira.

When Vicky eventually came over to see me it was well

gone twelve o'clock so I wouldn't have much time to talk to her.

"Sorry she said, not many staff in this morning and we had to do all the prep for the lunchtime menu."

"It's all right," I said. "I've been amusing myself."

"I wouldn't have thought you need to do that," she winked.

Was she coming on to me again? I was flattered, unlike the last time she flirted with me, and considered responding in the same way, but wasn't sure if she was just that sort of person and taking the piss, or if she really was interested in me. Even if she was interested it was not the time or the place.

"Funny girl," I smiled. "What's for lunch then?" I was trying to change the subject before it got too silly.

"Why, do you fancy anything in particular?" she winked again.

"No," I said firmly. "I'm meeting a colleague somewhere else. Actually I haven't got long."

She didn't seem bothered by that.

"Me neither," she said. "It's going to get busy soon, well, as busy as it gets these days."

"Fair enough then."

"Do you want another coffee or something?" she asked.

I shook my head. "Better not, I need to get on."

"Yeah, me too," she said.

"Anyway," I said. "I wanted to talk to you again to see if you could think of anything else regarding Moira Mason or the Facebook friend you told me about."

"I don't think so, no, I told you everything before."

"I wasn't expecting anything more really, it's just that I'm trying to piece everything together, trying to make sense of it. It's the first step to finding out what really happened."

"Some things never make sense."

"You're right, but maybe you can tell me again, perhaps you'll remember something else this time. It shouldn't take long."

"All right then. So, a few months ago I was contacted by someone who'd seen that I was a member of a group on

Facebook for ex-pupils of Elchurch High. Her name was Alice and she said she wanted to get in touch with Moira Mason who . . ."

"Hang on, did she actually say she wanted to contact her, or did she just want information?"

"No, she, if it was a she, said that she had to get in touch with Moira, some sort of family thing."

"Did she say it was a family thing?"

"Um, I'm not sure now, sorry."

"All right, carry on."

"We became Facebook friends and then she messaged me a few times, but as we found out yesterday, she seems to have disappeared."

"What about the messages, did you check if they were still there?"

"I didn't think to check that until this morning but no they're not. I didn't think you could delete messages on someone else's account so I was a bit puzzled."

"There are ways," I said. "But you have to be pretty clued up to do it."

"She might have messaged other people in that group as well," Vicky said.

"That's a good point," I said. "Ever fancied working for the police?"

"Ha ha, you don't know me very well do you?"

"That's true," I said, "I don't know you . . . yet." I couldn't resist a bit of banter.

She lifted her eyebrows. I couldn't make out if it meant she was flattered or repulsed by my stupid comment.

"Anyway," I said hastily. "I'd better get on, thanks again."

"Cool," Vicky said. "Let me know if you want to meet up for a cuppa, just in case you need some more detecting advice of course," she smiled playfully and stood up.

"Before you go," I said. "I wouldn't mind another chat with your housemate Raskal. Do you know if she's about today?"

"Yeah, I think so, but she was going to go to her studio this morning. It's in the Coachworks, do you know it?"

"Yeah, of course, that big red brick building near the

railway station."

"That's right, she's on the ground floor, you'll see her name on one of the doorbells outside the front door."

"Thanks."

"Anytime Mr Bones."

What was I doing? Was I kidding myself about how much Moira had meant to me? Why would I so blatantly flirt with someone else so soon after her death if she had?

Maybe meeting with Chunky would put things back into perspective.

SKIN

It wasn't going to take long to get to the pub that dull Tom had recommended, so we needn't have bought the snacks and paid the prop forward off, but at least we got a bottle of vodka out of it. The downside to the free vodka was that Mel started drinking it as we were driving up the valley.

"Hey," I said. "Take it easy, that stuff's deadly. We need to keep our heads clear today."

"Stop worrying, it doesn't affect me like that. I'm only taking sips anyway."

"All right, if you say so. What do you think of the views?" I asked, trying to distract her from what I was coming to see as self-destructive behaviour.

She looked up, and at the mountains. I thought they were majestic and sort of threatening at the same time, but most of all they were massive, a million times bigger than us, a reminder that we were just tiny ants on the surface of the earth.

"Yeah, the views are cool, bit grey though," she said

"I suppose so," I said, defeated.

"How much longer until we get to the pub?" Mel asked. "I could do with a drink."

"You've got one," I said.

"Yeah, but I'm bored," she said, taking another sip of the

vodka.

"We're almost there," I said.

A couple of minutes later we pulled into the car park of the Gorse Arms. It was a typical country pub, nestled against a hillside, with a fake old-fashioned look, whitewashed walls, wooden tables at the front and a gravelly car park out the back.

There were a few people scattered around the large lounge and a smiling middle-aged woman was waiting in full-on congenial host mode behind the bar.

"Can we see the food menu?" Mel asked abruptly. "I'm starving."

I raised my eyebrows and smiled at the woman, she reminded me of an older version of Mandy. She ignored me, grabbed a menu from a pile on the bar, and handed it to Mel.

"There you go love," she said. "But the food won't be ready for half an hour yet. Though you can order now."

"That's all right," I said. "We'll have a drink while we're waiting."

"Sure," she said. "What can I get you?"

"Just a lime soda for me please, I'm driving."

"I quite fancy a large red," Mel said. "Have you got anything decent."

"Yes. There's a nice Malbec I can recommend, would that be all right?"

"Bring it on," Mel said.

We sat down with the drinks.

"Let's see what's on offer," I suggested, reaching for the menu that Mel was still clutching.

She yanked her arm away.

"Let me choose," she said.

I shrugged, "Whatever."

She scanned the list of dishes and closed the menu in the time it took me to take a sip of the soda.

"There's only one choice," she said.

I waited.

"Veg curry and chips of course."

I winced, remembering where the last batch of curry and

chips had ended up.

"Are you sure?" I asked.

"Totally."

I took the menu back to the bar and ordered the food.

When I got back to the table Mel had pulled her phone out and was looking at the screen.

"Shit," she said. "It's dead. Can I borrow yours? I just want to check the news, see if there's any updates about poor Moira."

I unlocked my phone and handed it over.

"We can charge yours when we get back in the car," I said. "I've got a lead somewhere."

Mel was tapping frantically at the screen of the phone.

"Bollocks," she said, "there's hardly any signal."

"Perhaps they've got wi-fi, let me have a look."

I took the phone back, there was no connection of any kind. I went over to the bar.

"Excuse me, do you have any wi-fi here?"

"Ha, we're supposed to, but it never works. It's all down to geography and weather conditions apparently. They're good at making promises but not good at delivering them."

"Shame," I said.

"You might get a signal out the front if you stand close to the road."

"I'll try that, thanks."

I went back to the table and sat down.

"The woman said that we might get a signal outside, might be worth trying?"

"I can't be bothered now."

"I'll go and check."

Mel shrugged. "Whatever."

I was getting a bit pissed off with Mel's attitude. It hadn't taken long for our relationship to start disintegrating. Not surprising perhaps considering what it was based on, and what we were dealing with. I'd have to make an effort to be more patient, after all, she was still dealing with her childhood traumas after all.

I sat at the wooden table nearest the road and checked my

phone. There was a weak signal, but there was no mobile data available.

I sat quietly for a few minutes not consciously thinking about anything in particular, but the events of the past few days kept coming into my thoughts in snippets, as if I was looking at a photo album about a recent trip.

I was jolted back to reality by my phone ringing. It was still in my hand. Shit, it was Mandy. I'd been trying not to think about her. I took the call.

"Hi Skin," she said. "How are things? Where are you?"

I took a deep breath, I'd half-anticipated the call so knew I'd have to make some story up. "The stupid car's broken down. I was just heading back to the motorway after dropping a fare at the airport late yesterday afternoon when the exhaust exploded. I had it towed to a garage nearby. The rescue guy said the catalytic converter had disintegrated and got lodged in the exhaust, the pressure built up, and bang."

Where the hell did that come from? I half-remembered a similar story that one of the taxi crowd in Elchurch had told me, I hoped it made sense.

"Oh you poor love, are you all right?"

"Yes, it was a bit scary but no damage to me. The car should be ready later this afternoon. I thought I'd hang around here instead of dealing with the hassle of coming back and fore, so I booked into a bed and breakfast near the airport last night."

"That's a shame, but I suppose you've got to do what you got to do. Any other news? How's business been?"

"Good, very busy. Got a couple of good fares, at least they seemed good, but now with all this, we'll probably end up out of pocket."

The history I'd created with my lies started to seem true. I even believed it myself.

"I'll see you later then, don't stress, if there's any delays with the car I'll look after things back at base."

"Where are you now?"

"Still at my parents. I'm getting a train soon, should be home later this afternoon."

"OK, everything else all right then?"

"Yes, oh there was one thing, Bones phoned me, first time he's done that in years. He sounded knackered. Anyway, he was trying to get in touch with you, something to do with your statement. He said it wasn't important. He'd catch up with you another time."

I just about managed to stop myself from showing the panic that had overcome me.

"All right, fair enough, see you later."

"Yes, and Skin, I do love you, you know."

"Me too," I said automatically. "Bye."

I put the phone back in my pocket and put my head in my hands. Shit, what was I going to do? What was I going to say, to Mandy and to Mel? I didn't like the feeling of disaster that was suddenly overwhelming me. I felt like everything was falling away from me and I didn't have a clue how it was all going to end. It was terrifying.

Then I thought, why was I feeling like that? I was still a grown up, I could do what I wanted, I didn't have to let anyone else tell me what to do and where to go. Yes, fuck it. I realised that Mel was, in some way, playing with me, using me to help her to deal with whatever terrible pain she was carrying. I would have to be more assertive, yes, that's all it would take, and if she didn't like it . . . well, I had other options, didn't I?

I went back inside the pub determined to be stronger.

BONES

I walked across town to my meeting with Chunky. Just before I got to Taffies Club, as I was passing the Raj Mahal, my phone went. It was Shane. I still hadn't really come to terms with the idea that we were friends again, or even if we weren't friends we were at least not deadly enemies.

"Hello," was the only thing I could think of saying as I answered it. It would have felt too weird to say 'hello mate' or 'Yo!' or any other kind of friendly greeting, but a simple 'hello' was a good start.

"Hey Bones," he said. "Where are you? How's it going?"

"Yeah good," I said. "My enquiries are still ongoing."

He chuckled. "That's what they all say."

"I'm just on my way to catch up with Chunky, it's been an interesting morning."

"Good, how about we catch up later this evening? We could meet over a pint in the Carpenters, what do you reckon? You could get a cab."

"Yeah, why not. Around eight?"

"Perfect, see you then."

Shane's suggestion that I should get a taxi to the pub had sparked a train of thought that led to the idea that it might be an opportunity, or an excuse, to talk to my brother. I wasn't sure if he would respond well to that scenario but I could pretend to be a punter after a ride, and then, when he turned up to pick me up, spring it on him. It would be too late for him to object, and I might even persuade him to have a proper chat.

Chunky let me into the club through the back entrance and led me to the bar. There didn't seem to be anyone else there.

"Drink Boss?"

"No, I'm all right for now. How's it going?"

"With the investigation you mean?"

"Yeah, and with you, how's things with you, you and Jan?"

"Cool head Boss, you ok?"

"Yes Chunks, why are you asking?"

"I dunno, you just seem different lately, since, you know."

"Do you mean since Moira Mason was killed?"

"I suppose so, it must have affected you though."

"Cool head Chunks, you ok?"

"Very funny."

"But seriously, yes, I have been thinking a lot over the past few days."

"Aye, it does make you think doesn't it? What's it all about innit? You think you've seen it all in this job, then something like that happens and bang."

"True. Anyway, what about Adams? Is he behaving himself?"

"You know what Boss, I think he's dafter than he looks."

"Well, he's always looked as daft as fuck to me," I laughed. "But what do you mean?"

"Well, when we went to talk to Mason earlier, as soon as we arrived Adams sent me back to the station because he'd forgotten a file with his notes in it. Then when I got there I couldn't find it. I phoned him and he told me that he had it with him after all."

"It happens," I said.

"Yeah but, when I was on the way to Mason's, Adams phoned me and asked me to wait outside. I parked on the road opposite the front entrance where I could see through the gates. The front door opened and Adams came out."

"All sounds pretty straightforward to me."

"Maybe, but the weird thing was there was a woman, came to the door with him. He turned and kissed her goodbye, well, it looked like a kiss, but I was far away."

"Are you sure?"

Chunky shrugged, "Not really."

"What did she look like?"

"Like I said I was far away, but I'd say she was quite young, twenties maybe. Dark hair. I dunno though, maybe I was seeing things, I was knackered and Adams does my head in big time."

Fucking Adams," I said. "It doesn't make a lot of sense, but sometimes the sense comes later when all the pieces fall together."

"Fair enough Boss."

Chunky updated me on some of the finer details of the investigation. Jan turned up and made us all tea. She and Chunky looked so peaceful and comfortable together that I envied him.

"Better get on," I said. "Lunch break over."

"Fuck," Chunky said. "Me too."

"Catch up with you later?"

"Yes Boss."

As I was walking from Taffies I passed the Raj Mahal restaurant and remembered about the bloke Dave had mentioned. The one who's cousin Abdul used to work as a taxi driver in Elchurch. I checked my notes, ah yes, his name was Imran and he was a part owner of the Raj Mahal, allegedly. I couldn't remember him from my frequent visits there, but then those were usually late at night and quick.

The restaurant was open so I went straight in. Although it was lunchtime there were no customers. I couldn't remember if I'd ever been there in the daytime before but it looked very tidy and clean, not like the usual messy late night dump I was used to.

A man in his forties came in from the kitchen area.

"Good afternoon sir," he said.

"I'm not here to eat," I said. I'm looking for Imran. Is he around?"

"What's it about?"

"I'm Detective Inspector Barry Jones, with the Elchurch CID," I said, flashing my ID. "I just want a quick word if I can."

"I'm Imran," he said. "I was wondering if you'd want to talk to me."

"Oh, why would you think that?"

"Well, the murder isn't it."

"What would you have to do with that?"

"What? Nothing of course. I thought that . . . because of what happened a few months ago . . ."

"What's that Imran?"

"About the fight, with Bill Mason, that was just a misunderstanding. We sorted it out."

"Ah yes," I pretended I knew what he was talking about. "Who was the investigating officer now?"

"It was lucky he was off duty, he said, otherwise I'd have been arrested. His name was Adams, he's a Chief Inspector or something like that, he's a regular customer."

"OK," I said, "Can you tell me again what the fight was about?"

"Adams told me it would be better for me, and my family to forget about it. Let sleeping dogs lie, he said."

"What did he mean by that?"

"You know, about my cousin Abdul. He disappeared three years ago, he was working for Mr Mason at the time."

"Didn't he go to Pakistan?"

"Why are you asking me all this again? I've told Adams everything."

"It's always good to think again about things, you might have missed something the first time."

"Are you really a policeman?"

"Yes, I showed you my ID. Look, if your cousin is missing you must think that Mason has something to do with it. Is that why you were fighting with him?"

"It wasn't really a fight."

"What then?"

"I lost my mind and attacked him. I nearly got my hands around his neck, but the big man with him pulled me off."

"Why did you lose your mind?"

"I didn't believe him about Abdul."

"What did he say?"

"That my cousin was not really working for him, that he had helped him with some driving once but that's all. He didn't know where Abdul was, or what happened to him."

"Do you believe him now?"

"I have no choice. And Mr Adams promised me he would investigate Abdul's disappearance."

"Did he?"

"Yes, he came back a week later. He said it was going to take more time but he thought that Abdul didn't want to be found. He owed a lot of money and was hiding."

"Did you believe Adams."

"I knew Abdul owed money and he was very worried about it. I didn't have a choice."

"Do you remember anything else about Mason?"

"No, there's nothing else."

"That's great, thank you."

"Hey do you like onion bhajees?" Imran asked as I was

turning to leave the restaurant.

"Heck yes," I said, "who doesn't?"

"One of our customers ordered them earlier but ate too many samosas and didn't want them after all."

"I know that feeling," I laughed.

"Would you like them? They're still warm but they won't keep for long."

"Yes please," I said without hesitation.

Imran went into the kitchen for a minute and came out with a white paper bag. He handed it over to me, the smell of the bhajees made me hungry immediately.

"Thanks," I said. "That's very generous."

"They'd only go to waste otherwise."

A group of three men dressed in suits came into the restaurant and hovered near the entrance."

"Excuse me," Imran said.

"I'll let you get on now," I said. "Thanks again, and especially thanks for the bhajees. If you think of anything else about the disappearance of your cousin, please contact me directly."

I handed him my card and left the restaurant.

CHAPTER TWENTY

SKIN

When I got back to the table the food we'd ordered was already waiting for me. Mel had a freshly-filled glass of red wine in her hand and was lifting it to her lips.

"You took your time," she said. "The food came early."

"Yeah, I had to walk up and down a bit trying for a signal. No joy sorry," I lied.

"Never mind," she said.

She drank half the wine in one swallow, put the glass down and stabbed her fork into a large chip.

I didn't really fancy the curry after the previous night's antics so I started on the chips as well.

"Yuk," Mel spat the chip out of her mouth and back onto the plate.

I bit the end of an identical chip," It's not that bad," I said, "a bit tasteless but that's easily sorted. Look, there's a small table over there with ketchup and all sorts on it. I'll go and get some."

Mel swallowed the rest of her wine and put the empty glass down.

"That's better," she said, pointing at the glass. "Get me another will you."

I got the condiments and brought them back to the table.

"Where's my wine?" she demanded.

"I didn't get any, shouldn't you eat first?"

She stood up suddenly, gave me a stinking look and marched over to the bar. I made a show of eating the rest of the chip and watched as she shuffled impatiently waiting for the barwoman to appear.

"Is there any chance of some service?" she shouted loudly.

The few other people that were there stopped drinking and talking and stared over at her. One of them, a big man who looked like an older version of Tom the prop forward, stood up and hovered, as if he was assessing the need for some kind of intervention.

Mel shouted again, then tried to climb up onto the bar, shoving multiple trays and glasses out of the way as she did so. The barwoman reappeared and the older Tom lookalike moved swiftly towards Mel.

He put a restraining hand on her shoulder.

"Come on now, this is no good to anyone is it?" he said, in what I thought was a reasonable tone.

Mel turned around, swung her arm, and punched him on the side of his head. He absorbed the blow and tried to look as if it hadn't bothered him. He backed away.

"All right, he said. "You'd better go I think, we're not going to tolerate that kind of behaviour here."

I stood up and moved towards them.

"Fuck off, you patronising bastard," Mel screamed at the man.

I touched Mel on her arm. "We'd better go," I said.

She turned to face me. "You can fuck off as well, keep your fucking hands to yourself."

"Sorry," I said standing back.

I could see that she was fighting some great internal battle against her emotions, perhaps something had stirred the trauma she'd had to deal with since her childhood.

She was shaking with rage and fear.

"Let's go," she said suddenly, and ran towards the door and out to the front of the pub.

I turned to the other two. "Sorry," I said, "I'll have to go after her, I'll come back later to settle up and pay for any damage."

"I'd rather you just left," the woman said. "And please, don't come back – ever."

I found Mel sitting on the gravel next to the car. She was sobbing and couldn't speak.

"It's all right," I said. "It's all sorted. Come on, let's hit the road."

I helped her off the floor and to get strapped into the

passenger seat of the car.

"I'm still hungry," she said, as we drove away to God knows where.

I didn't respond, thinking it would be best to get a few miles down the road before talking about what had just happened.

Mel found some left over crisps and started crunching on them.

"Do you want any?" she asked.

"No thanks, not while I'm driving. But how about we stop somewhere soon and then we can have a chat? I'll have something then."

She continued to eat the crisps and I continued to drive for a few minutes until I spotted a decent looking grass verge on the side of the road. I pulled over.

"What about here?" I asked.

"Why not," she said quietly as if she was defeated.

"I need a piss," I said. "Will you be ok for a minute?"

"Yes," she dropped her head, "you go on."

I got out of the car and looked around. The grass verge was too open and I would be seen by any passing motorist, so I crossed the road and walked along it for about twenty metres where there was a clump of gorse. I stood behind it.

As I was zipping up, I heard the engine of my car start up and fearing the worst looked back to where it was parked. It started moving along the road in my direction.

I stepped into the road and waved my arms trying to flag her down but she just accelerated towards me. I had to jump out of the way, tripping in the process, and ended up on my knees on the side of the road.

Shit!

BONES

After the Raj Mahal I decided to walk down to Raskal's studio in the area behind the railway station. On the way I munched gratefully on the onion bhajees that Imran had given me. They were delicious, crunchy on the outside with a sharp bite of spice, and reminded me of the ones my mother's Bengali friend Sharaz used to make for my birthday sometimes, until my mother fell out with her and banned her from our lives.

I hardly noticed the walk, because of the bhajees and because I was thinking about what I'd discovered so far and whether any of it was relevant to Moira's murder. Every little detail and snippet of conversation that I'd had over the past few days was swirling around in my head but nothing was connecting. I shook myself. Best let it rest. I was still collecting information, I promised myself that I would sit down with my notebooks later and try to make sense of it.

When I got to the red brick building the front door was unlocked so I walked straight in and wandered along the corridors on the ground floor until I found a door with a handwritten sign scrawled on a piece of cardboard that simply said '*The Raskal*'. I tapped on the door and pushed it, it swung open. I stepped inside. It was a room about the size of a school classroom and almost every inch was covered with a mess of canvases, paints, half-built sculptures and boxes and containers of all kinds rammed with arty stuff. Along some of the shelves were what looked like half-formed life-size heads of weird looking people made from some sort of paper mache.

I couldn't see any sign of The Raskal herself, so I called out her name.

"Hello," she responded.

Her voice was coming from behind a free-standing shelving unit at the back of the room.

"I'm over here," she said, stepping out and staring at me. It took a second before she recognised who I was.

"Ah, it's you," she said. "Is everything all right?"

"Yes, of course," I said. "I was just hoping for a quick chat. Is that ok?"

"Of course, give me a minute."

She ducked back behind the shelf. I looked around the room while she fidgeted with something. I didn't get it myself. I could understand the paintings, even though most of them looked like random splashes of colour at least they were something you could use to decorate a wall with, but what was the point of making something that looked like a piece of driftwood and sticking a coat hanger in it?

"Right," Raskal said, as she came back into view. "Fancy a cuppa?"

"Yeah, why not." I was thirsty after the bhajees.

"Haven't got any milk, or sugar, sorry. Would black coffee be all right, and it's instant I'm afraid."

"That would be cool thanks," I said.

"Come over here," Raskal said.

I followed her to the space where she'd been working. As well as a table covered with what looked like tiny half made plasticine figures of people in various poses there was an old school desk and two small chairs. On the desk were an electric kettle, a jar of instant coffee, a teaspoon, and a stack of disposable paper cups.

Raskal pressed the switch on the electric kettle and put a spoonful of instant coffee into each of two of the cups. She stopped the kettle before it came to the boil and filled the cup with the hot water. A quick stir and she handed me one of the cups.

"Sit down if you like," she said. "I'm due a break anyway."

"Thanks. I just wondered if you could clarify what you told me before. When you said you knew Moira Mason from school."

"It was a long time ago," Raskal said. "In the final year of the junior school, and I didn't really know her very well, there wasn't much time really."

"What do you mean?"

"She joined the class late in the year, her family had only recently moved to Elchurch."

"Ah, did you ever talk to her, or become friends?"

"Not really, she was in the English side and I was in the Welsh, and then I went to Ysgol Elli, the Welsh school and she probably went to Elchurch High."

"But you do remember her?"

"True. If I remember right, she was a very delicate girl and used to sit on her own in the playground a lot. So I did go and talk to her now and again."

"Can you remember anything specific? Did she mention her family at all?"

"I'm not sure, she never talked about herself I don't think. Sorry, it was such a long time ago."

"It's all right. you were only a kid yourself at the time."

"Let me think. What can I remember about Moira? No, nothing there, sorry."

"Thanks anyway," I said, standing up, getting ready to go.

"Hang on, I think she used to talk about her friend, in fact, that's the only thing she did talk about."

"What sort of friend?"

"Someone she'd left behind wherever she lived before she came to Elchurch. Someone very close to her. A girl of the same age I assume."

"Did she say any more about this girl?"

"I don't think so. But I'd often see her crying, that's why I went to talk to her in the first place. She missed this other girl a lot by the sound of it."

"I don't suppose she mentioned her name?"

"Can't remember. Why don't you ask her father? I read about him online the other day, you know after what happened. If Moira was as close to this girl as it seemed then he should know who she is."

"Good point, thanks," I said. "It's probably not relevant but every little bit of information helps."

"No probs."

"Before I go, you said you were with my brother Skin. Just wondering how he was."

"Drunk mostly." she laughed. "Me too."

"Did he say anything about Moira Mason?"

"No, why, did he know her?" Raskal asked.

"No, but he was the last person to see her, he took her home in his cab. I think it affected him."

"Aw, that's sad," she sighed.

SKIN

Shit!

Mel had completely lost the plot. I wondered if she would realise what she was doing and come back for me. I wasn't even sure if that's what I wanted, but I didn't even have my coat on and everything was still in the car. All I had were the clothes I was dressed in and a decent pair of shoes on my feet thank god. I checked my trouser pocket, another bit of good news, I had my phone. I pulled it out, no signal, fair enough I thought, I was surrounded by mountains and it was a long way from civilisation. I put my phone back in my pocket, it should come in handy later.

I was worried about Mel's state of mind, she was being reckless. On top of that, she was drunk. I'd seen her drinking two large glasses of wine and nipping at the vodka she'd nicked, so she had drunk at least that much and she was on the run in my car belting through the narrow country roads. It would only be a matter of time before she'd kill herself or someone else. It might have already happened.

The only thing I could do was to set off in the direction she'd gone and hopefully flag down a passing vehicle. The road was quiet but not deserted and when I'd been sitting outside the pub I'd noticed some sort of car or van passing every few minutes.

It was getting overcast and starting to drizzle. The light wasn't too good either because of the time of year, so I was worried that I would look like some crazy lunatic or not be seen at all.

I started walking but the roads narrowed so much that I was afraid of getting run over, so I went back to the verge and stood as close to the road as was safe with enough of a soft landing behind me in case I had to jump back to avoid getting swiped.

A small green vintage van stopped almost straightaway. A man who looked like a version of Rhys Ifans as he was when he starred in Twin Town popped out from the driver's door and looked at me across the roof. It wasn't Rhys.

"You all right over there mate?"

I shook my head. "Not really. I've been dumped."

"Aw, sorry to hear that mate, but you'll get over it soon enough, been there myself mate, more than once."

"Not that sort of dumped, well, yes, that sort of dumped but also dumped here, like this. She belted it that way," I said, pointing in the direction the van was driving.

"How long ago?"

"Not long, a few minutes."

"Better get in then mate. We might catch her up."

"That would be brilliant thanks," I said. "Amazing."

We weren't exactly bombing it along those roads. According to the Rhys Ifans lookalike the van was so old it couldn't go over fifty, well it could but it would probably explode. I'd changed my mind by then anyway, and didn't really want to catch her up. I was going to need some time to think about what had happened and what I wanted to happen next, if I had any choice of course.

"Where you from then mate?" he asked.

"Elchurch," I said.

"What you doing up here for then?"

"Supposed to be having a break. it didn't work out. What about you? Are you from around here?"

"Aye, I am. It suits me. I'm a poet. You know, clouds, hills, and all that, inspirational isn't it."

"I suppose so. So do you do performance or do you publish books and stuff?"

"Bit of both, I came second in the Mid Wales Haiku Slam last year."

"Impressive," I said.

"Do you want hear my winning haiku?

"Go on then," I said, though I wasn't sure what a haiku actually was. I did know it was some sort of poem, I must have picked that idea up somewhere along the way.

"Well you know how the so-called traditional haiku goes in a pattern of three lines?"

I grunted as if I knew what he was talking about.

"And the first and third lines are five syllables each and the second line is seven syllables?"

"Aye," I said. "I know."

And of course by then I wasn't lying, I really did know, he'd just told me.

"Well it's not really like that you know."

"No, I don't know," I said, happy to concede that point.

"The original Japanese version was different, because the language is so different it doesn't work in the same way."

"Right," I said.

"So when you hear mine, don't expect the usual five-seven-five pattern."

"I get it."

"Right," he cleared his throat.

Sun shadow tree earth kisses
Sea river water
Mountain valley raindrop wind

"See," he said. "See what I mean?"

"Yes, it's different."

"Exactly. What do you think of it?"

"I'm not much of a reader but it sounded good to me, all those words, made me think of nature in a way."

"Exactly," he said. "That's exactly what a poem is supposed to do, a haiku anyway. That's why I won the prize, well, came second I mean."

"You should keep going," I said. "You've got something there."

"Thanks mate. Listen, I'm getting off this road soon, so I won't be able to take you much further. Will you be ok?"

"Which way are you going?"

"I'm off down towards the coast, going to see my missus, well my ex, and our kid."

"Nice," I said.

"Not really mate, I'm only allowed two hours once a week, long story."

"Shame."

"That's life mate."

"Will you be crossing the motorway on the way?"

"Yes. Probably have to stop for petrol at the motorway services."

"Would you be able to drop me off there please?"

"Whatever you want mate. What about your missus?"

"She'll be all right. Don't worry about her."

The next half an hour was a bit of an ordeal as Neil, as he was called, gave me a rundown of his life which started with his birth in a tent at the Glastonbury Festival in the early seventies, and how he'd had a very tough time growing up in the hills of rural Mid Wales.

"I've started my autobiography," he said, as I was getting out of his van at the service station. "It's going to be called 'Neil Down', do you get it," he laughed.

"Ha ha, I'll look out for it, sounds interesting."

"Good luck mate," he said and drove away.

I went into the services to use the loo, before positioning myself on the side of the road that led back onto the motorway and onwards towards Elchurch. With a bit of luck I'd get a lift quickly enough and I'd be home in less than an hour. Then I'd be able to tidy things up a bit before Mandy got back.

Christ, I might get away with it . . . except for the car, what would I say about the car? I stuck my thumb out. Hell, I was sure I could come up with a good story on the journey back.

BONES

It was time to look up the scumbag Jackie Mann again. A lot had happened since I'd duffed him up in the alley and I didn't want him to think I was keeping out of his way. He still needed to know who was boss. Besides I was sure he had more to tell me, especially after what Shane had said about

Mason and his connections.

I checked the time. Mr Mann should have regained full consciousness after whatever shit he'd ingested the night before and might even still be sober, but he was a slippery little git so there was no way of knowing what he would be doing or where he would be. I cut through Burry Terrace to pick up my car from my flat, it was only a ten minute walk from Raskal's place.

I drove to the Backfields, parked in the car park behind the library and walked deeper into the estate. I was taking a chance but I thought that if I wandered around for long enough I'd either bump into Jackie Mann or into someone who could tell me where he was. And if I couldn't find him then I'd probably come across another scrote to squeeze something useful out of.

If I'd thought about it I would have walked a different route through the estate but I didn't and I got a bit of a shock when I suddenly found myself walking past my old man's house. Shit, I'd been avoiding the place for years. I stopped dead in my tracks and for a moment I considered whether I should finally knock on his door and try to talk to him.

A car pulled up outside the house. I stepped back and tucked myself behind an overgrown hedge. A woman wearing a dark blue raincoat with the collar of a light blue blouse peeking out of the top got out of the car and walked up to the door. She fiddled with a small box that was attached to the wall next to the door. I recognized it as the sort of box that contained a keypad to allow entry through the door for carers. That meant he was probably in a pretty bad way.

I wasn't ready to deal with all that then, so I padded on into the estate. I wandered around for almost an hour and found myself pausing at various locations I knew from when I was a boy and thinking about some of the little and not so little dramas that had happened in those places, like the alley where I had sex for the first time with a girl called Samantha from the top site, or the junction where Mrs Roberts had fallen in front of a bus.

I walked the long way back to where my car was parked

behind the library so I could avoid going past the old man's house again, and on the way passed the row of shops in between the middle and the bottom sites.

I spotted the fucker Jackie Mann coming out of the chemist. He'd probably just been in there for his daily dose of methadone. At least he'd be in a good mood. I tucked myself into the corner of the doorway of the closed Chinese takeaway and waited. As he walked past I popped out and followed him for a couple of metres until he drew level with a lane that led to an area behind the shops. Then I shoved him into the lane and pushed him face first into the wall.

"Fuck off," he squealed. "Leave me alone."

"Keep your trap shut and listen."

"Ah it's you Mr Jones. You'd better let me go or they will fucking kill you."

"I'll let you go when you tell me who 'they' are, and if you don't, I'll bust you for dealing, right now."

"Fucksake Jones. It doesn't matter what I tell you, you're going to be a dead man anyway."

I cuffed the bastard and turned him around to face me.

"What's that supposed to mean?"

"You don't know who you're dealing with, these people have contacts, and money."

"Why would an idiot like you know people like that? You're just a small-time dealer on a council estate, there's litter-pickers earning more than you."

"The handcuffs are too tight, let me go."

"Who are these people you're talking about?"

"Nobody, all right. I don't know nobody, I was lying. And you're right, I'm an idiot."

His face crumpled and he slid down the wall until his legs were splayed out across the lane.

"I told the other copper the same thing. Why won't you leave me alone?"

"What other copper? What the fuck are you talking about?"

"I can't say any more, I don't know any more. Kick my head in again if you want."

His head slumped forward. I could see he was defeated, or maybe it was the methadone.

I knelt down, uncuffed him and left him there snivelling.

CHAPTER TWENTY ONE

SKIN

While I was waiting for somebody to give me a lift I thought about what I'd tell Mandy about my missing car. The only option I had was to tell her it had been stolen. I'd stupidly left the keys in the car when going into the petrol station at the motorway services and when I came out it was gone. There was CCTV of course and I'd tell her I'd already spoken to the police and they were on the case, there had been a spate of such thefts but they were confident my car would be recovered intact. I'd say I hadn't wanted to worry her, so didn't tell her immediately, and anyway my phone was playing up.

I'd say that I'd had a lift home with a friendly police officer. That last bit might be hard for her to believe, so maybe I should make the lift come from a sales rep or a minibus full of rugby players?

Then a builder's van pulled over. I opened the passenger door to get in but the seat was covered with the contents of a broken cement bag and the driver looked like the sort of cowboy I wouldn't trust to put a shelf up let alone drive me along a motorway.

"Sorry mate," I said. "I've changed my mind."

"Tosser," he said under his breath as I was closing the door.

He zoomed off. Another car had stopped behind the van. I turned towards it. Fuck me, it was Dai Honda. Dai drove the car forward so that the passenger door was right next to where I was standing.

The window rolled down and he leaned across.

"Get in then," he said.

I got in.

He waited.

"Thanks," I said.

"Seatbelt," he said. "You know the rules."

"Sorry, yes."

"Mask too please."

"Oops!"

I pulled my mask up, fastened the seatbelt, and sat back with a sigh.

"Been in the wars have you?" he said, "I thought I hadn't seen you for a couple of days. What happened? Been on a bender again?"

"What do you mean again?" I decided to play along with his assumptions, I couldn't think of anything better to say.

"Word gets around Skin, you know that."

"Yeah, I went on a stag do, bastards left me stranded."

"Whose was that then?" Dai Honda said as he was pulling away.

"Neil," I said, thinking of the poet who had just dropped me off.

"Neil? Don't think I know any Neils."

"Nah, you wouldn't know him, he's more of a family friend, lives in Cardiff."

"So I assume you're going home?"

"Yes Dai."

"You live in Bont Road don't you?"

"That's right, yes. Will you be going that way?"

"It's not my normal route, but it makes no difference. So I'll drop you off on the main road, by the Co-op. Is that all right for you?"

"Brilliant thanks, you're a star Dai."

"You'd do the same for me."

"Of course," I said, although I wasn't sure if I would. I changed the subject. "So, you're a bit far from base, are you coming back from a job?"

"Aye mun, bit of a pain, but worth it. She's a doctor, an eye surgeon, needed to get back to work suddenly, after an overdue break."

"Oh yeah. How's things in Elchurch anyway? Any more talk about, you know, what happened?"

"I've heard some stuff about your brother. Can't vouch for it, just rumours."

"Oh yeah."

"He's been suspended apparently, and getting into bother with some people he shouldn't be getting into bother with, if you know what I mean."

"Who's that then?"

"Don't say I told you, but looks like him and Big Bill are at it, either that or they've fallen out big time."

"Is that linked to Moira Mason?"

"Don't know, but you know that she and your brother had something going, don't you?"

"What? No, I didn't know that. Are you sure?"

"Well Bel told me, and she's usually on the ball."

"Fuck!"

I was already losing my grip on reality after the last few days and I had thought that going back home would help me to take a breather and ground myself again. But the idea that Bones had been in an intimate relationship with the dead sister of the crazy woman I'd recently screwed and who had abandoned me in the middle of nowhere was a total headfuck.

"You've gone quiet," Dai Honda said.

"Uh, sorry, I can't get my head around it. So, do you think he's involved in some way with what happened to her?"

"Sorry Skin, I haven't got a clue."

I started to doubt whether I actually had a brain at all, because I just couldn't put what I knew about the murder, my brother, Moira Mason, and Mel, together in any way that made sense. And after Mel's behaviour I didn't know if I could trust her version of events. And then the idea that Bones was involved in something like that was something I couldn't, or wouldn't, accept.

Maybe Shane would know more, or at least be able to figure it out, after all he was investigating Mason and his cronies, and he knew Bones from back in the day.

Dai dropped me off outside the Co-op as planned, and I

walked quickly back to my house. First thing I would do was to make myself a cup of strong coffee to kickstart my brain. After that I would look around the house for any remnants of Mel's visit and then if there was time I'd take a shower to clean away the physical and hopefully the mental shit that I'd accumulated.

Luckily the spare key was still sitting in the old tobacco tin under the privet hedge. I let myself in and closed the door behind me.

"Is that you Skin?" it was Mandy's voice coming from upstairs.

I almost shit myself.

BONES

Even though I'd been pacing myself, I felt like I needed to take a breather, things had been getting so intense since Moira Mason died that I'd forgotten who I was. I did think again about going to see my father but decided I wasn't quite in the right frame of mind, especially after my run-in with Mr Mann.

I knew that at some point, if I was to get enough information to put together a full picture of what was going on locally and how that might feed into the global criminal network that Shane was investigating then I would have to speak to fucking Adams or at least have some kind of contact with him because as far as I was concerned his name was in the frame after what Jackie Mann hadn't been able to say.

So, I needed to somehow get in the same room as fucking Adams and the best way to do that, as far as I could tell, was to start with Chunky.

I rang the fat bastard as I was approaching my car. He'd reply if he could, and if he couldn't he'd see the missed call and get in touch with me when he could. He answered.

"Hello Boss," he said, a little too formally.

That could mean that he was with fucking Adams and wasn't able to talk freely, but then surely he would have said

'Hello Mr Jones', or even 'Hi Barry' or even simply 'Bones'. So, I guessed it was actually something quite serious, in Chunky's eyes at least.

"What's happening?" I asked.

"You'd better get down here Boss, it's all kicking off."

"Get down where? What's kicking off?"

"Down to the station Boss. Your brother is going to be arrested. They're going mob-handed."

"Skin? Why?"

"The murder of Moira Mason."

"What the fuck?"

"I know. Anyway . . ."

"On my way," I said.

That woke me up. I ran the rest of the way to the car and was on the road to Elchurch Central with blue lights flashing and sirens shrieking in less than a minute.

The station was buzzing when I arrived, with at least a dozen officers, some of them armed, milling around waiting for the starting pistol. Fair enough, I suppose, a murder of that kind in Elchurch was a big deal.

Chunky was with Adams and a bunch of assorted officers including Sergeant Elena and DI Reb.

Reb was a very good officer with a good attitude. Shame she was working under Adams. There was a time when I thought we could be more than just work colleagues and I think she'd thought more or less the same thing. But times changed so quickly and we never got together. We still had a connection though. It helped that she was gorgeous, like a young Helen Mirren and just as intelligent, every cop's fantasy woman, well, mine at least. But Reb wasn't into me in that way. Shame.

Rebecca seemed to have it all under control. It looked like she had become the focal point of the investigation while fucking Adams sat back and took all the commendations and congratulations.

Chunky made his way over to me followed too closely by Adams.

"All right Boss?" Chunky said, as Adams pushed past him.

"Yes all good."

"I'm glad you're here Barry," Adams said. "I wanted to tell you about this myself."

Chunky held back. He raised his eyebrows and smiled at me, he wasn't as dull as he looked.

"I'm very sorry," he said, "but we are going to arrest your brother Harry."

"What?" I tried to look surprised. "Why?"

"He's being arrested for the murder of Moira Mason."

"Fuck off," I said.

"His car was found in a field a few miles outside Elchurch, not far north of the motorway junction. It had crashed into a hedge and been abandoned. There are traces of blood on the steering wheel. It's not the only evidence."

"Why are you telling me all this?"

"You've got a right to know. It's just common courtesy."

"This must be wrong, there's no way Harry would kill anyone, he's never done anything violent in his life."

As I was talking I remembered how he'd lost the plot with me that day by the car. I'd seen the rage he was carrying, and I'd felt it as he laid into me, and I should know from all my years as a police officer that almost anyone is capable of almost anything.

Adams shrugged and walked away.

Something was missing from the picture that was building up, it didn't make sense at all. I knew from experience that when something didn't make sense it was only because of a lack of information. So I needed more information and since Skin was about to be arrested I needed it fast.

I knew that Bill Mason knew a lot more about his daughter's death than he admitted to, and I knew that, according to Shane at least, Mason was part of a ruthless and well-connected organisation and I was convinced that he hadn't finished with me after what I'd done to him.

There was no other choice, I would have to confront him once and for all and get it sorted. But first there was one person I needed to talk to urgently. It was time to pay that visit to my old man.

SKIN

I didn't shit myself but I had to think, and act, very quickly.

"Yeah," I shouted. "When did you get back?"

"Hang on, give me five minutes. I'm in the shower."

"OK, I'll put the kettle on."

I didn't put the kettle on but instead ran around the ground floor of the house looking for any signs that might arouse Mandy's suspicions.

There wouldn't be much, because I'd already made an effort to cover our tracks before we'd left, but I had to be sure. It was lucky I did, because when I went into the living room I detected the distinct smell of strawberry and Pernod. I searched the room frantically and found an open half-used lipstick that had rolled under the sofa. I grabbed it and took it to the kitchen, where I wrapped it up tightly in a plastic ziplock freezer bag and buried it at the bottom of the bin.

Then I ran back to the front room and sprayed it with a good dose of the supposedly neutral cotton air freshener that we kept on a shelf near the television. It would have to do.

Mandy came down the stairs just as I was pouring the boiling water over the instant coffee, Mandy preferred a fancy filter brew, but I was useless at making that so I just made the instant extra-strong instead. She seemed to like that or at least had never complained in the past.

She walked into the kitchen wearing the dressing gown that Mel had been wearing just before we legged it. Thank god she didn't seem to have noticed it had been used recently.

I gave her my best fake smile. Well to be honest, it wasn't really fake, in fact when I saw her I experienced the feeling people talk about when they say their heart skipped a beat.

I moved towards her to give her a hug.

She backed away.

"You stink," she said. "And you look terrible. What have you been up to?"

"Nothing, it's been a weird day, that's all."

"You'll have to tell me all about it. I've had quite a strange time myself, starting with the offer of all that money from my parents of course."

The panic that had been building up inside me started to subside. It didn't look like she was suspicious, but I would still have to explain where the car was and why I was in such a state, but at least I could question her about the money and about whatever her strange time was all about.

"Yes, the money thing is surprising, tell me all about it. Did you ask them to help out financially?"

"Not really. Anyway, perhaps you should go and get a shower as well, and put your clothes in the wash please, I'm going to do a big one later, this dressing-gown is getting a bit grubby too."

She sniffed at the fabric of the gown and paused as if she was trying to identify the strange odour.

"More weirdness," she said.

"Listen Mandy," I said. "I need to talk to you."

"I know that, and I need to talk to you as well. Now, get upstairs and get clean. I'll do a bit of tidying up and when you come down, well, I think we've got a lot to talk about, it really has been a bit of a weird time."

Mandy winked at me. I laughed and went upstairs.

While I was in the shower I heard Mandy moving around the house, probably tidying up as she'd said she was going to do. I washed myself vigorously, scrubbing every inch of my body until my skin was almost red raw. I realised that what I was doing was trying to remove every last reminder of the madness that I'd succumbed to with Mel. Was there really a way back from that? I hadn't yet told Mandy about the missing car, I supposed she was assuming it was parked outside as usual.

After the shower I got dressed in a clean T-shirt and a pair of faded blue denim jeans that Mandy had bought me years earlier. The fading was genuine because they were my favourites, and they'd been worn and washed hundreds of times, at least once or twice a week.

When I got downstairs Mandy was waiting in the lounge, sitting on the sofa. I was scared that she might have found some incriminating evidence while I was in the bathroom, but she smiled at me and patted the sofa next to her. She looked so relaxed and happy that I couldn't help smiling myself.

I sat down.

"Well," she said, "did you miss me?"

"Of course," I said, with what I hoped was a convincing tone of voice. The truth was I didn't have time to miss her, it had been a totally crazy couple of days and I hadn't even come up for air.

"Hmm," she said. "Well, I really missed you. I'm sorry I went off like that, but you've got to admit that it turned out all right."

"I have really missed you too you know," I said, "and yes, the money from your parents is a proper lifesaver."

I leant over and put my arms around her.

"I love you," I said.

"I know," she said, kissing me on my cheek. "We should spend some time apart more often," she said.

"Not too often though," I said. "I never want to be without you again."

I heard my voice breaking with emotion as I was speaking. She heard it too.

"What's the matter Skin? Why are you so sad?"

"I'm really sorry Mandy," I said. "There's something I need to talk to you about."

She sat up suddenly and looked across at me suspiciously.

"What are you talking about?"

"I . . ."

I didn't get a chance to finish what I was going to say because somebody started banging the front door violently. I stood up instinctively on full alert. Mandy was doing the same as I moved quickly into the hallway. I could see the outline of several dark-clothed figures through the frosted glass pane. I knew it had to be the cops, but I didn't know exactly why.

I yanked the door open as Mandy joined me in the hall. There were four or five uniformed police officers crowding in front of the door. Two plain clothes men pushed their way through and stopped just inches in front of me. One of them, the bigger man was someone who I'd seen knocking about with my brother Bones, the other more senior and serious looking officer was someone I'd already spoken to recently, DCI Adams.

"Harold Jones," he said. "I'm arresting you on suspicion of the murder of Moira Mason."

I heard Mandy gasp behind me.

BONES

I watched the troops as they left the station on their way to bring Skin in. I thought about phoning him or Mandy to warn them but it would have been counterproductive and would cause more grief than it was worth. Plus I knew that there was no way that Skin was responsible for Moira's death so they wouldn't be able to hold him for long anyway.

After they left to arrest my brother, I drove straight to the Backfields and parked across the road from my father's bungalow. The carer's car had gone. The streets were quiet and very peaceful. I sat in the car and thought about what I was doing and about why I was so reluctant to do it.

So, I was about to go and talk to my old man for the first time in years, and I was going to tell him that his son, my brother Harry, was being arrested on suspicion of murdering the daughter of the biggest gangster in town, or even the country.

I didn't like my father, never had. I might have tried when I was younger but just couldn't get over the way he used to treat me when I was a child in the primary school. Unless I had some kind of false memory syndrome, he had been a shit father and to be honest my mother wasn't a lot better, even though there had been no direct abuse except for the odd smack when I was a toddler.

Maybe I did have a naughty streak but I could never think of any reason why he would punish me so much for doing so little, like the time when I was about seven years old and put salt in my little brother's fruit juice and he'd got very upset and puked everywhere. My so-called father smashed my bike up for that and I didn't have another one for two years. Most of my childhood memories were made up of stories like that.

But still, something inside me really wanted to make peace with him before he died, and my recent change of heart about Shane, and about Skin to some extent, seemed to lead naturally to making up with the old bastard.

I stood outside his front door for two or three minutes giving myself the chance to change my mind and abandon the idea of the meeting I was dreading. But the fact that I'd got that far was a massive breakthrough for me and if I didn't go through with it then I knew I never would.

I pressed the doorbell and tapped on the glass part of the door with my knuckles. I waited. I knew from when I'd seen him earlier that it would take him a good sixty seconds to get from the living room to the front door so used the time to try and relax by focusing on my breathing. It was a technique an old friend had told me about years before.

The door opened and my father lifted his head and stared at me.

"Hello Dad," I said.

He tried to speak but couldn't get the words out.

"It's ok Dad," I said. "Sorry to turn up like this but is it ok if we have a chat?"

"Yes," he said in a croaky voice. "I've been hoping you'd come. I've really missed you."

He turned and I followed him along the hallway and into the living room. He eased himself into one of the armchairs and I sat in the other.

"Give me a couple of minutes to get my puff back and I'll make you a cuppa," he said, struggling to breathe.

"Don't worry about me," I said. "Is there anything I can get you?"

He put his hand out and shook his head.

Neither of us said anything for a couple of minutes. I stood up and walked over to the sideboard, where besides the medicines and the remnants of envelopes and flyers, a few photos were displayed. Eric, my dad, with Sian – my mother, and me and Skin, together when I was about twelve years old and he was eight. Skin was looking up at me as if I had just said something important. And a pic of me in the first year of secondary school at eleven years old, and one of Skin in the first year of junior school at seven, both of us smiling innocently at the camera. I knew, by then I'd already given up on finding happiness, in that family at least.

I sat down again.

"I need to talk to you Dad, about something, but first I want to say sorry about the way I've been."

"You've got nothing to be sorry for Barry," he paused to take a few shallow breaths. "I know I was a useless father, but I did love you, and I am proud of you." He couldn't manage any more.

"Thanks. Listen, I'll be back to see you a lot more after this but I've got to tell you something."

"Go on then," he said.

"It's Harry, he's been having a bit of trouble. Don't worry, he's fine, he's not ill or anything."

"Didn't he go to Brighton?"

"I don't think so," I said. "Not that I know of anyway."

"Oh!" He waited.

"He got caught up in something and he's being questioned by the police."

"Did he do anything?"

"No, he was in the wrong place at the wrong time."

"Where is he now?"

"He's at the police station."

"Has he been arrested?"

"Um no, I mean, sorry, yes, he has been arrested."

"Why?"

"It's nonsense, don't worry, I'll make sure he gets out of there as soon as."

"What for?"

"Well technically it's suspected murder, but . . ."

He started coughing. I started to panic. He waved me away.

"I'm all right," he said. "Is it about the girl up by the motorway?"

I nodded. "Yes, how did you guess?"

"He was here the other day. He was quite upset about it."

"Listen Dad," I said. "I should go and find out what's happening and talk to him myself, not in an official capacity, just as brothers.

A tear came to my father's eyes. "Yes," he said. "Brothers."

CHAPTER TWENTY TWO

SKIN

I was handcuffed and escorted to one of the police cars that were parked in the street outside. Some of the neighbours were already standing outside their houses staring across and chatting. A very young police officer opened the rear door of the car and nudged me inside, he shoved me along the seat, followed me in and closed the door behind him. Another two officers stood guard, one each side of the vehicle. The other cops, there must have been at least six of them besides the plain clothes detectives, trooped into the house carrying bags and boxes of protective clothing and equipment.

"Can you tell me anything?" I asked the young cop. "I haven't got a clue what's going on."

Detective Chief Inspector Adams will talk to you in a minute I'm sure," he said. "I'm afraid I can't tell you any more than that."

"Is it something to do with my brother?" I asked.

"I don't know," he said.

"He's one of your lot, DI Barry Jones, do you know him?"

"I'm afraid I couldn't say sir."

"Can you get hold of him? I'm sure we can clear this up."

"DCI Adams will be able to help you do that."

I sighed. There was no point me trying to get him to open up. He was too young and inexperienced to take any risks, and he probably didn't know anything much anyway.

The door opened. The fat detective leaned into the car and motioned to the young cop to get out. The detective then got in and sat next to me. He closed the door behind him and turned to face me.

"How are you doing?"

I shrugged, "Look at me. What do you think?"

"I work with Bones," he said. "You probably remember me,

we've bumped into each other before."

"Yes, a while ago I think."

"They call me Chunky. Listen, don't repeat anything we talk about ok? If you do I'll only deny it."

"All right," I said. What choice did I have?

"I know you didn't do it, Bones does too."

"Where is he?"

"He's all right." he said. "Got himself into a bit of bother but he's ok now, and he's been taken off the case. He was too close to the victim."

"Moira Mason?" I asked.

He nodded. "Yes."

"What do you mean by close?"

"Ssh, I can't say any more now. Look, Adams is coming over. You'll be all right. Don't say anything until you talk to a good solicitor, ok? The less you say to Adams the better."

Adams yanked the door open.

"What's going on here?" he asked.

"Nothing sir," Chunky said. "I was just going to tell him about his brother."

"This is not appropriate. Leave it now, get out."

"Yes sir."

Chunky got out of the car and Adams leaned in. "Your brother has had some issues," he said. "That's all I can say. But don't worry, it's all right."

"What? How? When?"

"The sooner we get this over with the sooner you can talk to him," Adams said. "All you've got to do is to cooperate. Understand?"

For a moment I thought I should come clean. I should tell him everything including what Mel had told me about the abuse she'd suffered and about how her father had killed Moira by mistake. But I thought about what Chunky had just said and got myself totally confused.

"Um," I said.

"Not now, I'll see you at the station."

Adams moved away. The young cop got back into the car. Another officer got in the other side so that I was firmly squashed between the both of them. Someone got into the driving seat, started the engine and drove away from the house towards the main road.

BONES

By the time I got back to the station it was all over. Adams was back in his office, Skin was locked up in a holding cell and Chunky was helping Reb prepare for the first interview. I barged straight into her office.

"What the fuck's going on?" I said. "What evidence have you got? Whose blood was found in the car?"

Reb shook her head. "Sit down Bones. And calm down. Nobody really believes your brother killed Moira Mason."

"So, why arrest him then?"

"We didn't have a choice. Adams insisted, even though he didn't have a lot to go on."

"What about the bloodstains? He didn't have time to analyse them. And the car was abandoned? Could have been stolen."

"There was a notebook," Chunky said.

"What sort of notebook?"

"I dunno, tell him Reb."

"All right," Reb said, "a small notebook was found in the glove compartment of his car. It's mostly gibberish, but there were one or two mentions of Moira and Mason. It looks like it was her secret notebook."

"Whose?"

"Moira's. And it was in your brother's glove compartment."

"I don't get it," I said.

"Neither do I," Reb said. "It didn't really make sense, it's probably in some sort of code. But it does mean there's a connection, and that with the blood, Adams just wanted to go for it."

"Is anyone trying to break the code?"

"It's early days," Reb said. "It's going to take some time, as you know."

"And in the meantime," I said. "My brother is banged up in a cell?"

"Yes, Adams insisted."

"Can I see him?" I asked.

"Don't ask me," Reb said. "I'm on the same level as you. I don't have the authority."

It took me a second but I realised that she was letting me know that if I did go and visit Skin in his cell, she wouldn't interfere.

"Can I have a word with you?" I asked Chunky.

"Sure Boss," he said.

"You can talk to me on the way out," I said. "Come on Chunks."

Rebecca turned away and shuffled the papers on her desk.

I went into the corridor with Chunky.

"Take me to him," I said. "I want to go and see Skin now."

Chunky shrugged. "Follow me," he said.

SKIN

I suppose I must have been in shock because I was just staring into space wondering how I'd got to the point of being arrested for murder. I didn't feel upset or angry, just numb. I played out the events of the last few days in my head like I was telling myself a made-up story except I couldn't control how it ended.

Mel kept coming into my mind. At first with her beautiful smiling face, her lips and her playfulness, and then that beauty getting distorted by anger and pain and frustration closely followed by a distant emptiness.

Then Mandy and her different beauty, her warmth and consideration, and her lovely kind eyes looking at me with disappointment and sadness.

I hadn't said anything to the police about Mel. There was going to be a lot of explaining to do but other than that I was sure things would work out all right, though I still wasn't sure how it would affect my relationship with Mandy. I realised I didn't really care about Mel at all, she could be dead in a ditch and I don't think I would have been bothered.

The door to the cell opened suddenly, I looked up to see my brother Bones framed in the doorway. I stood up and waited. He moved into the cell and closed the door behind him.

"Sit down," he said. "There's nothing to worry about. You'll be out of here before you know it."

I sat back down on the bench and nodded.

"How are you?" he asked.

"It's been a crazy few days. I'm not sure what's going on."

"I don't know much myself," he said. "But keep your mouth shut until you've had a talk to a solicitor. I know a good one, his name is Leo, he was in school the same time as me, very clever bloke. I'll give him a shout if that's ok? Otherwise you'll just have to go with whoever's on the rota."

"Yes thanks, that would be great."

"You know I'm not supposed to be working on the case don't you?"

"Yes, your colleague Chunky told me. Because you were too close to Moira Mason, is that right?"

Bones nodded. "Yes. We were seeing each other, but that ended a while ago."

He seemed quiet and emotional. I wanted to ask him more about his relationship with Moira Mason and to tell him about my brief relationship with Mel but wasn't sure if it was the right time to talk about all that.

"Are you all right?" I asked.

He took a deep breath. "Yes, I am. But listen, I've just been to see Dad."

That was a surprise. "Wow," I said.

"I know," he said. "Things have changed for me lately and when I think about Moira's murder some things don't seem as important as they used to."

"I know what you mean."

"I want to apologise to you too. I've let you down I know that. I'm sorry."

"Ah, don't be daft. I know life isn't as simple as it seems. We've all got things we regret. It's not that big a deal. From now on is all that matters."

"Yes," he sighed. "From now on."

"I've got something to tell you too," I said. "It's about me and Mel."

"Mel? Who's Mel?"

"She's . . ."

The cell door opened again and Detective Chief Inspector Adams stomped in.

"Jones," he said to my brother. "What are you doing here? This is entirely inappropriate. Please leave now."

"But," I said. "We're just talking about our father, he's very ill."

"I'm sorry about that," Adams said, "but this is not the time or the place."

"But . . ."

"You'd better go now," he snapped at Bones. "We'll deal with this later."

Bones turned to me. "I'll give Leo a ring, you'll be all right."

He gave me a wink and walked out of the cell. When he'd gone Adams turned to me.

"We're going to need to conduct an interview with you soon. You're going to need a solicitor. We can arrange that."

"There's no need," I said. "My brother is sorting it out thanks."

It felt good to say that, my brother was helping me, I could hardly believe it.

BONES

When I opened the door to the cell Skin stood up with a look of panic on his face as if he was expecting to be led to the electric chair. I told him he was going to be all right and he sat down with a sigh.

I asked him how he was and he couldn't give me a sensible answer. He didn't seem to have much of a clue about what was going on. I tried to reassure him and told him I'd get in touch with Leo Jenkins, he was a good solicitor, someone I'd known since school. He wasn't my best friend or anything, we didn't even socialise together, but I respected him and he seemed to respect me despite our obvious differences, him being a posh boy and me being a bit more of a chavvy lout.

I told Skin I'd been to see the old man, he was impressed with that, then he tried to talk about Moira, he knew I'd had a relationship with her. I wasn't up to having that conversation then, so I tried to bat it away, but then he started talking about someone called Mel.

"Mel? Who's Mel?" I asked.

Before he could answer, fucking Adams came charging into the cell and asked me to leave. To be fair Skin defended me and told Adams we were just talking about our ill father.

Adams wouldn't let it go so I had to leave. I was pissed off because I'd wanted to talk to my brother about the kiss from Moira that Dave had told me about, and I still wanted to know who the hell Mel was.

Fucking Adams.

As soon as I got outside I phoned Leo. He was happy to help and told me he'd get the ball rolling his end, he would be free to go and talk to Skin in an hour or so, he said.

I needed to catch up with Shane and find out if he was anywhere near ready to move in on Bill Mason. Chances were he was not, because the type of investigation he was involved in could take years and even then end in nothing more than a couple of gigabytes archived on a hard drive. But, no matter where Shane was at I would still go ahead and find a way to bring the bastard Bill down and I was determined to stop at nothing to find out who had really killed Moira and still believed that Mason was at least complicit in her death.

SKIN

After Bones went I was left alone. I was confident that my brother's solicitor friend would be able to get me out so was surprisingly relaxed and even nodded off. I don't know how long I was out for but I don't think it was much more than an hour. I was woken by the sound of the door opening.

I sat up. A blonde woman in her thirties was looking down at me.

"Hello. I'm DI Rebecca John, a colleague of your brother's. Your solicitor's here," she said. "Follow me."

I followed her out of the cell and along the corridors. She led me to a tiny windowless room furnished with a small desk and four plastic chairs. A smartly dressed dark-haired man stood up from one of the chairs.

"I'm Leo," he said. "Your brother called me."

"Thank you," I said. "I don't know . . ."

"Hang on," he said. He turned to DI John. "Can you give us a minute please."

She smiled and left the room.

"The good news is that you're getting out of here, you will be de-arrested. Do you know what that means?"

"Never heard of it, but it sounds good."

"It is," he said. "But before you talk to anyone else, I just want to ask you not to say anything about whatever it is you've been doing. You will have to be interviewed at some point but for now you'll be free to go."

"All right," I said. "That's brilliant, amazing."

Twenty minutes later I was out on the streets of Elchurch wondering where to go. I headed for the taxi rank outside the jobcentre where I knew there would be a few drivers idling and waiting for business to pick up as it got later in the day.

Dave was there. I'd half-expected that and half-wanted it too. I felt like I should see how he was after everything. He had one of those free newspapers open on his lap and was staring down at it with a pen in his hand, it looked like he was doing one of his usual sudokus I tapped on his window. He looked up and wound the window down.

"Skin?" he said. "What's happening man? I heard you'd been arrested, and Dai Honda said . . ."

"Never mind all that now Dave. Can you do me a favour

and drive me home? I'll tell you all about it on the way."

"Heck yes man, no probs, jump in."

I didn't tell Dave all about it, far from it, but I did tell him that my car had been nicked and trashed and I'd been arrested on suspicion of the murder and then released because they realised it was a mistake. I told him that my brother Bones had sorted it out.

"I've been talking to him," Dave said. "He's not as bad as you told me.

"Huh!" I said. "Give him a couple of weeks."

Dave laughed.

"But seriously," I said. "I think we're on the way to being friends again, fingers crossed."

"Yeah, we were talking about how the murder must have affected you, especially after she kissed you. It's nothing to be ashamed of. That would have affected anyone."

I was already shocked into silence before he finished talking. Bones thinking that Moira had planted a passionate kiss on my lips plus the fact that I hadn't mentioned it to him was not a good start to our new friendship.

I asked Dave to drop me off at the top of the road to give me time to think before confronting Mandy. I would have to be very careful about what I said, at first anyway. I would definitely tell her the whole story very soon, but needed some time to let things cool down, besides, Mel was still out there as far as I knew, and after her antics I was afraid of what she might be capable of doing.

Before I left the police station I'd asked Leo to phone Mandy and let her know I'd been released without charge and would be home as soon as I could, to explain why I'd been arrested. I was hoping a call from a respected local solicitor would impress her enough to let me back in the house, because I didn't have any keys on me. I did have a spare set in a drawer in the office along with a spare mobile phone so if I got in the house I could start functioning again. I could even start working again by using the car that Dave returned when he left.

When I got to the house I tapped on the door, pressed the

doorbell and waited.

BONES

Since Shane had told me just how ruthless an organisation Bill Mason was involved in I had become even more wary of him. If I was going to confront him, and I was, then I would need extra protection, so I decided to go back to my flat in the Docks to get the gun, it had done the job before and would do it again.

I wondered why I was going to put myself in serious danger again after the last time. Up until then it had been about getting at Big Bill because of what I was convinced he had done to his daughter. But it had become even more personal than that, as personal as it got, my own survival, it was a case of getting him before he got me, If I was lucky then I could justify whatever I did, by arguing that it was necessary for Shane's operation. I was getting myself tangled up in knots. The simple fact was that I was in too deep and the best way for me to get out of it, i.e. survive, was for Mason to end up dead.

When I got back to my flat I made myself a sandwich and a cup of coffee and sat down with the gun at the breakfast bar in the kitchen. I unpacked and inspected the weapon while I was eating the sandwich. It seemed ok and hadn't suffered any damage after it was used against Mason in the car park behind the transport café.

I rang Chunky on his mobile to see where he was and what he was doing.

"I'm in the fucking office Boss, it's fucking doing my head in," he said. "The good thing is that they've let your brother go, without charge."

"That's great, was it Leo Jenkins?"

"Yeah Boss. I don't know what he did but he's a fucking genius."

"How did Adams take it?"

"Haven't seen him for ages."

"Is there any way you can get away?" I asked.

"Well yes, like I said, Adams has fucked off somewhere, Reb seems to be in charge of everything but she's got her own people and hasn't bothered me much."

"That's a fucking shame," I said. "If only she realised how good a cop you were you'd be at her side."

"Thanks Boss."

"Listen," I said. "I'm going to take Mason down. I don't care what Adams thinks or what Shane wants me to do. Big Bill's time has come and that's the end of it. Are you in?"

"Fuck yeah," Chunky said. "What's the plan?"

CHAPTER TWENTY THREE

SKIN

Mandy came to the door. She looked more suspicious than surprised to see me.

"All my stuff," I said, fumbling. What I was trying to say was that all my stuff was in the house and I needed access to it at least, even if she didn't want to talk to me.

She looked at me as if I was thick.

"Get in," she said, "I think you've got a lot of explaining to do. What the fuck have you been up to?"

"What have they told you?"

Mandy didn't answer but turned and walked into the living room. I followed. We sat down on separate chairs opposite each other across the coffee table.

"It's a long story," I said. "And I thought we were over."

"What's that supposed to mean? It was just a little bit of a crisis," she said. "And I know I let you down and messed up the finances, but from what I've heard you took it a few steps further."

"Sorry. What have you heard?"

"How about you tell me what you've been up to and then I'll tell you what I've been told."

I sighed. "Yes. But Mandy, you have to know that I love you. I know I haven't always shown it but I do, and what's happened lately has made me realise just how much I do."

"Words Skin, that's all they are. Where's the meaning? Where were you? Who were you with? What were you doing? I'm not stupid. This is important."

I sighed heavily, I didn't have any choice. "The woman I had in my car isn't the one that was found dead. The dead woman, Moira, was the sister of Mel who was my passenger. Mel thinks her father killed her sister by mistake."

"What? Are you making this up as you go along?"

"No. Mel needed help. She was scared stiff of her father."

"So where were you and why was your car found smashed up in a hedge?"

Over the next half hour I told Mandy almost everything, though not in too much intimate detail. I admitted that I'd slept with Mel but played it down, making out it was a drunken fumble and only then because I was so upset about us two breaking up. I didn't mention Raskal.

"But we hadn't broken up," Mandy said. "Not really. Oh shit, I don't know what to think, or what to do."

"We can work through this," I said. "Please, let's try?"

"I don't know," she said.

I sighed.

"By the way," Mandy said, "I'm pregnant."

"Uh? Wow!" I felt a rush of surprise and shock. I didn't know how to react.

"I was going to tell you earlier, but then you were arrested."

"Sorry about that," I said, still struggling with how to respond. "But that's amazing, how do you feel about it?"

"Sorry Skin," she said. "I don't know how to feel about anything at the moment. There's a lot to think about."

She was right, there was a lot to think about for me too. It was such a huge thing to take on board that I couldn't find the words to explain how I felt either.

"Yes," I said. "There is a lot to think about. How long have you known?"

"I took a test last week. It was positive. That's one of the reasons I was all over the place. Then, I did another test earlier today, after you were taken away. They're very reliable."

"What can I do?"

She shook her head. "Nothing. I don't want to think too much about it or about anything else really. Maybe just take things easy for a couple of days. Let things percolate."

"How about a little break?" I asked. "We could go away for a few days, find a nice hotel?"

Even as I was saying it, I realised that it wasn't an option. There was still an unknown amount of mess to sort out both in our business and in our personal life.

"Nah!" she said.

"All right, it might be best if I leave you alone for a bit. I need to see Bones and my dad anyway. I could stay somewhere else tonight if that's what you want."

"No Skin, that's not what I want."

"What then?"

"Well, I haven't seen your father for a while and can't remember the last time I saw Bones, so how about I tag along with you, we don't have to talk but if we do it might help."

"Sounds like a great idea," I said, though I didn't really think it was.

I checked that Dave's old car was still roadworthy and was fuelled up with diesel and we went to visit my old man. We parked outside his house next to a little Fiat with a big 'Doctor on Call' sign inside the windscreen.

"Shit!" I said. "What's going on?"

"Come on, we'll know soon enough," Mandy said, already getting out of the car.

I followed her and we walked along the path to the front door. As we were approaching it, it opened, and a woman with a medical bag came out. My dad Eric was behind her, he looked relaxed. The doctor walked past us and nodded. Eric's face lit up when he saw me and Mandy.

"Hi Dad," I said.

My father completely ignored me and smiled at Mandy. "Well, hello so nice to see you, you're looking good."

Mandy reached out and kissed my father on the cheek. "Lovely to see you Eric, how are you doing?"

"I'm good," he nodded, looking embarrassed. "Come in. Have you got time for a cuppa?"

"Fig rolls," Mandy said, producing a packet from her bag.

"My favourites," he said.

"I know," she said. winking at him.

"Yuck!" I said.

I hadn't eaten a fig roll since I was old enough to tell my father to stick them where the sun doesn't shine, and then later when I read about the little wasps that crawled inside the figs and died, that was the end of that, I would never eat them again.

Eric led the way to the living room. He seemed to be much more mobile than the last time I'd seen him, perhaps he was on new meds?

I made a cup of tea to go with the biscuits while the other two chatted.

"I've had some good news," my father said, as I laid out the teas and biscuits on the coffee table.

"Go on," I said.

"Looks like I'm on the mend," he said. "I thought I was getting worse but it was a chest infection. I've got some antibiotics."

"Wow!" Mandy said, leaning over and hugging him.

"Oops," she said, realising she'd embarrassed him with the kiss on the cheek.

"Stop worrying, it's all good," he said.

"Brilliant. Nice one Dad," I said.

Mandy looked up at me and raised her eyebrows. "We've got some good news ourselves, haven't we?" she said.

It was my turn to raise my eyebrows.

Mandy winked at me, and looked back at my father.

"We're going to have a baby," she said.

"Um, it's a bit early yet," I said.

"I can't believe it," Eric said, tears forming in his eyes. "I'm going to be a grandfather."

We drank the tea, they ate the fig rolls, and we all talked about having children.

"Why did you tell him that?" I whispered when my father had gone to the kitchen to get more sugar.

"I'm not sure," she said. "He looked so happy because he's getting better, I just felt it was the right thing to do, besides, now that it's out in the open it means that it's real. And, it means that I believe we can do this. What do you think?"

"Oh yes," I said.

We hugged. My father came back in from the kitchen.

"Now now," he said. "That's enough of that don't you think."

We all laughed.

My phone rang.

"It's Shane," I said, "I'd better answer it.

I stood up and moved into the hall.

"Hi Shane," I said.

"Where are you?" he asked. "I need to talk to you as soon as possible about how it went in the police station with Adams. Can you come to the B&B please?"

"All right, I'm not far away, could be with you in ten, maybe fifteen, minutes. I'm with Mandy so will have to take her home first."

"Great, I'll wait outside," Shane said.

When I went back in Mandy was already washing the dishes.

"We have to go," I said.

BONES

I picked Chunky up outside the car park entrance to the police station, it was already dark. I was hoping he'd be able to tell me more about fucking Adams, since he'd spent a few days in his company. I had serious doubts about the man, especially after what Shane had said, plus I was going to tackle Big Bill Mason whatever else happened, but if I could use Adams, or anyone else, to tip the odds my way then I would.

"Before anything else we should have a chat, a catch-up," I said when Chunky plonked his fat arse onto the front passenger seat of my BMW.

"Yeah Boss, and I'm hungry."

"You're always fucking hungry. How about we pop over to the Tinworks Arts Centre for a bowl of chips and a swift half?"

"Sounds good to me."

"We can have a chat there."

I drove across town to the Tinworks while Chunky moaned in my ear about how much of a fussy twat Adams was, complete with detailed descriptions of his obsessive behaviour, like making sure every single second of every single working day was meticulously planned and logged.

I ordered the chips first, just a regular bowl each. I knew I wouldn't eat half of mine but would use the rest to keep Chunky sweet. I wanted to keep my wits about me so I bought a half pint of low alcohol beer for myself and a pint of some local brewery's craft ale for Chunky.

"So, what's it been like?" I asked him when we were waiting for the chips.

"What do you mean Boss?"

"With Adams," I said. "What's Adams like, close up if you know what I mean?"

Chunky shook his head as if he was trying to forget rather than remember.

"Was it that bad?" I asked.

"I dunno Boss, honest. I can't work him out. Like I said, he's a fussy bastard, and he's got a weird attitude. I don't think he knows what the fuck is going on."

"Anything else?"

"He disappears a lot. Goes to meetings I suppose. and he's always taking calls on his mobile. He does fuck all, Reb does most of the work."

"Any ideas about where he's gone now?"

"He doesn't tell me anything. You could ask Reb, or even Elena, she knows more than me."

"What about Bill Mason then? Has there been much talk about how he might be involved?"

"Nothing official. But Reb thinks he's up to his eyes in all sorts, and there's some other investigation into Mason going on that she's been involved with, something to do with human trafficking and modern slavery I think."

"Hmm, yes, and there has been some talk of an investigation into a major cannabis farming operation that's associated with that, but I didn't know he was involved."

"That's it Boss, like I said, nobody tells me anything. I do keep my eyes and ears open though."

"I know Chunks, you're a star."

"Thanks Boss."

"I'll have a word with Reb, see if I can get anything more out of her," I said.

I was far away in my own thoughts when the chips were delivered to the table.

"Boo!" someone said as they plonked the bowls down.

I looked up. It was Raskal.

"Oh hiya," I said. "Thanks. How's it going?"

"Great," she said. "How's your brother Skin, after everything?"

"Good, I think."

Chunky was staring at Raskal.

"This is Chunky," I said to her. "My colleague."

"I'm Raskal," she said, holding her hand out to Chunky. "You're a cop too then?"

"Um . . . yes . . . Raskal . . . nice to meet you," he said, holding his hand out awkwardly.

"Good bone structure," she said.

"What?" he said.

"Sorry, I'm an artist, you've got distinctive features, you'd make a good model."

"Me? A model?"

I laughed. "Not that sort of model," I said. "Raskal is an artist."

"Enjoy the chips," Raskal said with a cheeky wink as she was turning to go.

Chunky was sitting open mouthed his hand hovering over his bowl of chips.

"Fucksake Chunks, get some of those chips in your mouth before you get lockjaw," I said. "She's too young for you anyway."

He snapped out of it, shook himself, and proceeded to stuff his huge gob. I picked at my food but didn't really fancy it. I shoved the bowl over to Chunky.

"Here," I said, "I'm not hungry. I think I'll go and phone Reb, ask her about the other stuff Mason's into. Wait here for me."

"OK Boss."

I walked out of the building and into the car park at the rear to ring Rebecca. She answered straightaway.

"Hi Bones," she said.

"Reb," I said, "I wondered if you could tell me anything about the investigation into Bill Mason, something to do with human trafficking?"

"Not a lot," she said. "It's early stages, just following up on some information from a contact of mine."

"An informer?"

"Sort of, though I think he may be playing me. He's a small time dealer from the Backfields estate."

"It's not Jackie Mann is it?"

"Um yes, how did you know that?"

"Educated guess," I said. "So has he told you much?"

"Not really. Though there has also been some intelligence suggesting that Mason has access to some warehouse space out of town somewhere. That's what I was going to look into next, it's just been so busy I haven't had time."

"Thanks Reb, that's interesting. "By the way, is Adams still missing in action."

"Ha ha, yes he is Bones, as far as I know anyway. But he might have gone to a meeting in HQ. He doesn't tell me everything."

"Can you do me a favour please?"

"You've done enough for me in the past so yes."

"Will you let me know when Adams turns up, and tell him I was asking a lot of questions about him?"

"Isn't that going to get him riled up?"

"Exactly," I said. "And tell him I was nosing about Bill Mason while you're at it. Might be good if you said I was asking about Mason's warehouse too."

"I don't know what you're up to Bones, but look after yourself."

"Oh I will."

While I'd been talking to Reb a plan had been coming together in my head. I'd connected the dots and realised that if Mason did have that warehouse space then it was probably near the place where I'd been taken when his monkeys had kidnapped me. If I could spook Mason, through Adams, into thinking I was on to his operation then I could be waiting for him, or better still both of them.

CHAPTER TWENTY FOUR

SKIN

I drove back to the house and Mandy got out of the car. She didn't mind me going straight back out again to see Shane, in fact I think she was glad. We each had a lot to sort out in our own heads and needed time to think. Mandy waved me away from the front door and went inside.

I put the car into gear and looked over my left shoulder. I had a hell of a shock when the back door opened and a shadowy figure tumbled onto the back seat and lay down. I knew straightaway who it was because of the strong smell of strawberry and Pernod.

"Mel!" I said.

"Drive," she said.

I obeyed and accelerated away up the street towards the main road. I pulled over before the junction and turned the engine off. Mel immediately got out of the car and came in again onto the front passenger seat. She looked dirty and her clothes were torn. Her eyes were bright but there was a distant look about her.

"What's happened to you?"

She leaned across, took my head in her hands and kissed my nose.

"Sorry," she said. "I love you."

Oh shit! I didn't want to say the same thing back to her, because I didn't love her, but I was worried that if I didn't tell her that I did, she would lose the plot and attack me or Mandy in some way.

"We have to get away quick," I said, trying to change the subject and making it sound urgent.

It seemed to work, she sat back and did a mock salute.

"Yes sir!"

I didn't know how to respond to that so I just stared.

253

"Sorry Skin," she said. "I'm only joking. It's just so good to see you. Where are we going?"

I could already feel myself falling for her again, I was going to have to watch myself. Jesus, my head was already in bits and she'd been back in my life less than a couple of minutes.

"I've got an urgent pick up. It's not just a pick up though, he's a friend."

"Can I come with you? I've got nowhere else to go."

"Yes," I said, mainly because I felt it was the only thing I could say.

I was playing for time. I'd already decided that she was unstable. I needed to work out the best way to handle her, I didn't want to hurt her and I didn't want to get hurt by her, emotionally or physically. There wouldn't be enough time to deal with her properly before meeting with Shane so he would just have to put up with it. He needed to know about the arrest but I wasn't sure if it was wise for Mel to hear about what had happened to me since she'd left me in those hills. I didn't think I had any other choice so I thought I'd better prepare the ground.

I started the car and pulled away from the kerb, heading towards the B&B where Shane was staying.

"I was arrested," I said. "When I got back."

"Shit!" she said. "Was it because of the hotel and the pub?"

"No, they thought I had something to do with what happened to your twin Moira."

She gasped.

"But they had to let me go after a couple of hours, it was all bollocks."

"Oh, you poor thing," she reached up and stroked my forehead.

"Did you tell them it was my father?"

"No, sorry, I was told, by my solicitor, to say as little as possible."

"Did you tell them about me?"

"No, I wasn't sure what to do about that either."

"Good, that's good," she said. "Thank you Skin. You did

the right thing. I don't want my father to know anything, yet, he still thinks he killed me, that I'm dead."

"What shall I tell Shane?" I asked.

"I don't know. That I'm a neighbour who needed a lift?"

"Hang on," I said. "I've just had a thought. Shane is not just a friend, he's an undercover cop. He's looking into organised criminals with local connections."

"Pull over," she said. "Quick."

I stopped the car. Mel leaned over and stared at me.

"Do you trust him? Has he got anything to do with my father?"

"That's what I was going to say. Shane is part of a team working undercover against multinational crime and your father is one of the people he's investigating."

"Why haven't you mentioned this before?"

"To be honest, I was never really sure it was true, I'm still not, but if it is, then perhaps he can help you. It might be worth telling him what's happened to you and your sister."

"Looks like I've got no choice," she said.

"Are you sure?"

"Yes," she took a deep breath. "Drive on."

Shane was standing at the side of the road when we got there. I parked right next to him and got out of the car.

"Hi Shane," I said. "Sorry I'm late. What's the plan?"

"We could go to the Carpenters, or you can come inside here," he suggested.

"I'm not sure. Listen, I've got someone with me, sorry. It's a long story, but she's had a hard time and needed to talk. I think you'll be interested in talking to her as well."

"Oh," he said. "Why? Who is she?"

"I think I'll let her tell you herself."

"Fair enough. But first, do you mind briefing me about the arrest first. It shouldn't take long. Just so that I can get the basics of what happened in the cop shop."

I shrugged. "Of course. It would have been nice to have a drink though."

Truth was, I was afraid of being left alone with Mel and I was hoping that by dragging someone else in, especially a professional police officer like Shane, I would be protected.

"There'll be plenty of time for that, and I'll be able to have a chat with your friend then, whatever it's about," Shane said. "Now, do you mind telling me about the arrest?"

He was right, it didn't take long. And I told him more or less the same story I'd told the other cops about what had happened to me, that is, someone nicked my car. He didn't seem satisfied. Then he kept pumping me to tell him more about the night of the murder, asking me if I saw anything or anyone else. He was so persistent that I almost cracked and told him about my time on the run with Mel, but with her still in my car I was afraid to say too much for her sake and for my own safety, since I was still very wary of her. Plus, we could tell him that story together, in the pub where I would feel much safer.

His mobile phone rang. He took it out of his pocket and looked at the screen.

"Hang on," he said to me.

He walked a few paces along the pavement and put the phone to his ear. I couldn't hear anything much but he did seem a bit wound up. He put the phone back in his pocket and walked quickly back towards me.

"I need a lift, now," he said. "It's urgent."

I shrugged. "All right, but what about my friend? I can't leave her, she's got nowhere to go."

"She'll have to come along then, we can talk on the way."

"Where are you going?" I asked.

"Hang on," he said. "They're sending a text message with the exact location, but it's in the Western Valleys, on the old A road, so if you can head in that direction I'll let you know as we go."

BONES

When I went back inside the Tinworks, Chunky had finished both bowls of chips and was tucking into a slab of chocolate cake. Raskal was sitting next to him with an open sketch book. She'd already drawn the outline of his fat head.

"What's going on here then?" I asked as I sat down.

"It's gluten-free," Chunky said, taking a mouthful of the cake.

I laughed.

"I'm going to be a model," Chunky said. "I have to watch my weight."

He winked at Raskal. She laughed.

"I'll leave you to it then," I said.

"Oh, not now," Raskal said. "I'm on duty, working in the café."

"Yeah Boss, I'm going to her studio tomorrow."

"I've got to get off anyway," I said. "Things to do, places to go and all that."

"What about me?" Chunky asked.

"I suppose you'd better get back to work, or twiddling your thumbs as it's better known."

"I'd rather help you Boss."

"Whatever," I shrugged,

Despite pretending not to be bothered, I was secretly very happy that Chunky was going to tag along. If I was successful in spooking Mason and possibly Adams and it led to a confrontation then the big man's presence would be a great asset.

When we got back to my car we sat in silence for a few minutes neither of us knowing what to do next. Chunky was messing with his phone and I was just thinking without focusing on anything in particular. But I was anxious and excited. It felt as if things were coming to a head. It had been a mad few days and I was expecting it to get even madder before things were resolved, whether that was for the better or for the worse.

I got out of the car, went around to the boot, opened it up and dug out the wrapped up gun from where I'd hidden it under the carpet. It felt solid in my hand, solid and deadly and that feeling made me feel strong and confident. Whatever was going to go down I was ready for it.

My phone rang. It was Rebecca from the station. I put the

gun down and closed the boot, just in case someone else spotted it while I was on the phone.

"Bones?" she said.

"That's me Reb."

"Adams turned up. I did what you wanted and told him you'd been asking all those questions about him and about Bill Mason."

"How did he react?" I asked.

"Well, when I told him you were talking about Mason's warehouse he looked horrified, made an excuse about needing the loo and disappeared. A couple of minutes later Elena saw him rushing out of the station."

Thanks Reb," I said.

"What's going on Bones?" she asked. "Is there something I should know about?"

I hesitated. All I'd wanted up until then was to find a way to get at Mason for what he'd done to Moira but now I had to face the reality that he was too big a fish for me to catch on my own. Despite what Shane had told me about the global crime network he was investigating I still didn't trust him and I didn't want him to interfere to protect his own investigation.

"Bones? Are you still there?"

"Yes, sorry," I said. "It might be a good idea to get a team on standby, I'm not sure of the exact location yet but will let you know when I am. We're dealing with a ruthless organisation but I'm not sure if anything is going to come of this tonight."

"I'm going to need more than that," Reb said.

"Fair enough, I'll be in touch when I get something more specific, but in the meantime it won't do any harm to do some preparation. It looks like you're the senior officer there so you've got the authority."

"All right then Bones, but let me know as soon as you can."

I got back in the car and started the engine. Chunky looked up from his phone.

"Where to Boss?" he asked.

"We're taking a little trip to the Western Valleys," I said.

"Cool, my uncle lives up there. He runs a pub called The New Polecat."

"I don't think we'll have time for a drink," I said.

SKIN

When I explained to Mel where we were going she decided to get in the back of the car so Shane could sit next to me. As I drove towards the valleys she leaned over from the back seat and started talking to him.

"What has Skin told you about me?" she asked.

"Nothing much," Shane said. "Just that you're a friend of his and . . ."

"A friend? Is that all I am Skin? Why don't you tell him how much we mean to each other? More than anyone else ever, isn't that what you said? And I feel the same about you."

She was laughing, but it alarmed me that she was still thinking about me in that way, especially after her irrational behaviour.

Shane chuckled. "None of my business," he said.

"No, it's not," Mel said.

"Skin also told me that I might want to listen to what you've got to say," Shane said.

"Oh! What did you mean by that Skin?" Mel asked me.

"You know, about who you are," I said.

"Yes," she said, "I was just messing, I love you really, you know that."

"So, let me out of my misery. Who are you?" Shane asked.

"Wouldn't you like to know?"

"Yes, I would, you look interesting."

"You don't look too bad yourself," she said in a flirty voice.

Shane laughed. "You seem like you could be fun," he said. "but Skin is more my type."

"You wouldn't be disappointed," Mel said. "I mean, with either of us."

"Anyway," I said. "Mel is Bill Mason's daughter."

"What?" Shane said.

"Moira Mason was my twin sister," Mel said.

Shane turned and stared at her. "Ah! Yes, I can see it now. I'm very sorry about your sister, but you disappeared a long time ago."

"You know?" I asked.

"Well I have been investigating Bill Mason for some time. I knew there was an ex wife and a twin, but they haven't been seen for more than ten years."

"My mother changed our names," Mel said. "My father is a monster. We escaped, but had to leave Moira behind. My mother died a few months ago, I've been looking for Moira ever since. I tracked her down to Elchurch. I wish I'd never done it now."

"Why?" Shane asked.

"It was my fault he killed her, he thought she was me."

"Who? Your father?"

Mel started sobbing. "Yes."

"Do you want us to stop the car?" Shane asked.

Mel shook herself and sat back, "No, I'll be all right thanks."

I drove on in silence for a few minutes.

"We're getting into the valleys," I said. "I'm going to need a location?"

Shane took a deep breath as if he was going to say something important but his phone rang.

"Yes," he said as he put it to his ear. "Right, thanks, hang on, let me repeat that. The derelict warehouses next to the pickle factory, is that right? Can you give me directions?"

"It's ok," I said. "I know where they are."

"It's ok," Shane said into the phone. "Thanks."

He disconnected the call and put his phone back in his pocket.

"Yeah," I said. "They started building this so-called warehouse park with European money years ago. It's been abandoned for more than ten years, silly location in the first place, I could have told them that at the time."

"How far?" Shane asked.

"Five, ten minutes, something like that."

"Go for it," Shane said. "It's urgent. But don't take any risks, and can you stop just before we get there so I can suss the place out before plunging in."

"Plunging into what?" I asked.

"It could be dangerous," Shane said. "I'm not going to lie to you. They're a nasty bunch."

"Who are?" I asked.

"We weren't ready to move in on them, but we've got no choice now. Your brother, Bones, he's jumping the gun, so we have to."

"What do you mean?"

"Listen, there's no time for this now. I'll explain later, in the meantime you'd both better stay in the car. No, better than that, drop me off, turn around and go home or somewhere, wherever you like."

I pulled over onto a small tarmacked lay-by and turned the engine off.

"It's just around that corner," I said. "There's an entrance on the left."

"Thanks," Shane said.

A car drove past going like the clappers, then a few seconds later another car whizzed past going almost as fast, it was too dark to be sure but it looked like a familiar black BMW to me.

"Shit! Is that Bones?" I said.

Shane jumped out of the car and belted it down the road towards the warehouses.

BONES

I headed straight to the location of the warehouses where I'd been taken after being kidnapped by Mason's monkeys. If my calculations were correct then that's where fucking Adams was heading and if he was then I knew he'd have warned Mason that his operation was under threat so he should also be making his way there. I was banking on them thinking it was just me, a lone wolf, who was onto them, because that would mean they'd take risks and expose themselves.

I was open to the possibility that I'd got it wrong and Adams wasn't actually in Bill Mason's pocket but I was still convinced that Mason was responsible for Moira's death. And based on what Shane had told me about his investigations I was also certain that the warehouses were an important location for the global crime network Mason was involved with.

Up until I'd spoken to Reb my plan to make sure Bill Mason got what he deserved for killing Moira had been simple and probably impossible to follow successfully. But things had changed since I'd dragged Rebecca and Chunky into my madness. I knew I'd have to play it by the book from then on.

As I was leaving the outskirts of town and moving into the valleys I saw Adams standing next to his car at a roadside filling station. He was just withdrawing the petrol pump from the tank of his car. He looked nervous and agitated. I drove on and stopped as soon as I could at the side of the road outside a row of terraced houses.

"What you doing Boss?" Chunky asked.

"Fucking Adams," I said. "He's in that petrol station back there. We'll wait here and follow him when he comes out. I know where he's going anyway."

I turned the engine and the lights off and sat quietly in the dark. My strategy seemed to be working. A couple of minutes later Adams zoomed past. I started the car's engine, put it into gear and followed him.

As expected, Adams turned off the road and into the warehouse site. I slowed down as we drew level with it. The tail lights of his car were disappearing behind a large unit set back from the road. I turned into the site and parked in a spot at the front of the same unit. I turned the engine off again and sat in the dark with Chunky.

"What next Boss?" he asked.

CHAPTER TWENTY FIVE

SKIN

I turned around to see how Mel was. She was sitting open-mouthed and staring through the window at the dark road.

"Are you ok?" I asked.

"Who was that in the car?" she asked.

"That was my brother Bones, the cop," I said. "It was his car anyway."

"He's your brother? Are you sure?"

"Yes. Why? What's the matter?"

"Nothing," Mel said, shaking herself.

She opened the back door, got out of the car and ran down the road in the same direction as Shane had gone.

I got out of the car and followed her. "Hang on," I shouted.

She stopped and waited for me.

"Let's do this properly," I said. "Be careful, you know what Shane said."

She gave me a fierce look, but nodded.

We walked slowly and carefully along the road until we got to the warehouse site. The entrance must have been protected with wide metal gates at some point but was now open to the road, I guessed that the gates had long since been nicked and sold for scrap. There was a car park just inside the entrance littered with rubble and broken tarmac. Just beyond the car park were two large red brick two-storey office buildings, their windows all smashed. A road passed between the two office buildings and led into the darkness where the warehouses were sited.

My brother's car was parked near the office buildings about sixty or seventy metres from where we were at the entrance. The doors and the boot of the car were open and two figures were shouting in each other's faces while another figure was standing a few metres away from them. Because

263

it was dark I couldn't see their features, but it was obvious it was Bones and Shane having an argument about something and from his build the other figure was probably my brother's sidekick Chunky. I could see that the taller man, Shane, was standing in front of the open boot and Bones was facing him.

Mel ran towards the three men. She put the hood of her jacket up and stopped twenty metres away from them. I caught up with her and we both stared at Shane and Bones who were still arguing. Chunky was still standing back as if he wasn't sure whose side he was supposed to be on.

"Fuck off Shane," Bones shouted. "This is nothing to do with you. This is personal. Get out of my way."

Bones launched himself at Shane, who fell back against the car but recovered quickly and held his ground.

"Don't be fucking stupid Bones," Shane screamed. "You can't do this yourself, you've no idea what's going on down there. And the armed response team are on the way. This has to be done properly."

Bones attacked Shane again and pushed him out of the way, Shane stumbled onto the ground. Bones grabbed something from the boot and stepped back. He lifted his arm, and I gasped when I saw that he was holding a gun and pointing it at Shane. He glanced over at us, peering in the dark to try and make out who we were.

"Is that you Skin?" he asked.

"Yes Bones," it's me. "What are you doing with that?"

"That's my business, keep out of the way. Why are you here? Go home."

Shane saw his chance while Bones was distracted talking to me and pushed himself off the ground and into Bones. Bones stumbled backwards and the gun flew out of his hand and slid across the broken tarmac towards where I was standing with Mel.

Chunky's eyes followed the gun but his reactions were too slow. Mel's body tensed and she ran towards the gun where it had come to rest halfway between Bones and us. She leant down and picked it up. She flicked her hood back from her head and pointed the gun at Bones.

"Don't fucking move," she screamed.

Bones stared at Mel. "Moira?" he said, "That's not possible."

He dropped to his knees, shaking his head in disbelief, as if someone had cut the bottom half of his legs off.

Mel ran on. Chunky stepped forward to try and intercept her but when she waved the gun at him he stepped back. I thought she was going to attack my brother and possibly kill him since she had a gun, so I ran after her, but she ran straight past Bones and Shane, waving the gun in the air, and then carried on along the road into the darkness.

I heard the sound of a helicopter overhead and suddenly the yard was lit up from above by a powerful searchlight.

"Stay where you are," a voice boomed through a megaphone.

Then I heard the sirens of approaching police vehicles.

I stopped in my tracks and waited.

Bones stood up and belted down the road after Mel, closely followed by Shane and a less fast Chunky. The searchlight tried to follow them but it was all over the place.

Shit! I'd have to go after them, I didn't want to be left on my own.

BONES

I must have sighed because Chunky asked me what was up.

"Just thinking that's all," I said. "Anyway come on we'd better get down there after fucking Adams. We'll leave the car here."

"What about Reb and the others?"

"God knows how long they'll take to get it together Chunks, you know what it's like, there's no time for faffing about when you've got dangerous bastards like Mason on the loose."

"Aye Boss, you're right."

We got out of the car. Chunky wandered off towards the

road that led to the back end of the warehouse site. I remembered about the gun in the boot. It wouldn't do any harm to grab it. I wouldn't have to use it but it would tilt the odds in my favour if it came to it. I opened the boot, took the weapon out and examined it. I was just about to shove it under my belt when suddenly I heard someone running towards me. I looked up and was staring straight into Shane's eyes, they were fixated on the gun in my hand.

Don't do anything daft Bones," he said, reaching his hand towards me like he was trying to stop a madman. That made me smile, perhaps that was what I was. But it also made me angry at being patronised, then I remembered that I still really didn't trust my old pal. I put the gun back in the boot anyway. As soon as I did Shane forced himself between me and the boot.

"What the fuck are you doing," I shouted.

"Take it easy Bones, calm down."

"Fuck off Shane. This is nothing to do with you. This is personal . . ."

I tried to shove him out of the way but he was too big.

"Don't be fucking stupid Bones," Shane shouted. "You can't do this yourself, you've no idea what's going on down there. And the armed response team are on the way. This has to be done properly."

I charged at the bastard and he fell down and stumbled onto the ground. I took the gun from the boot and pointed it at him. There was somebody else looming out of the darkness, two figures barely visible in the gloom but one of them looked like my brother Skin, the other was smaller and wearing a black top with a hood.

"Is that you Skin?" I shouted.

"Yes Bones, it's me," he said. "What are you doing with that?"

"That's my business. Why are you here? Go home."

While I was talking to Skin, Shane managed to get up and shove me. I lost my footing for a second and the gun fell out of my hand and across towards where Skin and the other one were standing.

The person in the black hooded top ran forward, jumped on the gun and picked it up. They pushed the hood off their head and pointed the gun at me. I stepped back instinctively.

"Don't fucking move," they shouted.

What the fuck, she was the spit of . . .

"Moira?" I said. "That's not possible."

All the energy drained from my body and I fell to my knees.

She ran towards me, I flinched but she carried on running along the road towards the rear of the site.

A police helicopter appeared above. A voice amplified through a megaphone told us to keep still and stay put.

The noise of the helicopter almost drowned out the sirens of the approaching police vehicles. I got myself to my feet and ran into the darkness following the woman who I was convinced was Moira back from the dead.

SKIN

I ran half-heartedly following the others. The road ahead of me disappeared into darkness and there was a turning to the right that led to a large grey warehouse that looked cold and empty. The shadowy figures of everyone else moved ahead of me towards the building.

Mel was first to get there. She opened a door, light streamed out onto the road illuminating a car park at the side of the warehouse that was crammed with vehicles, one of them, a large black MPV, was creepily familiar.

Mel went straight in and the door swung shut behind her. Seconds later the door was opened again and Bones dived into the building, closely followed by Shane and finally myself and Chunky.

There was no sign of anyone else in the long corridor that led off in both directions away from the entrance. Chunky turned left and I turned to the right, I don't know why, maybe it was some instinct I didn't know I had. I walked slowly along the corridor. I passed a heavy door that was firmly closed shut, yet I could hear voices inside. I hesitated but was too scared to push the door open, especially after Shane had told me to go home because it was too dangerous.

I carried on along the corridor, and came to a pair of large double doors that were half-open. I pushed at the doors and they opened wide revealing a large warehouse space. On the floor were several dozen makeshift beds, and lying on the beds and sitting against the walls there were at least twenty people. Every one of them stared at me, looking bewildered and trapped

Then at the other side of the room a door opened and Bones appeared. He scanned the room before running across towards me, he was followed by Shane and Chunky, there was no sign of Mel.

"Have you seen anything?" Bones asked.

"Back there," I said, pointing down the corridor in the direction I'd come in. "Heavy door."

I stepped aside. He rushed out. I followed, aware of the other two coming up behind me.

Bones stopped a few metres ahead of me and stared at Mel. She was standing outside the heavy door, pointing the gun at it. Further along the corridor I saw two tooled-up cops getting into position.

"Don't," Bones shouted.

The door to the room opened and somebody stepped out into the corridor, I couldn't see who they were. Mel pulled the trigger.

BONES

I was still in shock after seeing Moira's ghost. I knew there had to be a rational explanation for what was happening but at that moment I couldn't find it. I'd even identified her body and she was well beyond dead then. And whoever this one was why was she with my brother Skin? Maybe it was as simple as two brothers fancying the same kind of person and because it was dark and because I'd been so wound up about everything and . . .

Whatever was going on, the fact was that there was a young woman running around with a loaded gun in a place infested with crazy bastards. Someone was going to get hurt. I chased after her. I was losing ground when we got to a building at the end of the road. She ran towards it, pulled a door open and went in. The door swung shut behind her, I hoped it hadn't locked automatically. I was in luck, it opened easily, but when I got inside there was no sign of her.

I was in a long corridor that stretched away both to the right and to the left. I turned left. I slowed down and walked carefully along the corridor, after all there was an unstable person with a gun somewhere in that building.

I eventually came across a big double door. I pushed and it swung open inwards. I peeked inside and in the dim light I was shocked to see a couple of dozen anxious-looking people. I looked across the large room and saw my stupid brother standing in a doorway at the other end.

I ran across the room avoiding the mess of bedding and people. I was aware that Shane and Chunky were behind me.

"Have you seen anything?" I asked Skin.

"Back there," he said, pointing down the corridor. "Heavy door."

I pushed past my brother and rushed out of the room. Further along the corridor I saw Moira lift the gun and point it at the door. I stopped and edged forwards. She turned around sharply to face me.

"Stop," she said, pointing the gun at me.

I stopped.

She turned back to face the door. Further along the corridor I saw two armed officers levelling their weapons on her.

"Don't," I shouted.

The door to the room opened and Bill Mason poked his head out.

Moira pulled the trigger.

SKIN

The person who Mel had shot fell down like a sack of spuds and lay crumpled up lifelessly halfway in and halfway out of the room. Mel turned to face Bones and pointed the gun at his head. Behind her, further down the corridor I noticed one of the armed cops move.

"No!" Bones shouted.

There was a crack and Mel dropped like a burst balloon. The gun fell out of her hand and spun along the floor. Bones knelt down next to her. I ran over and knelt on the other side.

"Moira," Bones said.

"Mel," I said

She smiled at us. Her eyes closed. She went limp.

BONES

Mason was hit square in the chest. A bewildered look came over his face and he dropped lifeless to the floor. I was certain he was dead. I stared at the girl, she wasn't some random coincidence, she was Moira, she really was, there was no doubt about it. She turned towards me, the gun still in her hands. She lifted it up to point at my head. I noticed a movement coming from the officers who were crouching further down the corridor.

I knew what was coming next.

"No!" I shouted.

It was too late, I heard the bang of the gunshot and she crumpled to the floor.

I ran up to her and leant down.

I saw my brother kneel down opposite me.

She was lying on her back with her eyes open. There was a glimmer of life still there.

"Moira," I said.

"Mel," my brother said.

She smiled. Her head lolled and she lay still.

SKIN

The next couple of hours didn't seem real. Dozens of police officers, many of them armed, arrived and rounded up Mason's associates. The people who were effectively living in that warehouse were, I was told, taken to get looked after in some sort of temporary accommodation until they could sort their paperwork out.

The premises were going to be sealed off and forensically examined. Bones told me that Detective Chief Inspector Adams was up to his neck in Bill Mason's operations and had been arrested.

Mandy texted me at one point saying she was worried about me and we should talk. I texted her back to say that I was fine and would explain everything when I got home later.

The car I'd been driving was held for evidence. I was standing out the front in the near darkness with Bones, waiting for a promised lift home when Shane walked out from the building and came over to us.

"I'm sorry, that was a terrible thing to happen," he said. "I hope you understand . . ."

"Yes, yes," Bones said. "I know the score."

"She was very disturbed," I said.

"What do you know about them so far, what happened?" Bones asked Shane.

"Not a great deal," Shane said, "but we are almost certain that one of the twins killed the other one. We won't know who was the victim and who was the murderer until if and when forensics get an unambiguous result from the DNA samples."

"They were both victims," I said.

"So," Bones said. "Mel tracked Moira down and killed her, or got killed by her."

"Yes, and one or both of them wanted to kill their father and one of them succeeded," Shane said.

"I'm finding it hard to get my head around all this. What do you think?" I asked him.

"Haven't got a clue sorry, we'll just have to wait."

BONES

"What about all the rest of it?" I asked Shane. "The cannabis factory, the human trafficking, the modern slavery and all that?"

"After everything we've learned today is put together and followed through, it will certainly make a big dent in their operation, and a lot of people will be a lot happier, but you know how it is. There are plenty of dodgy bastards waiting in the shadows, we've just got to keep flushing them out."

Skin sighed and shook his head. "I'm still not sure about any of it."

"Well I'm sure of one thing," I said. "It was Moira, here tonight."

"I never met Moira," Skin said, "but I did get to know who Mel was, and I'm certain it was her."

Shane shrugged.

The End